I0739099

SNAPSHOT

by

rebel farris

Snapshot

Rebel Farris

Copyright © 2018 Rebel Farris
All rights reserved.

Published by Mad Lane Books
Austin, Texas, USA

Cover Design & Formatting by Mad Lane Design
Edited by Sandra Depukat of One Love Editing
Proofread by Jenn Wood of All About The Edits

A CIP record for this book is available from the Library of Congress Cataloging-ing-in-Publication Data

ISBN-13: 978-0-9997849-4-5

For my readers.

Thank you so much for all the love and support you have given me thus far. You guys are amazingly awesome. Each and every one of you that got hyped for this book. Those who were so excited about the duet, you had to share my stories with others. Those who spread the word: posting, sharing, and talking about my books. This book was written for you.

I will never stop being grateful that you took a chance on me.

PROLOGUE

I hear the crying from the next room over and try to ignore it. I'm not sure how I ended up in a place like this. I never imagined that this was what my life would look like.

Actually, I do know. Not only did it change my life permanently, but it's not the type of event that escapes one's memory.

You never forget the first time you see a dead body. If you're unfortunate enough to see one outside of a funeral, it's not a pleasant experience. There are things about the dead that they never cover in the movies. Smells, sounds, movements, the clearing of the bowels… all the disgusting stuff.

The crying gets louder, accompanied by the sharp rattle of wooden furniture. I know he'll take care of it, eventually, so I block it from my mind. Where was I? Oh, yeah.

My first time seeing death with my own eyes was on both the best and worst day of my life. When I think about it—even with years of distance—it's all shades of gray. A twisted mass of confused emotions and a racing heart.

Because it was the day I met *him*.

I remember being scared. At first, I thought he was the devil, come to claim me. Then I thought he was my savior. He was both and neither. But one thing was certain—he changed my life irrevocably.

The crying stops, and my shoulders release tension I didn't know I was carrying. But now—now, I can tell you my story.

CHAPTER ONE

Camera

Today was going to be a good day. I could feel it in the air as I walked out on my porch in the early-morning sun. The smell of morning dew and fresh-cut grass floated on the air.

Most people think that being alone is a horrible thing. I'd never really understood that. There was peace in solitude—a serenity in the quiet. In my experience, other people only served to bring about noise, distraction, drama… all things I could live without.

I released a contented sigh as I propped my boots on the railing of the porch. Leaning back in my lawn chair, book in one hand, coffee in the other, no sounds but the birds chirping from the nearby tree and the rustle of leaves on the wind, I could almost forget I had neighbors.

Almost.

It wasn't just that they were ten feet from my front door, within spittin' distance. I could tell the moment they woke up because their day always started with a crash. Then came the shouting: accusations of cheating, lying, being lazy, you name it. It was always the same. I wasn't even a paragraph in before they started. Living in a trailer park is not ideal for privacy. The walls are thin. Though, the way Billy and

Joanne Watkins went at it, they could be inside an airtight vault with twelve-inch-thick concrete walls, and the world would still hear them.

I huffed, stuffing my bookmark into the book and retreating back indoors.

Noise, distraction, drama... yep, definitely not missing out.

Looking around at my bare-bones furnishings, I settled on the twin-size mattress and box spring—what I called a couch—as my new cozy spot, nestling into the twenty or so pillows. Not that I'd much choice, since that and the wooden TV tray that sat next to it were the only furniture I owned, aside from my bed and a matching TV tray back in my bedroom. It wasn't much, but it was mine.

The bookmark dropped out onto my chest as I opened the book. *Hallelujah.* I was finally going to get to enjoy my day off. My first one in the last ten days. It had been that way since Tracey and Ronnie had quit last month, leaving the diner short-staffed. A grand total of three days in one month, and I was going to enjoy this one, Joanne and Billy be damned.

I'd finally gotten my hands on Dean Koontz's latest book, *Midnight*, and *The Queen of the Damned* by Anne Rice. And I was going to read these books before the month's end, come hell or high water.

It took me longer to get the newest *Vampire Chronicles* book because Jerry at the Book Shop didn't believe that female authors would sell if they weren't writing lusty romance novels. *Sexist pig.* But that's the price you paid for living in the country. You were subject to the whims of the local inhabitants. Unless you had the time and inclination to drive into the city—which I did on my last day off.

I'd just turned the last page on chapter one of the Anne Rice book when Billy and Joanne moved their incessant fighting outside. There was no escaping it. Now it was coming through *my* walls, loud and clear. Groaning loudly, I slammed the book shut, forgetting the bookmark. I frowned at it as I set it with the book on top of the TV tray. It was looking like reading would *not* be on the agenda today. But I didn't know what else to do.

I studied the bare walls as I ignored the screams and accusations happening outside. There wasn't much to look at, only one picture. One that had been given to me on my last birthday, by the girls at work. Actually, they were once my best friends, but things had been changing since we'd grown up. They had families of their own now and little time for me. So, we'd drifted apart. The picture was an Ansel Adams print, probably the most valuable possession in my home. And even if it was an incredibly nice gesture, part of it felt like a payoff for all the missing time together. It formerly hung in the window of the frame shop next to the diner. Every day, I'd stopped outside and stared at it. I'd always wanted to be a photographer. But it was just an out-of-reach dream, an expensive hobby outside my means to partake in.

Window-shopping was a specialty of mine. The other place I liked to stand outside and wistfully sigh was Big John's Pawn Shop. There was a brand-new Canon AE-1 35mm camera with a ton of accessories sitting there, calling my name. But I'd just finished saving up my emergency fund. It would be a good six months before I could afford it. If it was even still there when I was ready.

It might not be.

That was the moment I decided to throw caution to the wind. *Or maybe it's just my emergency fund burning a hole in my checkbook?* Spontaneity wasn't in my wheelhouse, but my mind was made up. I would get the camera, go to the drugstore for film, and find a pretty piece of countryside to take pictures. Just me and nature. I jumped up and tossed my purse on my shoulder and was out the door, narrowly dodging water flying in every direction. Joanne was standing in her front yard, threatening Billy with her water hose—again. I shook my head, not even understanding the point of being in a relationship where you obviously hated the other person. This happened every day like clockwork. And my own parents were a testament to the fact that love wasn't what they said it was in books and movies.

I dove into the front seat of my 1984 Pontiac Fiero, just as water sprayed across the windows. Somehow, I missed getting soaked, but a few drops still got in. Closing my eyes, I breathed deep to stop the impulse to say something. Bitch probably did it on purpose. She stuck her nose up in the air and turned her fire back on Billy, who looked unmoved by her antics.

Ten minutes later, I pulled into a parking space in front of the Big John's Pawn Shop. There it was, in all its black-and-silver glory. I walked in with confidence and looked Big John in the eyes as I told him I needed my camera. He smirked at me and went to get it from the window display. The rest of the time I was there, I avoided eye contact, carefully dodging his attempts at small talk. We'd gone to high school together. I knew he was an ass back then, and I was sure the same held true today. Taking over his family business probably didn't instill any more virtue in him.

Thirty minutes later, I was driving down the road with my new camera in my lap, four rolls of film in my passenger seat, and hope in my heart. Maybe this was it. Maybe today I would take the picture that would change my life.

CHAPTER TWO

Death

I drove for more than an hour down a farm-to-market road. There was nothing but trees, random cacti, and limestone boulders as far as the eye could see. Which didn't mean much, since I was in Hill Country, and the rolling hills impeded distant views. After not seeing another house for the last twenty minutes, I decided to pull over.

I loaded the camera with film and shoved all the extra lenses and filters into my purse, pulling out my Walkman. Eddie Thorpe—one of my regular customers—had made me a mixtape that I was thoroughly enjoying. He'd the best taste in music and the time to find songs outside of the incessant country music that permeated every radio station in the area.

I clipped it to my pocket and hit play. "Pictures of Matchstick Men" by Camper Van Beethoven rang in my ears as I pulled my long mahogany hair up into a ponytail. The manic violin hit my gut, springing goose bumps across my flesh. I bobbed my head to the steady beat and smiled.

My purse was a giant holdover from the hippie boom. I bought it from a garage sale a few years back. Made of brown leather, it had a slightly longer than normal strap and fringe on the bottom. Even after

I pulled it over my head, so the strap crossed my torso, it still hung longer than my cutoff jean shorts.

The books poked into my hip, so I reached in and adjusted them. I briefly considered taking them out. I had water, food, camera accessories, the normal purse stuff, and those books, and it was quite heavy. I pulled *Midnight* out and looked longingly at the cover before depositing it on my front seat. No sense in carrying two of them. Even if I found a nice cozy quiet spot to read, I wouldn't finish one.

I looked down at the toe of my boots. The brown leather of the hand-me-down cowboy boots was already scuffed and faded, so I wasn't worried about messing them up on the hike. It just seemed like I should thank them for protecting my feet before I set out to abuse them more.

Shutting my car door, I turned to cross the ditch to the barbed wire fence. It was old and in need of repair, and it sagged enough that I easily swung myself through it. I squinted at the tree line and remembered my sunglasses on top of my head, pulling them down over my eyes. Not seeing a clear path, I walked forward, my camera thumping against my chest with each step.

I made it three steps beyond the trees before my heart started racing. Shit. I forgot about the compass. I dug around in my purse, pulling out the new compass I'd bought at the drugstore. I turned back to face the car. My heart calmed as I saw the glints of blue-painted metal through the trees. I held the compass up, waiting for the needle to settle. *West-northwest.* I was heading east-southeast. I turned back and marched off in that direction, keeping one eye on the ground for snakes and the other on the compass, occasionally looking around and snapping pictures of the landscape and wildlife.

This was rattlesnake country—you couldn't be too careful.

I walked through nearly two rounds of my mixtape. I knew the second side was coming to an end as "Blister in the Sun" by the Violent Femmes started playing. My feet couldn't help the hop they did in response to the infectious beats, and soon I was all-out dancing as I approached a cliff.

The view was stunning. A rocky creek bed lay below, and from my perch, I saw the hills rolling out before me. The sun was directly above me, but as I checked my compass, I knew. The cliff faced due east. The sunrise here would be amazing. I made a mental note to leave something to mark the fence where my car was parked so I could find my way back. *I will get that sunrise shot.*

I took a picture anyway, and the film gave on the rewind, releasing the wheel so it spun freely. I'd filled my first roll. I changed the film out for a fresh roll.

My stomach growled loudly at that moment, in protest of my continuous journey. I looked around and saw a nice shady spot next to a tree, not more than a few feet from the cliff's edge. I untied the flannel shirt around my hips and laid it out on the ground, dropping my purse next to it. Enjoying the view and the silence, I ate my peanut butter and jelly sandwich and dug into the bag of Bugles. I flicked a few curious ants off my flannel when they wandered near, but I'd never been more content.

When I finished eating, I cracked open the book. I don't know how long I sat there, but when the sun dipped toward the horizon and I was no longer sitting in the shade of the tree, I packed up my stuff.

I looked longingly over the cliff for a few moments. I wanted to find a way down there when I came back. The steady stream of water had glittered in the sunlight when I first saw it. There would be some good pictures down there too. After the sunrise. If I didn't have to go back to work, I would be there the next day and then the next.

Reluctantly, I turned and made my way back to the car. I didn't bring a flashlight, so it would be a race against the setting sun to get back before night fell. I pulled my earphones on and hit play. Devo's "Whip It" came on and I let loose, dance-walking my way back to the car, only pausing long enough to snap a couple of cool shots in the fading sunlight.

When "Heroes" by David Bowie came on, I was lost in the rhythm of my own feet. Confident I was heading the same direction I came from, I didn't bother looking at the compass. The setting sun was guiding enough. I sang out loud, no one but the critters and trees to hear me.

And that was when I tripped over a cactus.

I could feel the spines sticking into the flesh of my shins. I caught myself with my hands, but not soon enough. My chin bounced on the rocky ground. The pain shooting through my head was immediate. I reached up and brushed my fingers over it. There was a tiny smudge of blood, but it wasn't gushing.

My earphones had fallen off with the jarring impact, David Bowie's voice sounding far-off and tinny. But the sound that really captured my attention was the loud buzzing of flies. The second thing to hit me was the smell.

Once, when I was a kid, my foster mom was driving past a sewage plant. We had the windows down. She ordered me to roll mine up quickly, but it was too late. The wretched smell had invaded our car. Up until that moment, that smell had stood out in my memory as the worst smell on the planet.

This smell had that one beat, hands down.

It was like shit and piss and something else that was metallic, mixed with a sort of sickly sweet. I breathed out quickly and looked up. In front of me was blue fabric—a shirtsleeve, stained with rusty brown splotches. Dread swamped my gut. I shoved up to my feet, forgetting the pain of the cactus spines or the throbbing of my chin. I gasped at the sight before me and immediately regretted it. The horrible putrid smell invaded my nose. I swallowed hard and held my breath through several heaves of my stomach. Then I breathed in through my mouth, trying not to taste the smell on the air.

The body of a man lay there, twisted like a discarded rag doll, eyes just as vacant. Flies swarmed around his body. I was surprised that his face wasn't bloated. I imagined that a dead body smelling like this would've shown more signs of decomposition. Yet his eyes were a clear bottle green, hair a dusky brown with gray patches over his temple. The cause of death: a bullet to his forehead.

But that man had been tortured. His tormentor... and I say tormentor because someone had cut and flayed most of his body. Those wounds looked much older than the one between his eyes. Some had festered and leaked a green, oozing pus, all in varying stages of infection.

I found myself fascinated. I stumbled, the dark thought rocking me to the core. But I was intrigued. Who would be strong enough to take this man down? He wasn't small, easily a foot taller than me. He was well muscled, though, not quite fit.

I don't know what compelled me to do what I did next, but I lifted my camera to my face and pushed the shutter release. The snap of the shutter blades made my muscles tense like it was the sound of a guillotine's blade. Flashes of guilt and intrigue warred within me like I'd just witnessed my first beheading. I took a step closer and clicked again. Again.

I only stopped when the hand wrapped around my mouth, cutting off my ability to scream, and I was pulled against a hard body. It was then that I noticed the shovel and the half-dug hole next to the body. It was so stupid of me not to be more aware of my surroundings when finding a dead body in the woods. I pulled up my feet to kick at him. *Fight.* I was sure this was the killer and I'd just signed my own death warrant.

Curiosity being the cause of my downfall was not surprising in the least. Especially as he dragged me backward through the trees, away from the dead man.

SNAPSHOT

CHAPTER THREE

Safety

"*Silencio*," a voice grated in my ear.

I didn't know Spanish, but I grew up in Texas. It's hard not to know some words. I knew he was telling me to be quiet. He wasn't the first person to make that mistake with me—to assume that I spoke the language of a Mexican based off my olive skin and my proximity to the country of my ancestor's origin.

"*Voy a dejarlo ir ahora. No grites o el asesino te escuche*," he whispered.

And though the meaning of his words were lost on me, the tickle of his breath on my ear and the tingle that followed its path rushed through me. The weight of his arm and the feel of his hard body pressed against my back calmed me a bit. It was like nothing I'd ever felt before, and the sensation stunned me.

His muscles relaxed. "*No voy a lastimarte. Estoy dejando ir ahora.*"

I shook my head, not sure if I was trying to tell him I still didn't understand him, or if I was trying to dislodge his hand. Both urges were forefront in my thoughts. The other urge that reigned was to hurt this fucker for having his hands on me in the first place. He was definitely going to kill me, but I wasn't going down without a fight. I'd been fighting my whole life to survive.

He released me and stepped back. I didn't scream. There wasn't anyone to hear if I did, and it would be a waste of precious time. I barely registered the widening blue eyes because in a blink I spun, throwing my weight into it when I flung my giant purse at his head. It hit him with a heavy thud, and he stumbled back, trying to regain his balance. I stopped thinking and turned on my heel, running. His heavy footfalls chased me.

His arm came around me again like a vise. He pulled me back and halted our forward momentum. I grunted, and his hand was back over my mouth again. He grunted as my elbow flew back into his gut.

"You do not speak Spanish, do you?" he asked in a murmur.

My eyes bulged at his stilted European accent. It was obvious in the way his voice rolled over the *P* sounds almost like it had its own syllable, but the rest of his words came out in a staccato rhythm. It sounded like a cross between the Russian and German accents I'd heard in movies before.

I shook my head as much as I could in his grip.

His lips grazed my ear as he spoke quietly. "You do speak English?"

I whimpered as fear flooded my system, but gave a nod.

His arms tightened before they relaxed a bit. "I will not hurt you, but you need to keep quiet. There is a man out here. The one who killed that man. Can you be quiet before you get us both killed?"

I hesitated because I didn't believe him, but gave a nod anyway.

He spoke in hushed tones. "I think he heard you sing, but did not know where you came from because your voice echoes through the trees. He went that way."

He used the hand from my mouth to point. Using the distraction, I bucked hard and fell away from his grip. I stumbled and turned to face him. His sandy-brown hair was cropped close to his head, not the usual mullet or short waves or long stringy hair that I was used to seeing on most guys. And his eyes. His eyes were a clear blue, like sea glass. He wasn't much taller than me, only a few inches, but I could see the hint of defined muscles underneath his clothes.

The corner of his mouth tipped slightly like I'd spoken my assessment out loud. I frowned at him, but I didn't run. There was no use; he'd only catch me again. And he didn't seem interested in killing me at the moment, so I waited.

"I will not hurt you. You come with me? I will show you."

He walked past me, motioning with his hand to follow him. I stood still. My mind warred with the intelligence of following a possible killer through the woods. He realized I hadn't moved and turned back to face me. Our eyes locked across the distance. I could hear the whirring of my Walkman as it still played, but as I looked down at it, I realized that I'd lost the earphones in the struggle.

I sighed as I hit the Stop button and unclipped it from my pocket, stuffing it into my purse. When I looked up, he was gone. Fear raced through my veins like wildfire. My heart kicked into overdrive as I spun in a circle. Expecting an attack, I brought my hands up in front of me. But when I didn't see or hear him, I lowered them. I didn't call after him. That would just be stupid. If he was the killer and he left me, then good riddance. If he wasn't and a killer was out there as he'd suggested, calling him over would be even worse.

The sun had set, but still lit the sky in shades of pink, orange, and purple. I could still see, for now, but I couldn't follow it back to the car. Plus, I didn't know how far offtrack I was after that encounter. I ran in the first direction my feet would take me, without thought. I pulled my compass out and moved quickly in the direction the car should be. Even if I was offtrack, I should be able to find the road. And I should be able to see my car.

Should. Fuck this shit.

This day had started out amazing; now I was traipsing around with a killer and a crazy man. And perhaps they were one and the same.

As soon as the road came into view, I pocketed the compass. Just as I was about to breach the tree line, a hand landed on my arm. I gave a startled yelp, and the other hand clapped over my mouth. Then his face was in front of me, striking blue eyes imploring me. Releasing my arm, he raised a single finger to his lips. *Quiet*, his eyes said.

He grabbed my hand and started leading me down the road, just inside the trees. He stepped carefully, making no noise, so I tried to do the same. I still didn't believe his story, but what harm could come from going along that would be cured by running? He'd catch me; I knew that well enough.

We walked about fifty feet before he turned to me and pointed at his eyes with two fingers and then pointed toward the road with the same fingers. I followed the direction of his gaze, and my heart stopped. There was a man walking around my car. He wore a green camouflage sweatshirt and jeans, with a baseball cap pulled low over his brow. Despite the cap, I could see that he was bald underneath, and what I could see of his face were hard frown lines burrowed deep in his skin.

A cold shiver ran down my spine. He was right. There was another person out here. But I wasn't stupid enough to believe that one was the killer and the other was not. They could be working together. Though I didn't know what this man's motivations were for helping me.

The man next to me released my hand and made hand motions, indicating he and I should walk the way we'd come, down the road away from my car. Under raised brows, his eyes begged for me to follow.

Shit. I couldn't make my mind up. I bit my lip as my brows furrowed, and I wrung my hands. I ran the scenarios through my mind, and in every one, I came up dead. But maybe I could give him a chance. If he was telling the truth, then it was my only way out.

Reluctantly, I nodded. He grabbed my hand, and we were moving again, at a much quicker pace. Hearing the door to my car slam shut behind us had us full-on running.

It's a horrifying thing to put your life in the hands of a stranger. I don't know how long we ran, but as we approached a clearing where a small farmhouse sat, the sky was an inky purple bruise.

"We should go inside in case he followed us," he said.

I halted, the sound of his voice snapping me out of the blind panic that had fueled my run. I was breathing hard and gasping for air. I was not in any shape to run anywhere, much less run through the wood at dusk from certain death. Or toward it.

A sharp pain in my shin made me hiss, and I suddenly remembered the cactus. I bent down giving myself a moment to think this through, looking at my leg which much resembled Pinhead from the *Hellraiser* movie. My hands hovered over it as I sucked in a breath, trying to decide which to pull first. I wasn't one of those bimbos in the horror movies that stupidly trusted the stranger and walked into his house without thought.

Gentle, long, lean fingers wrapped around my wrist, stopping me. "I have a first aid kit in the house. Let me take care of you."

His voice did strange things to my stomach, causing it to somersault inside my body. My lips parted, and I nodded. He pulled me to standing by the wrist he held and we started walking toward the house. Well, I was more or less limping, now that the adrenaline and shock had worn off. But whether I was headed toward safety or certain torturous doom… I would find out soon enough.

SNAPSHOT

CHAPTER FOUR

First Aid

The house was an old, dingy gray farm house, with a covered front porch and two stories to claim. It was small but still larger than my trailer. It sat in a clearing, flanked by a large red barn and a small shed-type building that sort of looked like it served as a garage. To my right, there was a fenced-in area that seemed to be a chicken coop with a small yard that was bare of grass or weeds, though it was quiet as night descended. But only a dirt drive broke the tree-line barrier that surrounded it from the outside world.

When we stepped onto the front porch, he walked right in, stopping only to brush off his cowboy boots on the wiry porch mat. No locks, no key. No shouts of "Honey, I'm home." He definitely lived alone, or knew that whoever else lived there wouldn't be around to call on.

I froze in the doorway. My knees locked up, and I watched from the porch as he walked to the kitchen to pull a wooden box from under the sink.

He opened the box, pulling out bandages and other first aid implements. Only once he had everything he needed did he look up to find me standing in the doorway. His clear blue eyes locked on me, and his eyebrows raised in question.

I couldn't bring myself to do it. To voluntarily walk in and trust a stranger was beyond my skill set. The more I thought about it, the more the fear of him and his house grew to match the killer behind me and the dead body in the woods.

"I don't know your name," I mumbled as an excuse, looking away.

My eyes took in the rest of the space. It was quaint and comfortable-looking. The little living room area had a brown tweed couch and a blue recliner, with a crochet blanket and a quilt draped over the back of each. The walls were natural wood clapboard, except for the kitchen, which had wallpaper with what looked like tiny ducks in flight. There was brown shag carpeting throughout, except where it gave way to the linoleum in the kitchen. A short hall led off the corner of the back wall of the living room, probably to the stairs that led to the second floor. It didn't look like the home of a psychotic man-torturer. Though I hadn't been in many of those, so I wouldn't really know.

I sucked in a breath, startled when my gaze tracked back to his direction, and I found him directly in front of me. He moved in silence, which sort of freaked me out.

"Xander... Novak," he said, holding out his hand to shake.

I eyed his hand warily, but eventually took it, answering, "Rosie Dominguez."

"Rosie." The way my name rolled off his tongue with that accent sent a chill down my spine.

If he never opened his mouth, I would've assumed him to be a simple cowboy. The Wrangler jeans and dusty boots, the flannel shirt and sweat-stained collar of his tee all fed into the illusion, but the accent was off. Hot European guys didn't usually move out to the bum-fucked middle of nowhere, Texas, to play cowboy.

"You want to come inside so I can get the needles out of your leg?" He struggled over the *W* in want, and it came out as a soft *V*, more like *vant*. But not in a Dracula way. It was definitely a German sound. *A German cowboy?*

"Huh?" I jumped a little and met his gaze.

His eyes held a hint of laughter, though he remained stone-faced. I was ogling him without forethought. My embarrassment had me stepping over the threshold while there was still that voice in the back of my head screaming at me that I shouldn't. He shut the door behind me and locked it. The sound of the deadbolt sliding into place made my shoulders relax a smidge, until he brushed past me, grazing my shoulder. My stomach gave a little flip at that.

I hardened my resolve and followed him back to the kitchen.

"Hop up," he said, patting his hand on the counter next to his medical supplies. Refusing to put my purse down, I struggled for a moment before Xander stepped in. "May I?" He motioned to my waist and waited.

My lips flattened out to a thin line as I pressed them between my teeth. I nodded.

His hands circled my waist, and he lifted me up like I weighed nothing. Whenever he decided to kill me, I was so dead because he didn't bat an eyelash or show any signs of strain at lifting another human, and I was a good buck thirty-eight.

"Turn sideways and rest your legs up here." He gestured to the expanse of counter next to me.

I got stuck on the soft *V* of sideways. *Sidevays.* Then I snapped out of it and did as he asked, tucking my purse in my lap and resting my arms on it like it was a shield.

"I'll do the big ones first, but this will probably hurt. How about…" He opened a cabinet, pulling out a bottle of some kind of dark alcohol. He walked back, turning the label to face me. Jack Daniels. He raised his eyebrows. "You want to steel your nerves?"

I didn't know if it would have any effect on the pain or nerves, but it would probably calm my racing heart. He unscrewed the cap and held it out for me. I pressed the bottle to my lips and tipped it back. The liquid burned down my throat, warming my belly. After the second drink, I could feel a numbness spread over me. I was a such lightweight. I handed the bottle back to him, and he bent over my leg.

His warm palm cupped my knee, pressing it gently against the counter so I wouldn't jerk. He worked quickly, pulling them out with deft precision. Either his whiskey helped, or he had some skills. I barely felt the pull, and it was more relief to get them out than leaving them in. When he got down to the tiny microscopic hairlike spines, I could feel his breath roll over the skin of my leg. Goose bumps rose, causing those to hurt more. I sucked in an audible breath.

"What were you doing out there?" I asked, to distract myself from his work.

He kept his concentration and focus on my leg as he continued to work. "I walk the property every day. Not much else to do. Chicken husbandry and car repair can only hold your interest for so long."

"That's all you do every day? Where do you work?"

"I do not work. I am retired."

My mouth formed an O as my brows rose. I looked around.

"You don't have a TV?"

"I do in the bedroom," he answered. "But I've watched all my tapes more than I care to admit."

A slight blush colored his cheeks, but it was gone just as quick. I blinked several times, thinking I imagined it.

"There. All done," he announced.

I looked down at the rectangle of gauze taped onto both shins. He did a nice job, almost like he was a pro at this. I relaxed a little. A killer wouldn't patch you up before killing you, right? It was then that I noticed the phone hanging from his kitchen wall next to a door I assumed was a pantry.

"We should call the sheriff," I say.

"Sorry. We cannot do that. The phone line does not work. It has been down for a week now. I am waiting on the phone company to send someone out to fix it. It is hard to get anyone out this far."

I studied his face, looking for a hint of a lie, but found none. "I imagine so."

I was tempted to jump down and grab it to see for myself, but that would be rude—if he wasn't a killer.

"You have a car, then. Could you give me a ride?"

His brow furrowed, and he shook his head. "My truck is not working."

"You're stuck out here? Alone?"

"Normally, I do not mind it so much. It is what I moved here for. To be alone."

I thought back to Joanne and Billy—what brought me out here in the first place. It was quiet. Peaceful. We weren't so different, were we?

"I am sorry. I can help you get back to your car in the morning. You are welcome to stay in my guest room. There is a lock, from the inside, if you do not feel comfortable with me. You will be safe there."

Fear twisted my guts, but I nodded out of habit. What other choice did I have? This man was being nothing but kind. And my only other option was to set out on my own, in the dark, with a prayer that the other possible killer wasn't still at my car. I'd a feeling this was going to be the longest night of my life.

SNAPSHOT

24

CHAPTER FIVE

Fear

My eyes were glued to the window as he disappeared into the back hallway of his house. The window faced the front porch where the porch light lit the weed-pocked dirt patch that was his front yard. My eyes unfocused as I tried to keep an eye out for any movement. I could hear the thumps of his footfalls as he walked, as if he was trying to make his every move known. It was slightly more comforting than when he was moving quietly.

He rounded the corner into the living room, and I turned away from the window. He held out a stack of clothing with a toothbrush and toothpaste on top, still in the packaging.

"If you want to use any of it," he said as I took the proffered items, "you can. If not, just leave it in the guest room. I'll show you where it is."

He motioned to me to follow him. His footsteps were quieter as we turned the hall. There were two doors, and when he opened one, it revealed a steep and narrow set of stairs. I assumed the other door was his room where he retrieved the items from. The fact that we would be separated by some distance eased my mind a little.

At the top of the stairs, he flipped a switch. The light flickered, revealing a short hall to the left, leading to two doors, and a small bathroom to the right. He walked down the hall, then opened the door to a nice-sized room. A window unit air conditioner sat low in one of the windows. The air up there was stale and musty, like it had been years since someone had used them. He walked over to the air conditioner and turned it on. It hummed to life, sputtering a few times.

"Sorry, I do not get many visitors."

I took in the room. It was sparsely furnished with a queen-sized four-poster bed against one wall, a rocking chair near the window without the AC unit, and a small nightstand. All the furniture looked antique. The bed was covered with a quilt that looked handmade. It wasn't a typical bachelor pad, for sure, but it wasn't decorated either. It looked like a functional room in a farmhouse.

I forced a smile. "Thank you."

"Bathroom is down the hall. Did you see it?"

"I did."

"I will leave you to it, then," he said, backing out of the room. "I will be down the stairs, if you need anything."

I blinked, and he shut the door between us. I listened to his footfalls retreat down the wooden steps, and I rushed over and locked the door. I didn't think I'd be able to sleep there, but the room offered some relative illusion of safety. My shoulders relaxed for the first time in hours. They ached from my constant state of alert. I walked over to the window in front of the rocking chair. It overlooked his front yard.

I watched the yard for movement, but there was none. I sat in the chair. It was quiet in the house, but all the quiet did was expand the other sounds. A creak had me snapping my neck to search the room, my gaze running over every shadow until I was satisfied I was still alone. It was just the old house. Each splutter of the air conditioner as it kicked on and off, ratcheted my nerves higher. Every dip of a branch in the wind had me scanning the shadows outside. Looking for an arm, a leg, a face. Eyes watching me back. Waiting for the killer to make his move. To come after me, if not us.

Everything had me on alert. I was on the edge of tears. It was too much.

Yet, the tears would be a relief because my eyes refused to blink. They felt dry and sticky. My head pounded. Distant laughter. Male laughter. The killer laughing at the silly girl glued to a window like it would save her. It was all in my head.

I was sure Xander had gone to sleep. No one could be that quiet for that long.

Unless he was as scared as me, jumping at every sound like a skittish animal. But somehow, I doubted he was. He seemed as cool as a cucumber, which was the most sketchy thing about him. I contemplated leaving. Sneaking past his room, slipping out the front door. But in my mind, the second I was out there, so was the killer. The walls between us felt safer. I wrapped my arms around myself, leaning forward to see more of the area outside.

It was still dark out, and the clear sky was littered with more stars than you could count. A pale moon hung low in the crowded sky. The man in the moon's face seemed more sinister than ever before, or perhaps that was my imagination.

I was startled by a loud bang. I jumped from the rocking chair and it rocked back so far I thought it would clatter to the floor. It only rocked back into place, shuffling across the floor with a loud *rhump-rhump*. Stilling it, I looked out the window and saw something near the chicken coop. A shadow. My heart thundered loudly, echoing in my ears. There was someone out there.

A light tap at the door broke the silence of the room. Glancing around for a weapon, the only thing I could find of use was an old ewer on the nightstand. I plucked it up and tiptoed to the door, trying to move as silently as possible. Very carefully, I twisted the lock on the old doorknob that looked like the large end to an old skeleton key. Then I waited, determined to get the drop on whoever tried to enter.

The door parted from the frame silently, not even a creak. Then his head poked in, turned away, looking toward the bed. It was so dark, with only the faint light from the porch leaking into the room,

I couldn't tell who it was. With the ewer held high, I brought it down with all the strength I could muster. He reacted faster than my eyes could track, catching the ewer in his hand and stopping my assault. I backed away.

Fear rushed through me. There was no way I could survive. I could only beg for mercy. Would he even have it? Time slowed until my heartbeat sounded like a slow *whhhhhhuuuuuummmmppppp-whh-hhhhhuuuuuummmppppp* in my ears. His posture straightened, and he reached out to lay a gentle hand on my shoulder. I whimpered.

"Are you okay?" His voice sounded strange and garbled, like I was underwater listening to his muffled soundwaves reach through the thick barrier. "I didn't mean to scare you."

Slowly his voice became more clear, like I was finally breaching the surface. I blinked. His accent was almost nonexistent. I blinked again.

"I just wanted to be sure you were okay before I check outside. Lock the door behind me." And the accent was back.

My eyes tracked him as he went, my brain still seeming to operate like it was stuck in tar. I didn't move otherwise. When I heard him hit the bottom of the stairs, I snapped out of it. I took the two steps to the window in one large step and watched for him. He came out seconds later, with a shotgun ready at his shoulder, swinging it around like Chuck Norris in *Delta Force*.

When he turned the corner near the chicken coop, his arm moved faster than I could track, but my ears caught the faint *snick* as he cocked the gun. My hand flew up over my mouth. I wasn't particularly religious, but in that moment, I prayed. I prayed that if the killer was over there, Xander would take him out. Even though I didn't entirely trust him, it was better the devil I knew than the one I didn't.

I held my breath when he disappeared out of sight. Tears welled in my eyes from lack of oxygen. A startled shriek escaped me when the gun went off. Time stretched out into an eternity as I waited for anything to happen next. When he finally came back around the corner, I collapsed to the floor. I couldn't hold myself up any longer.

I couldn't see anymore, but I heard him enter and lock the front door and take the stairs in less steps than should be possible. Then the knock. I jumped up and flung open the door as fast as my shaking hands would let me. When it was no longer between us, I flung myself at him, crashing into him so hard, he stumbled back a step before finding solid footing. My arms wrapped around his waist. Relief felt thick in my veins.

His smell invaded my senses. Cedar trees and fresh air, with hints of something metallic. *Gunpowder.* I sucked in a breath, and a sob came crashing out of me. I felt out of control. I was clinging to a stranger and crying into his shirt hysterically.

His arms wrapped around me. One around my waist, while the other curled up my back, his hand cradling the back of my head.

"Shh, shh," he cooed into my ear, leaning his cheek against the top of my head. "I didn't see anything. I only fired a warning shot in case the coyotes were after the chickens."

I relaxed into him, finding his comfort soothing. More soothing than one ought to find a stranger. When my breathing slowed, I pulled my head back. His shirt was soaked with tears and snot. *Good God. I'm a wreck.* I sniffed, but found I couldn't breathe from my nose.

"Have you gotten any sleep?" he asked.

I shook my head.

"Okay."

We stood there for a moment, still wrapped in each other, neither of us willing to move. There was no discernible emotion behind his eyes, but he appeared to be thinking, processing. Then suddenly he moved.

He swept me up and walked into the guest room, depositing me on the edge of the bed. Then he turned and left the room, only returning moments later with a wad of toilet paper, which he held out for me. I took it from him and blew my nose. Such a simple gesture, but it shook me to my core. I set it on the nightstand once done, and he nodded to the bed.

You should lie down, his look said.

When I did, he pulled the quilt up over me. I turned onto my side to face him.

"I will sit in that chair and keep an eye out, if you will go to sleep. I won't let anything happen to you." His eyes pleaded with me to trust him. "Can you? Please."

I watched him for a second, trying to make my mind up. I think in any other circumstance, I wouldn't have let myself trust him. But I was exhausted, scared, and out of options. And it looked like we were in this together, for better or worse.

I nodded, and his shoulders relaxed. An audible breath left him like he'd been holding it, waiting for my answer. He retreated to the rocking chair, turning it so it angled into the room, but he could still see out the window. He sat, kicking his legs out in flannel pajama pants. His hand came up and covered the tear stain on his shirt as he turned his head to face the window.

"I will protect you for as long as you are in my life," he mumbled into the darkness of the night, as if he were talking to no one.

I closed my eyes then and let sleep take me.

CHAPTER SIX

Kilometers

When my eyes opened, sunlight filtered through blue-and-gray-checked curtains that had been pulled shut. I didn't know what time of day it was, but Xander was gone, the rocking chair empty. I stretched lazily before the sleep finally cleared and the unease started to set in. I sat up slowly, surveying the rest of the room.

It had to be late in the day, but I couldn't believe I had slept that long. I felt better, having rested, but as my memory of yesterday caught up with me, I felt less and less sure of that assessment.

I threw the quilt back and slid out of the bed, deciding to use his donated toothbrush to freshen up. I grabbed my purse and went into the bathroom at the end of the hall.

It was quiet, except for the *plink, plink* of a leaky faucet. I looked around and realized that the tub faucet was dripping. Rust stains colored the iron tub where the water hit and trailed to the drain. I jiggled the handle and it stopped. I found myself lost for a moment, just staring at the faucet head, waiting for the next drop to fall. It didn't, but in that moment, I saw it. The cliff—the sunrise spot—the warmth of the sun, then the horrible smell, the frozen waxy face, the panic, the running, the fear... It all came crashing back into me. It raced through my veins and stole my breath. I didn't know I'd moved when my back hit the wall, and I slid down it, wrapping my arms around my knees.

I wasn't sure how long I sat there, but slowly familiar sounds that I'd only heard when visiting an auto shop pulled me from the trance. I blinked. *Was that a compression wrench?* I dated a mechanic once. Jeff. *I think that was what he called it.* It was short-lived, as with all my relationships.

That thought pulled me starkly from my reverie, and I quickly finished what I'd come in there for. I moved down the stairs. The silence of the house was punctuated by sounds drifting in from outside. Music. He was listening to music while working on his car. I walked into the kitchen. A foil-covered plate sat in the center of the counter with a one-word note: *Eat.*

I pulled back the foil to find a scrambled egg sandwich on toast. My stomach gave a growl at the smell. I hadn't eaten anything since my PB&J on the cliff. I plucked the sandwich off the plate and took the first bite. It was delicious. The eggs were buttery and fluffy. It sated the hunger pangs quickly. I was down to one bite when I saw something out of the corner of my eye. The phone.

Taking the last bite, I walked over to it. My heart pounded in my ears as I reached out and touched the cool plastic of the Trimline phone. My hand hesitated before I pulled it from the base and brought it to my ear. Silence. No dial tone, nothing. He wasn't lying. It didn't work. I checked the cords, but it was plugged into the wall correctly. It just wasn't in service.

I placed it back on the base and turned back to the room. That's when I heard him singing. I followed the sound of his voice, which wasn't bad. He was actually quite good, though his accent got in the way of reproducing the heavy twang of the country song he was singing along to. I found him out in the garage. His feet stuck out from under the truck.

"You don't have to call me darlin'..." he sang.

I watched his feet jerk with the movement of his hands and listened to his voice. The music was coming from a record player that sat on a row of cabinets against the wall. There was something so domestic and innocent about the whole scene. It brought a smile to my face, despite everything.

When the song got to the part about the mom and the train, I giggled. Even if it struck a nerve within me, he was singing it with such seriousness, plus the mixture of his accent and the silly words forced it to bubble out of me. He rolled fluidly out from under the old truck he was working on with wide eyes.

His cheeks pinked, and a shy smile played at his lips. "Sorry, I didn't know you were up."

"It's okay. You're a good singer." I smiled and looked away to the chicken coop.

The rooster was strutting around the small yard while the hens pecked at the dirt. Xander stood up, and though I wasn't looking, I could feel his closeness like an energy radiating between us.

"You want to go to your car?"

I nodded.

"Let me go clean up, and I will take you back there."

He was covered in grease, up to the rolled-up sleeves of his flannel shirt. He looked better, almost happy, in the full sun, though there were dark smudges underneath his eyes, belying his lack of sleep. Guilt welled up in me. There was a black smudge on his skin near his collar that made me consider wiping it off, but I turned away, nodding again. He went back into the house, the screen door slapping against its frame as he entered.

I watched the chickens wander in the yard for a moment longer before my gaze drifted, taking in the space. Near the record player, there was an old milk crate on the floor, filled with albums. I wandered over to it. Flipping through it, I found the same that you would find at most people's houses around here. Merle Haggard, Hank Williams, Willie Nelson, Johnny Cash, George Jones... I pulled out a Tammy Wynette album and flipped it over. I remember my mama singing a song by her, often. I read the song list on the back. Sure enough, it was there.

I walked over to the record player. It had turned itself off, so I set the record over the one that was already on the spindle and pulled the arm over. I listened to her lament about how hard it was to be a woman. How you should stand by your man, no matter what. A cold shiver ran down my spine. Thinking about my mama, I cringed. Such a horrible sentiment. Exactly why I vowed long ago that I never wanted a relationship. I wouldn't be one of those women that idly complained when my husband screwed up or screwed around.

The song ended.

"You ready to go?" he asked.

His voice startled me in the quiet lull after the music ended. I spun around to find him leaning against the frame of the garage door, watching me. A smirk played at the corner of his full lips. The way the sunlight hit his back while his face stayed in the shadows of the garage gave him an ethereal look. *Though even Lucifer was an angel.*

I snapped out of my thoughts. "Yeah, sure."

"We can take the road. Your car is about two kilometers down."

I tilted my head, not sure how long kilometers were, but eventually brushed it off and walked past him. We walked up the dirt drive, for what felt like forever, until we reached the road and took a right. The walk down the road was equally as long before he stopped. His brow furrowed.

"This should be it." He pointed to the ground.

There were two trails in the gravel shoulder of the two-lane road, but they weren't tire tracks. There was no tread pattern. They were just two curved smudges in the dirt. I looked up and down the road, but it all looked the same. There was no landmark to say this was the right place. Then something white fluttered in the ditch, catching the sunlight. I walked over and picked it up. It was a hardcover copy of *Midnight* by Dean Koontz. *My* copy of *Midnight*. Which meant he was right—this was where my car had been. I'd left this book on the driver's seat. And someone tossed it into the ditch before they took my car. Not someone—the killer.

I clutched the book to my chest and looked around. There were no other people nearby or any signs of civilization. We were well and truly in the middle of nowhere. *Shit.*

36

CHAPTER SEVEN

Fixed

It wasn't really hot out that day, being that it was November in Texas. But the stress of walking in the full midday sun still caused sweat to bead up on my skin. I pressed my sunglasses farther up my sweaty nose with a finger and looked up to the sky. Buzzards circled in the air overhead. Not likely for our benefit, but I already knew what was calling to them like a siren. In my mind, I imagined that the killer was busy carting off my car to God-knows-where and making plans to return tonight to finish his disposal of the body and to dispose of me—us. But somewhere out there, that body was rotting away under the shade of the trees. Likely pulled apart by coyotes and mountain lions.

The thoughts had my step quickening, and soon I was leaving Xander behind. He didn't talk much, and I think that was what I liked most about him. When he said something, it was something that needed to be said. He didn't waste time on idle chatter.

When we got back to his house, I walked right in and sat at his kitchen table, tossing my purse on the ground. He paused at the door before following me in. Maybe it was presumptuous of me to think he'd welcome me back into his home for a second night, but I was frustrated and scared. I just wanted to be home more than anything right now. Even if Billy and Joanne were going at it again, it would be more comforting than being stuck out here, waiting for death to come for us.

He sat in the chair at the end of the table and kicked out the chair next to me to prop his feet in. He leaned back, pinning me with a stare. I looked away, uncomfortable with his scrutiny.

"I can't tell you when I will have the truck repaired. I do not know." He scrubbed his hands over his face. "I will give you a ride to your home as soon as I can. You are welcome to stay here. Make yourself a home."

I snorted. "It's make yourself *at* home." I smiled to take the sting out of the correction, but it was cute. "Thank you."

"Of course," he replied. "Make yourself at home."

We sat there in silence. I didn't think either of us knew what else to say.

"I should get to the truck. But please, use whatever you need."

"I will," I said with a nod.

He got up and left, the screen door clapping loudly to mark his exit. I looked around the room, trying to figure out what I'd do with myself. The funny thing was that I could go days on this earth without talking to people, without watching the news or caring how the rest of the world fared. But being this far removed from everything, and with all that had happened, I was restless for contact. No phone, but he did have a TV. The problem was—it was in his room.

That would be awkward. I'm sure he didn't mean *make yourself at home and go watch TV in my room.* What were the odds that he had cable or even an antenna? I tried to force my mind to something else, but it kept bothering me. I needed some connection to the outside world. Just to make sure it hadn't ended. Fire and brimstone could be raining down everywhere else and we'd never know. I couldn't take it anymore.

I jumped from the chair and walked toward the hall, looking back over my shoulder to make sure he was busy outside. I couldn't see him, though; I assumed he was. I peeked around the corner, and there was an antenna—rabbit ears—sitting on top of the small TV set.

His bedroom had a king-sized bed with a slatted headboard and footboard that looked handmade from rough cuts of cedarwood. The cedar smell lingered in the air. It smelled like him. A mismatched wood chest of drawers sat in the corner opposite the lone nightstand. The TV filled a low table opposite the bed. It was neat and tidy. The bed was made, the corners of the quilt tucked in neatly. Two doors flanked one wall, leading to what I assumed was a bathroom and a closet, but I didn't look. I turned my attention back to the TV.

I turned the knob, squatting down in front of it. White noise and static filled the screen. I turned the station dial to a local channel number. Dropping to my knees, I reached for the antenna, wiggling each metal stick side to side, trying to catch a signal. Faint faces faded in and out, but nothing solidified.

It seemed to work better if I moved it closer to the wall. I nudged forward, leaning over the TV. Suddenly, loud, breathy moans filled the air. I leaned back. On the screen, a dick penetrated a pussy. *Whoa.* It was so loud; I must've turned it up, trying to turn it on. I grabbed the volume-power knob and quickly quieted the noise. Porn. *Why is there porn on a local channel?*

With the volume down, I could hear a whirring noise. Its source was the VCR on the floor. I must have bumped it with my knee and turned it on. I sat back on my haunches and watched.

Though my ears were tuned into the sounds outside, I watched with utter fascination. It was a fairly typical porn. Well, I assumed it was. I didn't have much experience watching them myself, but the people in it were just having sex. After they panned out of the close-up, there were bouncing breasts and open mouths. The leading lady was blonde, and her pubic hair was neatly trimmed.

My thoughts turned to my own dark hair and ungroomed area. But if he liked blondes, then I was definitely not his type. My dark skin and Latina heritage ensured that.

My thighs began to ache from clenching, and I felt myself growing wet. I heard the hood of his truck slam down, or maybe it was the door. I really didn't know. I scrambled to rewind the tape back to the close-up shot and turned it off. I turned the whole thing off and jumped up from the floor, hauling ass out of the room.

The light was fading outside, and I knew dinner would need to be made soon. Maybe I could find something to cook? Make myself useful to him somehow. Repay his kindness. I rushed into the kitchen and started looking for ingredients.

It took me a moment to find what I needed, but there was a package that looked like ground beef or sausage in the fridge. Pasta and jars of preserved tomatoes were in the pantry. I could do this. I'd make spaghetti and meatballs. Hopefully, the food prep would take my mind off the porn. And thoughts of him watching the porn. Then maybe he wouldn't notice the look on my face when he came in. He wouldn't know that I knew what was in his VCR. Or had very graphic visual images of what he did while watching it. No, I'd forget while making spaghetti and everything would be totally normal. It only took about twenty minutes to make it, so that was plenty of time.

When I heard the screen door slam shut, my spine straightened. His boots thudded across the linoleum floor, stopping just behind me. I could feel the heat of his body even though he wasn't touching me. He smelled of cedar, fresh air, and motor oil, almost overpowering the food cooking in front of me.

"Smells good," he said in a low tone.

Tingles travels up my spine, leaving a wake of goose bumps behind.

I cleared my throat. "It'll be done in a few minutes. But here, have a taste."

I dipped the wooden spoon into the sauce and held it over my open palm. I turned to offer it to him, but he stopped me with a hand on my wrist before it collided with his chest. My eyes met his. An image of him on the end of his bed, watching the video and stroking himself popped into my mind, unbidden. My face started heating up, and I looked away.

What the hell is wrong with me? Why can't I stop thinking about this?

"Delicious." His voice held a tone that made me think that maybe I wasn't the only one with not-so-innocent thoughts. *Or maybe that's my imagination?* "I will go wash up before it is ready."

I nodded and turned back to the stove.

As he left the room, my legs gave out and I had to catch myself on the counter. It was obvious that the shock was wearing off, and I was attracted to this man I was stuck with for the foreseeable future. And that porn seemed to light a spark in my hormones. This was bad. This was so bad.

SNAPSHOT

CHAPTER EIGHT

Rebuild

I pushed the empty plate away from me after the last bite. The food turned out well, but it feels like a lump of stone in my stomach. I've spent the entire meal avoiding his eyes. I felt guilty for snooping around in his room. I shouldn't know what kind of movies he enjoyed watching. And if I would've read my book or showered or something, things wouldn't be as awkward.

"Have I done something to offend you?" he asked.

"What?" My voice came out shrill and thready. I cringed. I tried to laugh it off, but it only made it worse.

His brows rose in response, but he withheld comment.

He reached across the table and grabbed my empty plate. At the sink, he made a quick job of washing the dishes and placing them in the drying rack. He came back, but he didn't sit in the chair across from me. He pulled out the chair next to me and sat. I leaned back to counter his closeness and met his eyes. They were this crazy shade of indigo blue.

"I have bad news for you." He spoke hesitantly, as if testing the waters of how I'd take it.

I constructed my face into a neutral mask. All the previous awkwardness was shoved aside by the serious look on his face and the reminder that our situation wasn't ideal. There was a killer on the loose, and I doubted he'd let us live. He knew we were here. He took my car. He would return. It wasn't a question of *if*, but *when*. I nodded for him to continue.

"The carburetor on my truck is shot. I will have to dismantle it completely and machine the parts. It might take a few days or weeks. I am sorry. I wasn't expecting any of this to happen. I have no other way to get you back to your home."

I blinked several times to stave off the tears I felt brimming to the surface.

"Do you have friends or family that will look for you? Did you tell anyone you were coming out here? We can place something by the road to get their attention."

I shook my head. "No, I live alone. I didn't tell anyone. Other than my boss and coworkers, no one will miss me. But they'll just think I left town or something. They've got their own lives to worry about."

The tears finally did fall. My life was a sad state of affairs. And I'd gotten myself into a situation where I'd nothing to save me. Nothing but a stranger in the middle of nowhere, who was being way more kind than he had reason to. I pulled my knees up to my chest, resting my heels on the edge of the chair.

I'd never looked at my self-imposed isolation as a bad thing until that moment. The moment when I'd nothing left.

He reached out and wiped the tears from under my eyes.

"I will help you. If you want, we take our chances and hike to the nearest town. It will take a few days to get there, but I will go with you. Or we can stay here. I have enough provisions to get through the winter."

My eyes cut to his sharply. "You'd do that?"

"Yes. I think the chickens will survive without me for a few days." He laughed.

I gave a halfhearted laugh to try and match his. "Give me a moment."

I had to think it through. Staying there meant that the killer would come back, and we would definitely have to face him. But we would have food and shelter. Even though he never brought it upstairs, I knew he had a shotgun. So, our chances were pretty good.

Leaving to walk to the nearest town would ensure that I got home faster, but at what cost. I knew the Texas countryside as well as any local. There were coyotes and mountain lions out there, not to mention the rattlesnakes, copperheads, water moccasins, banana spiders... and a killer who could find us at any moment.

At least here we had some shelter. Some control over how he came after us. We had a better chance at fighting back. Of surviving. I could wait. All that was waiting back home was my need to find a new job. I knew Oscar wouldn't wait long to look for a replacement. I was supposed to be there, working.

"I think we should stay," I said. My voice was quiet and shaky; it didn't hold the conviction of my decision it needed to have. But I wasn't quite sure I was making the best decision, just the best decision based on the information I'd at my disposal. "But I want to help you. Whatever you need done around here, I'll do it. I don't want to just sit around and eat your food and fret about when he might come back for us."

His smile was hesitant at first but grew quickly. All white teeth set in a squared jaw peppered with a five-o'clock shadow. Lips that curved up at the corner in just the right way. I realized that moment was the first time I'd ever seen him smile. Really smile. It was beautiful. He was beautiful. No—beautiful wasn't the right word, but handsome didn't cut it.

I was staring at him again—no, I was gaping at him. I closed my mouth and looked away to hide my embarrassment.

"I have something for you. Tomorrow," he said with a nod, like he just decided something. "But you can take care of the chickens for me. Maybe cook and clean. Dinner was delicious. Much better than the eggs I make myself daily. I never have time to make more."

"I can do that. I don't know the first thing about chickens, but it can't be that hard. Cleaning is in my skill set. Do you need me to do laundry?"

"We are going to get along just fine." He smiled again, rising from the chair. "Tomorrow."

"Tomorrow," I repeated, my brows pinching together because I didn't know why we were saying tomorrow. The sun had only set an hour before. He couldn't possibly be going to bed...

"Good night, Rosie."

My flesh prickled in response to my name from his lips. I watched him as he turned and left the room. The subtle swagger of his hips distracted me.

I called out too quietly. "Good night, Xander."

His door clicked shut. I looked around trying to decide what to do with myself. A shower. I needed a shower. I turned off the lights and tiptoed to the upstairs bedroom. The clothes he'd given me yesterday still sat at the foot of the bed. I scooped up the T-shirt and prayed he at least had soap in there— shampoo and conditioner might be too hopeful. Pulling the shower curtain back, I stared at the tub below. On second thought, a bath was in order. I needed to relax a bit. I turned the water on and toed off my boots while it heated up. When I sank into the steaming bath, I felt a bit better about my decision. Staying was the right thing to do. I just had to hope he could get his truck fixed, sooner rather than later.

CHAPTER NINE

Sleep

I'd been sitting in the rocking chair for hours. I tried to lie in the bed and sleep, but every noise, every shadow, had me springing out of the bed to the window. The woods at night seemed to be alive—the restless wind stirring up trees, the distant yips of coyotes and yowls of mountain lions, the glow of the moon and sway of the trees—none of it giving comfort to sleep. It felt more like a medley designed to mask the movements of the killer. A killer that was coming for me.

Finally, I relented and sat in the rocking chair. Pulling out the Anne Rice book, I attempted to read in the dark. The light wasn't going to work because then I couldn't see outside.

Nothing eased my mind but staring out the window. So I watched over the yard, wondering if I'd ever get a good night's sleep in this house. Something out in the hallway creaked, and I sat still, listening. After several minutes of silence, I leaned back. It was no use. Blinking weary eyes, I came to terms with the fact that I wouldn't get any sleep.

Unless...

Sleep had come easier the night before when Xander stayed in the room with me. It could've been the exhaustion that finally took over, but I was placing bets on him. It was my only hope.

Frustrated, I grabbed the pillow and quilt off the bed and opened the door. Taking slow, measured steps, I cautiously made my way down the wooden stairs. I paused each time a creak threatened to expose my movements. It was a slow journey until I stood outside his door, debating whether to knock or just sneak in and lie on the floor at the foot of the bed.

In the end, sneaking won out. Embarrassment toppled the debate. I wasn't used to needing people. I didn't need anyone—hadn't needed anyone since I was a young child. Admitting defeat and my need of a stranger was harder than I thought it would be. I turned the knob and the door creaked quietly. I froze. I waited, but the only sounds from the room were from the low hum of the air conditioner. Even in sleep, he was the definition of quiet.

I took a deep breath to steel my nerves and shuffled in, silently pushing the door closed behind me. I went to my knees, crawling to the foot of the bed. I spread the quilt out and placed the pillow at one end. Lying down, I covered myself.

The light from a lamp switched on. I stilled, closing my eyes, as if that would hide me from the shame that he knew I was there.

"What are you doing?" his voice asked from somewhere above me.

I cracked one eye open to find him standing near my head. His hair was ruffled and his eyes half-mast, like sleep still rode him. He was shirtless, with only low-slung flannel pants that seemed to cling to the bulging outline of his cock. My pussy pulsed. I'd never responded that strongly to a man before. It scared me, but it didn't overpower my need to not be alone. It didn't abate the need for sleep.

"I couldn't sleep." I sat up on my knees, the blanket falling to the floor behind me. Something shifted in his eyes. "I did last night when you were in the room, so I thought I'd just sneak in and sleep here on the floor. I didn't mean to bother you. I'll leave. I'm sorry." I looked down at my hands resting in my lap, twisting my fingers together.

"Get in the bed," he said, causing my brown eyes to meet his dark blue ones. "I will sleep on the floor."

"No," I answered. His eyes shifted again, not physically, but something within them. Indiscernible thoughts. "I'm not gonna run you out of your own bed."

I gathered up the blanket and pillow in my arms and stood. He moved as if to grab me, but his hand stopped in midair, and my eyes stuck on it. Neither of us moved for a moment.

"Please, take the bed." His voice was a plea, but there was something else that rode the edge of his tone.

I shook my head. We were at an impasse.

"Then share my bed. It is big enough for the two of us."

My eyes snapped back to his face, tracing the furrow in his brow and questioning his intent. The rhythm of my heart kicked up. I looked to the bed. It was mostly untouched. Still neat and tidy, except for the small area near the lamp and nightstand that was rumpled. The king-size bed was huge. A vast sea of blanket and mattress would separate us. The blanket tumbled out of my hands as I nodded. He laid it over the footboard and watched me as I moved to the other side of the bed, still clutching the pillow. It was only when I bent to pull back the blankets and felt the cool air of the air conditioner kiss the back of my thighs that I remembered I was only wearing the plain white tee he gave me—his shirt.

I moved hastily to dive under the covers and hide myself. *What was I thinking?* I wasn't—I was just scared and exhausted, the fear carrying my numb mind to drastically invade his privacy. He shut off the lamp and climbed under the covers on his side. The blanket of darkness between us felt like a blessing, and my body relaxed, as did my mind. My jaw cracked on a yawn, and I snuggled farther under the covers. I still clung to the pillow that separated us.

"Thank you," I whispered into the dark abyss. "Good night, Xander."

"Good night, Rosie."

Butterflies tiptoed around my stomach as he said my name. He shifted to better find sleep, and I let my eyes drift close, giving myself over to dreamless rest.

CHAPTER TEN

Tease

I blinked my eyes open to find the early-morning light had colored the room in shades of brown and orange from the diamond-print curtains that covered the window. As the fog of sleep cleared my mind, I realized I was warm yet uncovered from the waist up. Correction, I was snuggled into something—somebody warm. My spine stiffened.

Xander and I were in the middle of the bed. Like two magnets, we were drawn to each other in our unconscious states. He was on his back, his arm stretched underneath me, curved around my waist where his hot palm sat at the top of my ass. My ass that was only covered in cotton bikini panties. Half of my body was on top of him, and his opposite leg pinned the leg I'd slung over him. I was trapped.

I knew the second I tried to move that I'd wake him. There was no way to get out of this without being embarrassed. Especially when his dick was hard, pushing against my hip through his flannel pants. I knew it was normal for guys to wake up that way, but his thigh pressed up between my legs addled my brain and gave credence to thoughts better left alone. My heart beat a steady tattoo as I fought the urge to move my hips—to utilize the pressure and relieve the feelings he was stirring in me. I could feel my heartbeat in the throb between my legs. It echoed in my head like a warning siren, screaming at me to move—away or against, I didn't know.

I just sucked it up and went for it. Feigning a stretch as I woke, I arched into him, using his thigh to relieve the pressure. I was going to hell for this. I bit back the moan that tried to escape. His hand resting on my ass flexed and followed my movements. My body froze when his other hand came down, sliding up my rib cage. His hand stopped just as his thumb traced the curve under my breast.

Tingles raced through my veins, sending a shiver throughout my body.

"You are enough to test the will of a saint by standing across the room." His voice was deep and gruff. "If you don't want to break my will, you should stop."

My mind warred with itself. *Move. Don't move. Move away. What to do.* In the end, it was too much. The level of need I felt for his presence at night coupled with a need for his body. I gave in to one; I couldn't give in to the other. I slowly began to pull away.

In a blink, I was on my back and he was between my legs, hovering over me but not touching me. His cornflower-blue eyes searched mine. My chest heaved as I struggled breathlessly for air. He opened his mouth to say something, then closed it. Closing his eyes, he shuddered and when he opened them, he spoke.

"We should see to the chickens first."

Then he was gone, the door to his bathroom shutting behind him before my eyes could catch up. I grabbed the pillow and the quilt, rushing upstairs before he could read the embarrassment on my face.

CHAPTER ELEVEN

Chickens

I'd been a country girl since the day I was born, having lived in seventeen small Texas towns in my twenty-three years of life. But I'd always been poor. So, while I've known many people with chickens and farms, never had I been near one. And that's what was going through my head as Xander opened the gate to the chicken pen, motioning me to go ahead of him.

I stepped inside the empty area and suddenly felt nervous at the idea that I had to care for something living. Xander handed me the bucket of chicken scratch. At least that's what he called it. It was a mixture of corn and seeds and tiny brown nugget-looking things.

"You need to open up the coop and let them out, first thing," Xander said.

He walked over to the coop and pulled a pin that locked down the little door. As soon as he did, the rooster was there, waiting to strut out and down the ramp to the yard. He was followed by the hens. The hens were pretty, with black coats of feathers covered in white speckles. They started walking around me, pecking at the ground like they expected the food to be there already. It spurred me into action, and I reached into the bucket, tossing a handful of scratch on the ground.

One hen ignored the food on the ground and looked up at me expectantly. My brows furrowed. I bent at the knees to reach down and touch her.

"That is Laney. I named her for my sister."

My eyes found blue ones, watching me. Two questions struggled to come out of my mouth at once. I settled on one. The easier one.

"You name your chickens?" I laughed.

I found it hard to believe that he could tell them apart. They were all mottled in black-and-white feathers. There wasn't anything that I could see that distinguished one from another. He smiled with a nod. That beautiful smile where white teeth gleamed at me. His front two teeth were a little crooked, an imperfection in an otherwise perfect face. It made him seem more human.

"Yes, she is Laney because she is fearless and curious, and seeks out love more than the others. She reminds me of my sister."

There was such love and pride in his eyes as he spoke. A small part of me was jealous. No one would ever look like that when they spoke about me. One of the many downsides of being alone in the world.

"That one over there is Adéla"—he pointed to a chicken by herself at the far reaches of the feed I'd tossed out—"because she reminds me of a girl in primary school that used to spend her time alone on the edge of the playground, never playing with the kids. These three are Ilona, Darina, Květka… three girls who lived on my street growing up that I would see every day, together, always whispering. The rooster is Blažej—it means babbler, because he never shuts up. Always crowing."

"Where're you from?" I asked, curiosity overwhelming me.

He smiled. "I grew up in Prague."

My eyes widened. What would bring someone *here* after growing up in such an old city with a wealth of history and culture? So many questions ran through my head.

"Czechoslovakia?" I asked, and he nodded. "Why—how'd you end up here?"

"You do not know much about my country, do you?"

I shook my head. I didn't think I could even point it out on a map. Really, I only knew the city Prague was there because of some long-ago geography lesson I'd had. Just like I knew that it was a history-rich city with museums and beautiful architecture, because that's what I was told in school. But that's about all I remembered. He nodded, lips pinched like he expected as much.

"I wanted something of my own," he said simply, spreading out his arms, palms up. "We do not get such choices back home."

The way he said *home,* with such longing spiked into the word, sent a shiver down my spine. I wanted to ask why it was important enough to live half a world away. What happened to his family? Were they still there? Why would he choose a lonely life on a farm? But in the end, I asked none of it because I didn't want to pry.

"You remind me of Laney, a little bit."

My brow furrowed in confusion. "Huh?"

"Not in the way you look. My sister is blonde with the same eyes as me, but you both have the same quiet curiosity."

That was... that was very insightful for a man. Most guys my age had never looked closely enough at me to notice that. It made me wonder...

"How old're you?"

His brows rose at my random question. "I am thirty-two. You?"

"Twenty-three," I answered.

The question of if that nine-year difference bothered him niggled in the back of my mind in the ensuing silence. But why would he care? Why did I care? There wasn't an age limit on rescuing someone from a murderer. He reached down, petting the Laney chicken as she approached him.

"After you feed them, you have to collect the eggs," Xander said, breaking the silence.

He motioned for me to follow him and walked around the back

of the chicken coop. There was another latch there, and he lifted the whole back wall up. Propping it up with a board attached to the inside of the coop, he ducked under the wall. I followed.

A strong hit of ammonia, laced with something... just not right, surrounded me. It was overwhelming. Who knew chickens smelled so bad? I held a finger under my nose as I held my breath. There was a row of hay-filled nests, an egg, sometimes two, in each one. He reached out for the empty feed bucket in my hands, and I gave it to him. We filled the bucket with the eggs, and I began to see why he ate so many eggs. If we got that amount every morning, we would never run out.

"That is all there is to it," Xander said, ducking out from under the propped-up wall. He closed it. "I should get to work on the truck."

I nodded in agreement as he took a step back. He turned and walked out the gate to the chicken yard. He held it open for me, and I jumped through before a hen escaped with me.

"You don't have to clean the house. But I do look forward to dinner." He smiled, and my legs trembled a bit in response. He hesitated for a second, like he'd say something else, but never did. He pursed his lips and left in the direction of the garage. I watched him for a moment, before turning on my heels and walking back to the house, bucket of eggs in hand.

CHAPTER TWELVE

Routines

I found a boom box radio in his closet. I was, of course, looking for his laundry to put into the washer and dryer. But it was like the clouds parted and heaven shined down on my activities that day, because I could—at last—listen to good music. I was no longer stuck with the old country crap he listened to. I got enough of that everywhere I went—this was Texas, after all.

The only downside was that I only had one mixtape with me and there was no signal to a decent radio station. Beggars couldn't be choosers, however. I carted that thing all over the house with me. Jesus Christ, there was dust everywhere. You would think that no one had lived here in ages, it was so bad in some places.

Otherwise, Xander was a neat freak. All his dirty items were in the hamper. His closet was organized by type of item, color, and length. He'd put *a lot* of thought into where his clothes should hang. And that wasn't even touching on his dresser organization. He folded his underwear. I was not a slob by anyone's standards, but I didn't see the point in underwear folding. Was anyone going to see me in my underwear, notice a wrinkle, and turn their nose up with a cringe and call me a bum? No.

It was getting close to lunchtime, so while I pulled the warm clothes from the dryer, I thought to stop and make him a sandwich. I set the laundry basket on the end of the counter, the radio snuggled into the bed of clean clothes, playing "Kiss" by Prince. I bopped around the kitchen, pulling out the things I needed, and dancing. Which was more like a reenactment of the words to the song, but whatever.

I'd borrowed a cable-knit sweater of his that was way too oversized, but it kept me the right amount of warm. It was long enough to cover my cutoff shorts completely and hung off one shoulder. My hair was pulled up in a shitty bun on top of my head, but it was doing the job of keeping my long hair out of my face. It was very *Flashdance*, though I didn't have an ounce of dance talent in my body. Except my hips. They swayed with the sexy beats of Prince's music.

I was spreading mayo and making kissy noises like a champ. I located the potato chips and dropped some on the plate, then stopped for a dance break, singing along with the impassioned climax of the song. I bent over, grabbing the pitcher of sweet tea I'd made earlier and turning to set it on the island, when I saw him.

He was leaning against the wall that divided the kitchen from the living room. Arms folded over his chest and smirk on his face, he was watching me. I came to a complete stop, the tea sloshing over the edge of the pitcher.

I looked down to my socked feet, speckled with tea. I knew my face was red. I could feel the heat radiating off it.

"I made you a sandwich," I mumbled. "Let me get you a glass for your tea."

I set the pitcher down and hustled to the cabinet that held the glasses, but as I reached up, his hand beat mine to the nearest one.

"Thank you," he said, his other hand grazing my hip.

He was right behind me. I could feel the heat rolling off him. The smell the engine grease and cedar lingered in the air around him. All my muscles locked up and I found myself frozen, half leaning over the counter in front of him, my hand still up in the cabinet.

Touch me.

My cunt throbbed as I imagined him pushing me down on the counter and thrusting inside of me. The sound of the clinking ice as the tea filled his cup was a faint background to the porn in my head. I heard his plate clatter as he set it down on the dining room table, and I snapped out of it.

I quickly moved to grab the clothes basket and sat across from him, folding his clothes and towels. I even folded his damn underwear. He watched me, but I didn't dare meet his eyes. He probably knew what I was thinking and thought I was just a silly girl. And if he didn't, he would read it on my face. *I'm a horrible liar.*

Maybe if I tried changing the subject—not that there was a current subject outside of my wayward thoughts—but if I could get my thoughts on track... *Thanksgiving.* The holiday should be the next day—assuming I hadn't lost track of the days in my restless state. I was scheduled to work that day, since most of the other waitresses had families to celebrate with. I usually picked up holidays to help them out. Plus, there was bonus pay involved, so it wasn't totally altruistic.

"Thanksgiving is tomorrow," I said, offhandedly.

"Ah, the American holiday."

I'd forgotten he likely didn't celebrate it. "Yes."

"Did you have plans?"

"No," I answered, pausing to gather my thoughts. "Well, I was supposed to work, but I won't be. I was just thinking that we could celebrate. But I wasn't thinking about..."

"What do you need?"

I steeled myself to meet his eyes. "We don't have to—"

"I really want to." He nodded earnestly. "I would like to learn the local customs."

His genuine interest made the awkwardness fade into the background.

And making a traditional dinner would take my mind off the killer and get it on something more productive. This was a good plan.

"Well, I was looking through the pantry today and it seems like we have the makings of a full meal. Except one thing—a turkey."

"Thanksgiving is a meal?" The pinched line between his brow brought a smile to my face.

"No, there are other things."

He raised a questioning brow.

"There is a parade and football game on TV. We all say what we're thankful for at dinner. It's really just about being with family."

"So why do you not have plans to be with yours?" His deep voice was flecked with earnest curiosity.

"I don't have a family." I ducked my head, looking at the shirt in my hands. "Haven't for a long time."

The pregnant pause and questioning look was enough for me to know that he was asking without asking. I didn't want to talk about it. I could count on one hand the number of people that knew my story. But I wasn't sure why I had the urge to tell him, lingering in the back of my mind. A haunting urge.

"My mama was sent to prison for killing my stepdaddy. My real dad didn't even know I was conceived. And I have no siblings. I've been on my own since I was twelve."

"You are an impressive woman."

My head snapped up. His look wasn't teasing—it was serious. He was being serious.

My jaw hung loose as I searched for a response. "That's—that's one I haven't heard before."

"To have lived through that and still have the joy for life I've seen when you think no one is looking. You have grace under pressure. And a healthy dose of caution and instincts. Strength and courage. I'm not surprised that you have made it this far on your own... It is impressive."

My mouth opened and closed a few times, struggling for a response before I settled on "Thank you."

"An honest assessment doesn't require thanks, but you are welcome, Rosie."

He smiled as he got up and went to wash his dishes, leaving them in the rack. I sat there, stunned. Not moving, not blinking. No one had ever made me feel like where I came from was a source of strength before. Gathering my wits, I grabbed the basket and pulled it toward me to finish folding the laundry. He paused at the door.

"I promised that I have something for you today. When you finish up in here, come meet me outside."

His face was an unreadable mask, but he watched me as if waiting for an answer.

I nodded. "Sure."

The screen door clacked shut, and he was gone. I leaned back in the chair, almost as if I were melting.

SNAPSHOT

CHAPTER THIRTEEN

Sharpshooter

After I finished the clothes and put them away, I made myself a sandwich while taking inventory of what Xander had that I could make for our Thanksgiving dinner. The pantry in this old house was large. There were lots of home-canned vegetables in glass jars, and a few store-bought items. I was ecstatic to find a can of pumpkin pie filling. I wasn't expecting that he would've had something like that. He didn't seem like the baking type. My only thought was that someone else had stocked this pantry. But who?

I took the last bite of my sandwich and went outside to the garage, following the tunes of Xander's country music. There was a loud clang, followed by what I could only guess was a string of curses in his native language. He was bent over the engine with his back to me. He was shirtless and sweaty, with his T-shirt tucked into the waist of his jeans. I watched, mesmerized, as his back muscles rippled with the strain of whatever he was doing under that hood. Then I swatted the thoughts away like an annoying fly.

"You wanted to see me?"

His head bolted upward and banged into the open hood above

him. I tried to smother my laugh and the resulting smile as he turned to face me.

"Yes. I did." He smiled sheepishly, walking over to the counter and wiping the grease from his hands.

I watched him as he walked to the back wall and opened a tall two-door metal cabinet. He pulled out a small metal box and brought it over to the counter. I met him halfway as he set the box down and clicked open the latch. He made no move to open it. Instead, he reached over and turned off his record player.

"I do not know if you will be comfortable with this. I thought it might help you feel more safe."

He opened the box, revealing a small handgun. It was silver with a black handle. Near the black part, a little circular emblem read Astra in a sunburst design, and along the barrel, the word Terminator was engraved. He pulled it out of the box, clicking it open to reveal the six-holed revolving chamber. Barrel, chamber, trigger... I knew those from the movies, but I was sure all the other parts had actual names too.

"Have you ever used a gun?" he asked, loading the holes with bullets that were also in the box.

I shook my head, fascinated and more than a little scared. I'd never been this close to a real gun.

"That is what we will do today. You can learn how to use it, and you can keep it with you. You will feel more safe. Yes?"

I didn't know about that. I could be in danger from myself with that thing, but I nodded anyway. It was something other than feeling helpless and scared all the time.

"Good. Take this." He handed the gun to me after he clicked it shut, fully loaded. It was heavier than it looked for such a small gun. "Follow me."

He led me down a well-worn path between the house and the garage. A huge old oak tree shaded most of the space back there, and what was left in the sun was a fenced-off vegetable garden. It looked well-tended but was dormant for the winter. My grip tightened on the gun as my palms began to sweat.

"Stand right here," Xander said, and he continued around to the other side of the garden.

He picked up old cans riddled with holes off the ground and lined them up on the garden's fencing. He'd definitely done this before.

Of course he had. He owned the gun.

But it crossed my mind that he was placing a whole lot of faith in me. He gave me a loaded gun and was standing directly in front of me. If the situation were reversed, I wouldn't be so casual about walking in front of him if he had a loaded gun in his hand. And the thought crossed my mind that maybe that was the point—he wanted me to feel more comfortable. Not just with a killer that could show up any second, but with him.

I realized as I watched him walk back that I did feel more comfortable with him. I wasn't sure if it was that moment, or something we'd been slowly growing toward, but I wasn't afraid of him any longer.

"You will want to hold it with both hands, straight out, like this—" He demonstrated like he was holding a gun. "Make sure you tighten your arm muscles when you pull the trigger, because it will want to push back. You don't want it to hit your face."

"No, I don't think I'd like that." I smirked at him.

He grinned back. I held up the gun like he demonstrated and aimed it at the can on the far left.

"Squeeze the trigger, do not pull on it." He stepped back.

I tried to will myself to squeeze the trigger, but I was afraid of what would happen if I did. I was not known for being one of the most graceful human beings. I didn't want to accidentally shoot a poor defenseless squirrel or bird, and with the luck I was having of late, I probably would. I dropped my arms when they started shaking.

"I can't." I shook my head.

Xander tilted his head, his stare penetrating through me. Then he shook his head. "You will not hurt anything you don't want to. It is not that hard. Here." He walked up behind me and pulled my arms up.

My heart started at a gallop as his smell of cedar and fresh air and engine grease wrapped around my senses. He pressed against my back, bending his knees so his chin rested on my bare shoulder, and spoke softly. His breath tickled over my skin, springing goose bumps to life.

"Line up the sight at the end of the gun. Aim it at the can, and tell me when you're ready."

I gave a garbled gasp as my head bobbed in response. "I'm ready."

My body tensed as he sealed our bodies even closer and his hand wrapped over mine and gave a gentle squeeze.

Bang! The gun went off and I gave a startled yelp, which I didn't really hear because my ears were ringing. We didn't hit the can, but we also didn't hit anything else. My heart was pounding so loudly it battled to drown out the ringing in my ears. But it wasn't fear that thrummed through my veins; it was this heady mixture of excitement and relief.

"Oh, my God," I breathed out. "I wanna do it again."

I felt more than heard his deep chuckle as it rumbled through his chest, sending vibrations through my shoulder where his chin still lightly rested.

"Do you think you can do it on your own this time?"

I didn't want him to move, but I couldn't bring myself to say the words. There was something about the way his arms felt around me. I didn't have the words to describe it, but I'd never felt anything like it. And I was pretty far from a virgin. Never settling down and not having a moral stance to stop me from sexual pursuits had left me with a fairly sordid history of brief flings and one-night stands. I shook my head as an answer.

He'd stepped back after the gun went off so there was a gap of space between us, but it was so thin I could still feel the heat radiating off his body. When he pressed against me, I felt his own answer to the excitement of the moment. I bit back a moan and fought the urge to press farther into it. I wasn't sure if I was ready for that. I knew that I wanted him, but being stuck out here with nothing else to do, it could be a distraction that would definitely hamper his work and my ability to get back home. It wasn't a good idea.

I bit down on my lip and gave him a nod. "Ready."

His big hands swallowed mine again. *Bang! Clang!*

"We hit it!" I squealed and bounced on my toes in celebration, belatedly realizing that with us pressed together, I was basically rubbing myself up and down the front of his body.

Xander was off and backing away from me like I'd burned him. I turned slowly to face him, afraid of what I might see. He wasn't looking at me anyway; he was staring off the way we came—from the garage. His back toward me, he wasn't moving.

He cleared his throat. "I should get back to my work on the truck."

His words were stilted and robotic-sounding, but I wasn't sure if that was a smothering of some kind of emotion or just a byproduct of his accent. Either way, with that, he set into motion, leaving me alone with a loaded gun and a box of bullets in his backyard. I watched him take a few more steps, then raised the gun, aimed at the next can, and pulled the trigger. *Bang! Clang!*

My laughter pealed through the space between his house, the garage, and the trees. I looked back to him, and he paused at the edge of the garage, just before he turned the corner. But he didn't look back, only rubbed his thumb over his forehead and then went back into motion. Turning the opposite way, he moved toward the house, disappearing from sight.

My brow furrowed a bit that he went inside, but I shook it off and pulled the gun back up and aimed at the next can. *Bang! Clang!* I fucking rocked at using a gun. And that was the most freeing thought since this whole incident began.

I felt like I could float up through the treetops. I'd never be a helpless damsel in distress again. I was a dangerous badass with the aim to prove it. After the last shot, I pulled the gun up toward my face and blew on the barrel, feeling like that was just something I should do before I reloaded. *I probably watch too many movies.* I could feel the heat radiating off the gun onto my lips, making them tingle. I dared the killer to come after me now.

68

CHAPTER FOURTEEN

Preparations

I was in the kitchen prepping the sides for the Thanksgiving dinner when it happened. A shot echoed through the trees from somewhere in the woods. My heart rate went from steady to thunderous in a split second. I reached for the handgun that Xander had given me. I had it sitting on the edge of the counter and gripped it tight while I moved against the wall to the window, peeking out to see if Xander was still in the garage.

The way the garage angled away from the house didn't help matters—I couldn't see him. I'd have to go outside or wait and see if he came out. I decided to give it a few moments. He'd likely heard the shot too, and would come out to inspect. Or I hoped he would. But there was nothing. No sounds. Not even his god-awful country music twanging away as usual.

I was going to have to go out there. I needed to check and make sure he was okay. I wasn't sure why I felt responsible for him, but we were in this together, so it was the right thing to do. *Right?*

I darted toward the door and stood against the wall near the edge of the frame. It was open, unlike the windows that were shut and locked, with only the wooden-frame screen door keeping intruders out. It wasn't cold or hot enough to bother shutting it, and it actually helped regulate the temperature.

I listened carefully before making my move, and when I turned and pushed the door open with my knee, I brought the gun up in front of me, the way Xander had shown me. I turned back and forth, looking both ways off the porch to make sure I wasn't being blindsided. Then I stepped off and dashed to the garage, keeping the gun sight centered in my field of vision, my eyes sweeping across the area for the source of the shot.

Xander wasn't there. He wasn't in the garage. Blood rushed through my ears with the sound of a tsunami making landfall. It was both deceptively quiet and intensely loud, overwhelming my senses and making the world feel like it was tilting. I stumbled and bumped into the side of the truck as I turned back to face the garage door opening. After making sure there was no one in the garage with me, I melted back into the shadows as I heard the chickens chatter. Something had stirred them up.

I shuffled along the darkened wall, soundlessly, toward the door to see what they were fussing about. Just as I was about to peek around the corner of the door, a shadow fell across the dirt yard. It moved with determination, not skulking in the shadows like I was, and that scared the shit out of me. I pressed back against the wall, focusing on controlling my breath. All that focus on being quiet hadn't deterred the pain from ripping through me. A dull throb radiated out of my chest, and I pressed my free hand against my sternum.

Jesus Christ! I'm having a heart attack. Would I be the first to die of a heart attack at twenty-three?

The shadow moved away from the garage, and I got a second to breathe. I'd be fine. As the pain receded, I moved closer to the door to see where the killer went, but I only caught the door to the barn swinging shut.

Curiously, I hadn't given the barn a second thought until this moment—what was in it or why the killer would head there rather than the house. And still no sign of Xander. *Could he be in the barn?*

I couldn't imagine why he'd be in there. But if he was, the killer could have him, and it was up to me to save him. I owed him that much.

I ran across the yard, gun held in front of me in case the killer stepped out of the barn. Hopefully, I'd catch him off guard.

When I got to the door, I halted and threw myself against the outer wall, next to the door. A loud thump from inside made me jump, and my heart set to racing even faster. Xander filled my thoughts. He could be hurt already; they could be fighting. I didn't know how I'd save him if he was hurt badly. Maybe go in search of the killer's car? Though I'd no idea where he would've left it. It certainly wasn't here in the yard.

Another thump had me moving. I pulled the door open quietly and slipped through the thin opening before softly closing it behind me, my gun held at the ready. It was dark in the barn, and my eyes took a few seconds to adjust. When they did, my insides twisted. I felt the urge to vomit churn in my gut.

Xander was standing toward the back of the barn, just to the inside of a wall that once separated out a stable. He was covered in blood splatter and held a dripping, sopping mess of flesh that belonged inside a body, not out of it.

A gasp escaped me. His head whipped in my direction. Blue eyes burned through me as he froze on the spot. *Oh, God. He's the killer. Xander is the killer.* I stumbled backward, confusion still locking down my brain functions, but the basic instinct of getting away forced my feet to move. I had to get out of this barn of death.

Xander's eyes widened a fraction as he stepped in my direction. I raised the gun to aim at him. The flesh fell out of his hand with a wet splat. His other hand raised in surrender, yet the glint of the butcher knife in it did nothing to quell my panic. His eyes tracked mine. The knife clattered to the floor.

"Rosie—"

"No, you stay away." I nudged the gun in the air, threateningly, and kicked the door open behind me.

The sunlight washed over me. I couldn't see his form anymore in the dark shadows, so I turned and ran. I ran straight for the house. I knew I couldn't outrun him. We'd played that game before. I'd no clue what I would do, but I could lock myself inside and shoot him if he tried to come in after me. That would at least buy me some time. Enough time to think of a way out of this clusterfuck.

72

CHAPTER FIFTEEN

Standoff

With the door bolted shut behind me, I slid down until my butt hit the floor. Tears welled in my eyes. It felt like a loss. Like someone I knew had died. Who really knew who he'd killed and was butchering out there. But the thought jumped into my head that he had a gun. Probably the same shotgun I'd seen him with only days before. Back when I thought he was a good guy. And why did the thought that he wasn't good hurt so much?

Scooting away from the door, I moved over to a side wall. Behind the door seemed too obvious—a likely place that he'd shoot as he tried to get back into his house. I waited.

I wanted to run upstairs to get my purse and be ready to leave at the first opportunity. But going upstairs would allow him too much time. He could break in and overpower me before I could get back downstairs to react to his intrusion.

I listened for the sound of his footsteps hitting the porch, but nothing came. Though knowing him, he'd do it so quietly, I wouldn't hear him. Slowing my breaths, I strained to hear some sort of movement.

"Rosie," he called out. His deep voice booming across the yard sounded muffled from inside the confines of the locked-down house, but I could tell that he was loud. It was in the way he called out my name.

"I'm not goin' out there, Xander, and you're not comin' in here."

"I should have warned you. I should have told you about—"

I laughed darkly, loud enough for him to hear. "I don't think warnin' that you were a psycho would've helped, but thank you for not killin' me immediately. And for giving me the gun. But I'll shoot you if you try to get any closer."

"No, Rosie. Please look at me." He paused. "Look out the window. Any window. I'm not going to hurt you."

"Not fuckin' likely. I know you have a gun. And I'm not dumb enough to make myself an easy target."

"I don't have the gun with me. It is in the barn. Please, Rosie, just look at me."

I sat there for a moment, not moving, mulling over the possibilities of what he might want me to look out the window for. But in the end, it all boiled down to the fact that he couldn't aim at every window, and there were several to choose from. I crawled across the floor, taking extra care to be slow and quiet. Passing the obvious one near the door, I made my way to the one farthest away.

Would that be the least obvious one or the most obvious? I paused in front of the middle one and turned back to look at the one closest to the door. *It really depends on what he thinks of me.* If I was smart, I'd go the least obvious route. If I were dumb, or perhaps even sly, I'd choose the one closest to the door. But what were the odds that we would both choose the same of the three?

I was pretty certain he thought I was smart. But how smart? I could sit here all day and debate this, so I gave up and just moved toward the middle window, taking my chances.

Xander stood in the middle of the yard with both hands raised in surrender, but from one hand dangled a half-plucked turkey, dripping blood onto the dirt from the hole where its neck formerly was. The look on his face was half distress, half amusement. Then his eyes locked on mine, and his smile grew. He was shirtless under the black rubber apron and still speckled with blood, but he was so happy I couldn't help the smile that grew on my face in reply.

"You said you needed a turkey for dinner. I had a couple that escaped the pen in a storm a few weeks ago. I went hunting and found one for you. I am sorry I did not warn you."

I shuffled off the ground and moved to the door. Unlocking it, I threw the door open and stepped outside. He stepped up onto the porch at the same time. He took another stride in my direction before his hand darted to my side and his momentum stopped.

I looked down and realized that I still had the gun gripped tightly in my hand.

"Xander, I—"

"I am truly sorry. I did not account for your distress in this situation."

I shoved the gun behind my back and ducked my head. "I'm sorry for not trusting you."

"You have no reason to, Rosie. I get that."

I peeked up at him through my lashes, and his body lurched toward me, but he stopped himself. Dropping his free hand, he looked down at the turkey and the mess of himself. He took a step back.

"I should finish this, so you can put it on to cook. He was bigger than I remembered—it will probably take long."

I nodded.

"Xander, I'm sorry."

He shook his head, taking another step back and off the porch without looking. If I tried that move, I would've landed on my ass. But he was all grace and strength.

"It will make for a good story, no?" A smile lit up his face. "One day, we will laugh at this."

Perhaps we would, one day, but shame settled over me like a wet blanket as I watched him walk away.

CHAPTER SIXTEEN

Turkey

After he finished prepping the turkey, he brought it in and left me to season it. After a few minutes of rubbing it down with butter and herbs I found in the pantry, I got it in the oven. No sooner was it cooking than I heard a strange voice. I leaned around the corner to find Xander had moved the TV out of his bedroom. The signal from the local channel was clear and broadcasting the famous New York parade. I listened to Willard Scott, in his brown hat and tan leather coat, talk about the floats and marching bands; then Alf appeared as tears welled into my eyes.

Xander did that for me. No one ever did stuff for me. Well, at least not without expecting something in return, and I didn't get the vibe that Xander expected reciprocation. A giant Big Bird floated across the screen, wearing a blue-and-orange-striped sweater. I turned around before I lost it and made a fool of myself even further. Blinking several times, I cleared the haze from my eyes.

"Thank you," I called out, without looking.

"It is not a problem, Rosie."

I smirked at his failed attempt at a common phrase. It was sort of adorable. I felt his nearness and turned to find him towering over me in that way he couldn't seem to control. It was just his presence that filled the room. An ingrained quality that drew the eye and made him seem larger than everything around him. He smiled as he backed out the door.

"I will go back to work and leave you to the cooking and parade." He nodded toward the TV and then disappeared through the door.

After the parade was finished and the traditional Texas rivalry game was over, the timer dinged from the kitchen. I made my way over and opened the oven. The smell of the herbs and turkey were mouth-watering. I turned to grab the pot holders, but they weren't on the counter where I'd left them. But I did catch the large form from the corner of my eye. I turned to find Xander standing there with the oven mitts on his hands. He shrugged.

"Allow me?" he asked softly.

I nodded and stepped out of the way.

He inhaled deeply with an appreciative grunt as he set it on the top of the stove. A variety of delicious smells from my work permeated the house, and thankfully, our standoff that morning hadn't led to any burning or neglected ingredients. I was still embarrassed to look at him after the way I'd acted.

"Did you want to carve it?" I asked in a whisper.

He froze, not looking at me, for which I was thankful, but nodded once.

"It needs to rest for a bit, but you're welcome to do it. I'm sorry for this morning."

"It is okay, Rosie. I do know how it looked. And with what you are going through…" He shook his head. "I understand."

He still held the handles of the roasting pan through the oven mitts, but I could see his grip tighten in the way it pulled at the cloth. I busied myself with setting the table. He could say that he forgave me all he wanted, but it was obviously bothering him. I felt bad to be the cause of his distress; he'd been nothing but kind and welcoming to me. And that was why I stayed away from people. I wasn't a particularly adept person with social interactions. I fucked up more often than not.

An hour later, we found ourselves in sated silence, the food mostly eaten. I probably went overboard, but we could reheat the leftovers, and turkey sandwiches were always a great after-Thanksgiving treat.

"This was the best meal I have had since leaving home. Thank you, Rosie." He leaned back in his seat across the table, kicking his legs out and relaxing.

My face heated as I looked down at my empty plate. "You're welcome," I muttered. "It's actually the first Thanksgiving I've had in years. I'm usually working."

He nodded but didn't comment. I was grateful.

We'd left the TV on with the volume low. It didn't stop me from noticing that the nightly news was on. But what really caught my eye was the headline below the guy who was speaking: Czechoslovakia Minister of Defense. I hopped up and turned up the volume. The guy was speaking, but the sound was overpowered by a translator narrating his speech.

"...the army would never undertake action against the people. I call for an end to demonstrations," the translator intoned in a style that lacked the conviction written all over the man's face.

My eyes darted back to Xander. "That's your country."

"It is." He nodded, his attention fixed on the television.

The screen switched to an American commentator, who talked about what this could mean for the people of Xander's home country. The end of communist reign, they speculated, but under possible peaceful conditions—certainly a first for a world that had seen many violent transitions of power over the last few decades.

I looked back to Xander and studied him. His reaction was quiet, guarded. But he looked sort of peaceful, and if I wasn't mistaken, there was a tinge of hope in his eyes. This news meant a lot to him.

"I know just what we need." He jumped from his seat and went for the cabinet that I knew held his liquor.

Pulling out a bottle and a couple of glasses, he stopped next to me, kicking out the other chair on my side of the table. He sat facing me and placed the short glasses between us, pouring two fingers in each. I raised my brows as I connected to his gaze. He nudged a glass in my direction and picked up the other.

His lips quirked up on one side. "Last week was a holiday for my country. I never got to celebrate."

"Oh?"

"International Students Day." His smile grew.

I didn't know what was amusing him, but I'm sure it was at my expense. "What exactly does International Students Day celebrate?"

His smile dropped. "It commemorates the Nazi storming of the University of Prague to break up a protest. They killed a student and a worker, which started the protest. The student leaders of the protests and some teachers were executed, and over one thousand were sent to concentration camps." He paused, looking at the floor. "My country hasn't known true peace in quite a long time."

Well, that sounded like a fun holiday. "No wonder you drink to celebrate. Though, I guess I did just force you into celebrating a holiday that initially celebrated the slaughter of indigenous people, after they invited a bunch of pilgrims over for a meal."

He laughed. It started as more of a snort and quickly turned into a chuckle, which then led to a full belly laugh. I really had no idea I was that funny, but it was infectious, and I found myself laughing too. Downing the rest of his glass in one swallow, he stood. He marched over to the couch and pushed it across the room until all the furniture was against one wall, leaving an open space in the middle of his living room.

He walked over to the stack radio and put a record on, turned off the television, then turned to me with his hand out. My jaw dropped.

"You want me to dance with you?" My brows raised in question.

A smirk grew on his face, and it was as if a thousand dirty thoughts sprung into my head in response to that look. It was dark and mischievous but still felt like more of a question.

"It is one thing I want." His voice dropped to something deep and soothing, unfurling the strangest sensation in my belly.

I downed the rest of my drink in one gulp. It burned, and I cringed. He laughed at that as I rose from the kitchen chair and placed my hand in his. He tugged me to him with a fluid grace and spun us around the room, making my feet move where he wanted them. He made it seem like I could actually dance. I was so stunned, it took a moment for the sensation of being pressed against him to fully sink in.

His arm wrapped around my waist, and the stubble on his cheek grazed mine as he leaned in and sang along with the country crooner. His voice was amazing, and his feet moved with expert precision. When his fresh cedar and soap smell invaded my senses, my head spun. I felt drunk, but I knew my tolerance was high enough that it wasn't the whiskey that warmed my insides. It was him.

"You always good at everything you do?"

"No. You might be surprised at how bad I am at some things."

"I can't imagine what that is."

He let out a breath, like he was considering whether or not to talk about it. When he spoke, it wasn't what I was expecting.

"People... you make that easier." He stopped speaking, while his feet kept perfect rhythm. And I wished I could see his face and guess at what his thoughts were. "I think it is because you fascinate me. You make yourself vulnerable, but you carry that vulnerability as a source of strength. I don't know how to do that. To allow another in."

I snorted. "I don't normally do that. It just seems to happen with you."

"Then maybe this is where you belong." He squeezed me tighter, our bodies sealed together as he swept me around the room in time to the music.

I felt lost, tumbling into a deep abyss. I didn't think—I just went on autopilot and followed what felt natural. Turning my head, I pressed my lips to the corner of his mouth. His feet finally faltered. He stopped moving as his head turned in to my kiss. His tongue trailed along the seam of my lips, and I opened with a sigh. He tasted like whiskey and pumpkin pie.

My mind fizzled out to nothing more than base instinct and sensations. I could feel him everywhere, even in the parts he wasn't touching. He was consuming me. I slid my hands up the back of his shirt, his work-hardened muscles a stark contrast to the silky smooth of his skin. There were small bumps and odd raised strips around his torso, but my mind refused to consider what they could be. I just reveled in the feel of him.

His hand skimmed up one side of my body, coming to a stop just below my breast, his thumb brushing back and forth. It was so close but not enough. I whimpered as my knees went weak. I broke the kiss and stared at his swollen lips as I fought to catch my breath.

"Xander, I'm going to need you to fuck me now."

His chest rumbled with a masculine growl, and he hoisted me up in his arms with ease. My legs wrapped around his waist as he carried me back to the bedroom. Holy fuck! There wasn't an inch of this guy I wasn't attracted to. It should've scared me, my reaction to him, but my brain had shut off with the first taste.

Once in his room, he set me on the ground and stepped back. The low light from his bedside lamp cast shadows around the room, but my focus was on him. His eyes remained fixed on me as he pulled his shirt over his head.

Now I could see what my fingers had explored before. He had a multitude of scars across his body; they were faint, just a shade lighter than his fair skin. Which was probably why I never noticed, the few times I'd seen him shirtless in the garage. All were in various shapes and sizes, no pattern or obvious cause. It didn't detract from his beauty. He was beyond perfectly constructed, a work of masculine art. The scars only added to his story.

I watched, fascinated, as he folded the shirt and set it on top of his dresser. Biting my lip, I clenched my fist to stop from reaching for him. I wanted to have my hands all over him, but he was watching me with a look that said he was waiting for me to make the next move. I popped the button on my shorts and let them fall to the ground, then pulled the borrowed T-shirt over my head.

A dark shadow passed through his eyes. "It has been a long time since I have lain with a woman. I'm not sure I can... please you."

His honesty shot through me like a bolt of lightning and cracked something inside of me. I breathed in deeply and blinked a few times. He swallowed. His Adam's apple bobbed in his throat, making me want to lick it.

"You really can't do it wrong. I just want you."

"I want to see the rest of you." His voice was gruff and commanding.

I felt the wetness pool between my legs in response. Unhooking my bra, I let it slide down my arms to the floor. His gaze never strayed from his slow perusal of my body. My panties hit the floor next, and he watched. The feral hunger and undisguised lust, the erection straining against his pants—I was too distracted to even bother with being self-conscious. It was obvious he liked what he was seeing.

"Lay back on the bed and spread your legs for me."

I backed up until I felt the edge of the bed and let myself free-fall into the mattress. I wanted to be touched so bad, I couldn't help toying with my nipples and running my hands down my stomach before using my hands to spread my thighs apart. I squirmed a bit at his rapt attention to the apex of my legs. He hadn't moved an inch.

"Touch me," I whispered.

His hand went to his belt but paused as my hands strayed. I spread the lips of my pussy open for him and let the other hand circle my clit. My eyes closed of their own accord as a moan broke from my lips. I dipped a finger inside myself.

I'd never been this brazen before in my life, but the alcohol, him, the look on his face was a heady mix that had me acting out my wildest fantasy, for him. When I opened my eyes, his pants and boxers were neatly folded on the dresser with his shirt. He was closer, stroking his cock. My mouth watered at the sight of it. Even his dick was beautiful.

Those indigo eyes had gone black with lust as he watched me. "Add another finger."

I did as he asked, feeling how slick I was, my fingers gliding in and out of myself proof of my overwhelming lust for him. He hooked his hands under my knees and spread me open further.

"Perfect," he muttered, trailing his mouth from my knee, but pausing midthigh, he bit down. I cried out. "Is that okay?" he asked, smoothing over the tender spot with his tongue.

"Yes, more," I gasped.

"Keep touching yourself. I want to watch you come for me."

He wrapped his hand around his cock again and thrust his hips into it, like he was losing himself as he watched me. It was so honest and shameless, it had me edging closer to release.

I'd never met a man confident enough to fuck his hand while ordering me to get myself off as he watched. It was like I woke up in a sexual fantasyland, so far out of normal everyday encounters. His muscles flexed with each thrust, darkening each line that sculpted his body. It was hypnotizing.

"Now, Rosie."

"Xander, fuck me. I want your cock," I pleaded. "I'm coming."

He shoved my hands aside, but I didn't get what I asked for. Instead, his face buried between my legs—licking and sucking, biting and lapping up my release. All the while, his hips kept thrusting into his hand like he couldn't stop himself from following me. I gripped his short hair tight and ground my hips on his face. Darkness edged in on my vision as bliss rolled over me in waves.

"Come with me, Xander. Show me how much I turn you on."

His mouth released from me with a pop, and he rose to his knees, his free hand stimulating my bundle of nerves and drawing out my climax as he came. On my breasts, my stomach. And as I came down from the high, his hand withdrew from me. He leaned over, lapping up his own release and cleaning it off me with his tongue. His eyes watched for my reaction as he moved up my body.

When he got to my mouth, he hovered there for a bit, as if asking if I was okay with it. I gripped the back of his head, pulling him to me. The taste of both of us on his tongue had me moaning and pressing against him for more. Xander groaned, pulling away from me. He rose on the bed and sat back on his heels behind me.

"Come here," he said.

He motioned for me to sit on his lap, but when I tried facing him, he spun me around facing away. He positioned me so the hard length of him pressed against me from ass to clit. The heat alone made me throb with excitement. When I was seated, he pulled my ankles so that my knees aligned with his, straddling his legs. Just when I was thinking this was the hottest thing I'd ever done, he pulled my back against his chest, capturing my chin and directing my gaze to the space in front of me.

We were positioned so that we were directly in front of the mirror attached to his dresser. We painted a stunning vision of pornographic pleasure in naked flesh. My dark skin contrasted his fair, highlighting the strong arms wrapped around me. I could see the swollen red crown of his cock, straining where it pressed against my cunt. My gaze followed the movement of his hands. The one on my chin drifted down to cup my neck, while the other cupped my breast, his fingers toying with my nipple.

My body shuddered at the contact, and my hips moved, seeking friction on his hot, hard dick. I moaned, my lips slightly parted. My eyes were half-mast, my hair a rat's nest, but I'd never looked so wanton in my life. There was a burning need in my eyes that shocked me. And it clicked that he wanted me to see what he was seeing.

"I want you to remember this moment. To remember that I gave you a choice. Rosie, if I take you—you will be mine. You need to be sure you are okay with that before you ask too much of me. I already know that I won't want to let you go."

He pinched and twisted my nipple and I gasped, pressing down harder against the length of him. Rotating my hips, I tried to get the angle that would allow him to slip inside, but his hold on me was firm and my movement too limited to reach my goal.

"Do you see that, Rosie?" My eyes met his in the mirror. "No one has ever looked at me with that level of desire. No one has ever responded that strongly to my touch."

His hand slid down and his fingers pressed against my bundled nerves. My body jerked in his hold, the small touch nearly sending me over the edge. My head fell back against his shoulder as he kissed mine, trailing bites and licks up my neck to my ear.

"So beautiful. You are the most tempting woman. But are you ready to give yourself to me?"

Thoughts. Thoughts sprang up in my mind, and I fought to keep them at bay. I wanted to live in this state of mindless ecstasy forever. I knew that whatever he did, it would ruin me. Nothing would ever compare, and as much as it scared me, I couldn't not take the chance. He had me in thrall. Even if I only had him once, the memory would be enough to last me a lifetime, knowing that I had one perfect night.

I know he wanted me to think about the consequences of making the decision, but I couldn't do it. I didn't want to.

"Do it, Xander." My gaze snapped to his. "Ruin me."

In one smooth move, he lifted me up and pulled me back down, impaling me. There was no friction because I was so wet for him already. But the size... He was so much larger than I expected, the invasion so shocking, I cried out.

CHAPTER SEVENTEEN

Haunted

The sun peeked through the curtains in just the right way that unfiltered streams of light blazed right in my eyes, waking me the next morning. I recognized the familiar sensations of being entwined with Xander, since we woke up every morning in this state like we couldn't help ourselves. I'd been sleeping in his bed every night since my second night here, but...

Flashes of memories of the night before played in my head like a well-produced porn. Thanksgiving dinner, the dancing, the fucking... It was beyond everything, but in the light of day, it scared the shit out of me. I couldn't do this. I didn't do relationships because relationships didn't work. They never did. It might be exciting or heady now, but what happened when one of us lost interest, or we fought? Then it would all fall apart. One would be left hurt, while the other found comfort elsewhere.

The roles weren't gender-specific, but the result was inevitably the same. I'd decided long ago that I'd take no part in it because the chances of finding something that worked were akin to winning the lottery. And I was never lucky.

The look on Xander's face was nothing less than ownership, but not just that he claimed me. It was as if he let me know in those looks and touches that I owned him. It was heady in the moment. I was able to brush away the scary facts of life, but I couldn't set aside reality forever. I wasn't capable. I lived in my head and relied only on myself. This situation had already pushed me beyond my comfort zone.

I slid out of bed, careful not to wake him. I didn't want to confront that reality yet. I made my way upstairs and showered, then snuck back down and set to making breakfast. Looking back, I should've known better. Quiet as I was, there was power in the sense of smell to wake someone. I shouldn't have been surprised when he appeared in the kitchen.

I was, however, shocked that he did so stark naked. And that his first destination was me, as he wrapped me in his arms.

I stiffened.

He pulled me in tighter, his hands roving over me. I couldn't stop my body's response, as hard as my mind fought him. When his fingers slipped past the hemline of my shorts, he knew the effect he had.

"Fight it all you want, *zvonová sklenice*. I see you."

He toyed with me some more, slipping his fingers fully inside and grinding his palm against me until I fell limp against him. I let out a moan. I could feel the pressure building and responded by thrusting into his hand. I was on the precipice of release when suddenly he was gone. His hand and his body had vanished. I would've fallen if the kitchen counter wasn't in front of me.

I fought to regain my composure, and when I could stand straight, I thought about finishing what he started. But before I could, he returned fully dressed and stopped at the front door.

"You will wait to finish that." He paused, opening the door and pressing a palm to the screen. "Tonight." His voice carried an edge that was less of a command and more like a dark promise. I shivered in response.

I jumped as the screen door clacked shut in the wake of his exit. My flight response pressed in on me heavily. I'd normally bolt at this point with any guy, but my options were limited here. This was a mistake of epic proportions. I let my hormones fuck this situation, royally, and I'd no one to blame but myself.

All day, I was tense. I couldn't relax. My mind kept roving over the fact that I couldn't get away. And he'd warned me—he'd given me the chance to back out. I'm the one who stupidly said yes. I let myself get carried away. It was almost like I was losing myself and becoming someone else. It scared me more than the prospect of not leaving.

I went outside to shoot. The whole house was spotless, though I hadn't moved on to the second floor yet. I couldn't concentrate to read, and music hadn't been able to hold my focus either. I needed to get my mind off this shit.

It wasn't that late in the day, but because it was winter, the sun was already below the treetops. It was bright but shady throughout the whole yard. I set up the cans and shot off round after round until the large box of bullets Xander had given me was a little over halfway empty.

I was getting better, only missing every third shot at first, but by the end, I was hitting at least ten in a row. And the more I concentrated on getting it right, the less I thought about everything else. By the time I was ready to go back in, I was feeling pretty good.

And that's when it happened. I heated up some leftovers. Xander came in, we ate, watched the news and an episode of *The Outer Limits*, then went to bed. He didn't touch me or make a move. He stayed a normal distance away, giving me the space I was accustomed to. It was an unremarkable night. We lay down in the bed, and I listened to his breathing, focused on his every move, waiting for him to touch me. He didn't.

He acted as if the night before, or even this morning, never happened. And while half of me was grateful to not have to come up with an excuse why I didn't want to, the other half was curious as to why. I wanted to ask what he was thinking, but I didn't want to break the spell. Was he purposely giving me space? I sighed. I wasn't going to ask, so I closed my eyes and drifted off to sleep.

The next morning was the same—waking with the sun in my eyes, realizing that I was half-lying on Xander, our legs entwined. The only thing different was that he was awake. His fingers skimmed the bare skin where my shirt had bunched up in my sleep.

I could admit in the light of day I was slightly confused by his behavior. He had me on the edge of release, backed off with the promise of more, then nothing. My mind warred with indecision, trying to understand it all. Ask what his motives were? Play along and forget it all happened? It almost felt like a test, but he wasn't watching me closely enough to glean anything from my actions. Or maybe he was?

I liked to consider myself emotionally enlightened. I knew where my hang-ups came from. I knew the history in which my actions were grounded. But I also knew that I was powerless to stop myself from following that path. Xander called it a source of strength, but the fact that I ran and hid from all relationships when they became too heavy—that wasn't strong. Until that moment, I was okay with that. I was content.

But why was I content with being weak? I hadn't accepted weakness in any other area of my life. Up until now, I'd always looked at my independence as my greatest asset. This whole situation was fucking with my head. I wanted to pull my hair in frustration. I jumped out of the bed faster than I'd ever moved. Xander startled, but stayed in place.

"I need to go for a walk. I need to think. Alone." I looked up and met his eyes. "I'll take the gun."

He searched my eyes as if he was reading something in their depths and nodded once.

I pulled on my shorts and grabbed the borrowed sweater I'd been using from the closet. Needing out of the house right away, I quickly stomped to the door, shoved my feet into my boots, and was outside in a couple of seconds. I didn't bother with a hairbrush or toothbrush—I couldn't care less. I needed space. I needed to breathe—to think.

My boots crunched across the limestone gravel until I was under the shade of the trees. The white rocks were covered by a mixture of sparse grass and fallen leaves. Central Texas was beautiful in the way that it was unique. The rolling hills were speckled with verdant plant life mixed with more arid desert-dwelling plants. How they existed in the same place was beyond my knowledge, but the mix lent itself to familiarity. I could look at a sturdy oak tree with a cactus nestled at its base and I knew I was home.

It was the only part of that word—home—that recalled fond memories. Home, as in the house I grew up in, was a far cry from a fond memory. The house I grew up in was a tiny three-bedroom trailer that looked identical to three others on the street. In fact, they were identical, aside from the families that lived in them and the secrets they contained.

From the outside, we looked like a normal family. Two parents, one child. And my stepfather and mother were good at putting on a show. They had tons of friends; every family on the street would stop by in the evenings to sit in lawn chairs in the front yard, having a beer, chatting some, sharing lots of laughter, before the sun would set and they'd head home to go to bed and start the day over again.

And most days, it worked like that—but then there were the days that it didn't. Fred would have one too many beers, or he'd switch to the harder stuff, and when everyone left, the fighting would start.

My favorite part of our home was my closet. I don't know if that's weird for a child to think that, but it was my safe haven. I don't remember if my mama had ever told me that was where I was to go, but as soon as I heard raised voices, that's where I'd be. I'd shut off the lights in my room, sit in the floor of my closet surrounded by my stuffed animals, and pull out the flashlight and book that was always in there. I'd try to block out the screams for help from my mother. The thumps of flesh hitting flesh. The crash of furniture toppling over.

Tears would stream down my face, but I wouldn't dare make a sound. Never.

I do remember her telling me that. To stay quiet and out of the way. *You don't want to draw his attention, and I'm not sure I can protect you. I don't know how bad he'd hurt you when he gets like that.* The fights never started the same. It was a wholly random thing. Sometimes the food at dinner didn't taste the same as the last time. Sometimes the house wasn't clean enough. Sometimes it was the sound of her voice or the look on her face.

I never understood the lure of living in abject terror. Why she stayed. Even when we escaped and ended up in the women's center after a particularly vicious night—why did she go back? I'd asked her once...

"Why do you do it? Why don't you leave him for good this time?" my eight-year-old self asked.

My mother sighed and looked out the window of the car. "Because I love him. When he's not in one of his moods, he's good to us. He takes care of us and supports us. We need him."

I knew right then that I'd never let myself need a man. No one would ever have the power to make me love them when they were so horrible. I couldn't wrap my mind around a love like that. But the fact was that the older I got, the more I knew that my mother wasn't the only one. It happened more often than anyone ever talked about.

I'd seen women at work who'd come in with makeup caked over bruised faces. My neighbors were a prime example; the only saving grace to them was that I was sure that Joanne dished it out to Billy just as bad, if not worse, than he ever gave to her.

But what was the point in learning to outfight your man? Wasn't life just easier without one?

CHAPTER EIGHTEEN

Diction

I'd stumbled upon a stream, perhaps the same one that ran in front of my cliff. I couldn't tell. Streams and creeks were a common thing out in Texas Hill Country. I sat on a log on the edge of the bank, tossing little pebbles into the mostly still surface of clear water.

The sun was high in the sky as my stomach gave a growl of protest. I hadn't eaten anything since last night, and it was likely lunchtime. I needed to make my way back soon. I looked down at the pistol where it rested on the ground next to my feet. I didn't bring any extra bullets, only the six that were chambered. Not that shooting would be a bright idea. Xander would surely panic and come after me, and I'd likely end up shooting him.

Which brought my thoughts back to why I was out here in the first place—Xander. He didn't seem like the other men I'd met throughout my life. He had a screne calmness to him and wise eyes that held a history he left unspoken. I knew what he meant when it came to letting people in. I really didn't know much about the subject. I'd pushed everyone away, ever since my mother... I shook my head. I wouldn't let my mind stray there again. I'd given her and the past too much air space today. It was time to let it go.

Not that I hadn't let it go years ago. Or maybe I'd just deluded myself. The fact that I still let it control my actions was a definite signal that I was still letting it get to me, perhaps too much. Maybe I needed to suck it up and give someone a chance. Xander hadn't done anything to deserve my runaway routine. Not that I'd run away. I couldn't, but I knew that if I'd had the chance yesterday, I would've taken it.

The facts were, he was sweet and charming, he gave me my space, and asked for very little in return. Actually, the only thing he'd asked of me since I'd arrived here was to be sure I was ready to be with him. Which wasn't beyond normal expectations of human interactions. In fact, it was more considerate than anyone I'd ever been with. Most of the guys I dated were thrilled at the idea that I'd granted them access. They didn't waste a second making sure I was really ready for that step.

Maybe I owed him the benefit of the doubt. Maybe he was the freaking unicorn of men and I'd just won the lottery. Though now I was picturing him as a Lisa Frank unicorn, complete with rainbow colors and glittery sparkles. I laughed and shook my head. Tossing a last pebble into the stream, I stood and grabbed the gun off the ground.

I hadn't wandered too far from the house before stopping; it wouldn't take me too long to get back. I knew that it was easy to get lost out here, even with a good sense of direction. Even though I had to retrace my steps, every step closer to the house had my mind retracing the memory of our night together. Not just the sex, though that was beyond great. We had off-the-charts chemistry. But the rest of it. The thoughtfulness of him moving the TV into the living room for me so I could watch the parade. The laughter in his eyes as we danced around the living room.

He was unlike anyone I'd ever met, and not just the fact that he was from another country. We seemed to get each other. Like we operated on the same wavelength. My heart grew heavy. I needed to stop letting the past control me. I was pushing away a rare chance at happiness and all for some painful memories that were best left forgotten.

My mind was made up. I was going to stop dealing with this in the usual manner. I'd try and trust him.

As I breached the clearing that was his front yard, I found him immediately. Perhaps because he was in the place he always was, day in and day out—the garage. It looked as though he was just setting things up for the day. He wasn't covered in grease yet, and he still had on his flannel shirt, rolled up to his elbows.

As my boots crunched on the gravel below me, he froze, but he didn't turn to face me. He was giving me space to make my decision. My heart melted a little more at that, and my feet picked up their pace. He'd been watching me this whole time without looking, and he was very observant, constantly taking cues from my mood and giving me what I needed. Why hadn't I noticed that before? Or at least given him credit where it was due?

"I still need a few more days, but I am getting close to finishing it. You can leave soon."

I halted. I hadn't expected him to say that.

"That's not why I came over here."

"No?" His hands gripped the grill of the truck in front of him, knuckles whitening under the pressure.

"No. I came to tell you I'm sorry."

His grip didn't loosen, but his shoulders dropped a fraction. I stepped up behind him, letting my hands trail around his trim waist until I was wrapped around him, pressed against his back. His body shuddered underneath my touch. It felt empowering, like I held some tiny bit of power over him. My fingers found the edge of his T-shirt. I slipped my hand underneath, trailing my fingernails lightly over his stomach, tracing the waistband of his jeans. His grip curled around the edge of the grill a little more.

"I believe I owe you an apology," I whispered. "Let me make it up to you."

I stepped back, and he turned to face me. I reacted on instinct and fell to my knees, though I couldn't meet his eyes, still scared of the vulnerability I was offering up. I winced as the rough concrete floor of the garage dug into my knees. He stepped in front of me, but then his hand was held out in my line of vision.

"Stand up."

I placed my hand in his and let him pull me up. My gaze fixed on his eyes, trying to understand what he wanted. They were unreadable.

"Take off your shorts."

My eyes stayed on him as I kicked off my boots and popped the button on my cutoffs. I pulled them off with my panties, letting them fall to the floor. His eyes left mine to look down. A hint of a smile played at the corner of his lips. The sweater still covered all the scandalous parts, but I assume he thought my addition was amusing. He looked back up to me.

"Perfect." He smirked, probably at my addition to his request. "This is how I want you every day in my house. This is how I know that I am free to touch you when I want. If you put them back on, I will know that you need space. Does that work for you?"

I swallowed. He was full of keen insight. I really didn't think there was a more perfect solution. I wasn't good with talking about my feelings, and he understood that without me saying it. And he was offering me a visual cue. Tears pooled in my eyes, and I blinked rapidly to keep them away. I nodded.

"Yes, Xander. That works for me."

He let his full smile free, and my stomach tumbled in response. "Good. My penis has been hard since your knees hit the ground. I plan to take you up on your offering."

My lips pinched together, fighting a grin as my shoulders shook in silent laughter. His brows drew together. I decided to put his mind at ease because he likely didn't know why that made me laugh.

"It's a dick or a cock, but don't ever call it a penis again if you expect those shorts to stay off."

His eyes tracked to the chicken coop and back to me as his grin took its place back on his face.

"I know, I didn't make the rules. That's just the acceptable language here. But if you call it a penis, it's more like talking to a doctor, or listening to a health class lecture in high school. And believe me, the last thing you want to do is conjure images of old Mrs. Belfry in the moment. It won't work well for me."

He let out a smooth, deep chuckle that had my thighs clenching together. "Noted."

My gaze dropped to the subject at hand, and I could see the outline of him, straining against his pants. My mouth watered as my mind flooded with all sorts of filthy thoughts. I licked my lips and startled as his crashed into mine. He pulled our bodies tight together, and I could feel it pressing into my belly. Everything in my mind converted to a sordid playground. But at the center of it was him. It was always him who had the ability to turn me into this wanton creature, mindless with need.

His tongue tangled with mine in a way that felt like he was welcoming me home. It was hard to describe—I felt relief course through both of us, in the way that his body relaxed, pressing into me, and mine answered in kind. When he broke away, I stared into those indigo eyes as if they held the secrets to the universe and life. Maybe he did, but I wasn't sure he'd ever tell me. And that was okay. He gave me my space, and I could give him his.

"Use your shorts to cushion your knees," he said, his voice a rough growl.

I did as he said, but not because it was phrased as a command or that I felt like I should do what he said. He was a man of few words, but when he did speak, it was almost as if he was reading my mind and giving me permission to do what I wanted. I sort of loved that. My body definitely loved it as it responded with a pool of wetness, building between my legs.

I wasn't normally keen on oral sex, but I wanted to taste him. I didn't know why. It was just this urge that overwhelmed me. Out of all the ways we were together the other night, we hadn't done that. He fucked me in several different positions and gave me multiple orgasms.

He was attentive and focused on me the entire time. I hadn't ever experienced anything like it my entire life. And perhaps that is why I had the sudden urge to please him. I didn't dwell on it too deeply as I watched him slowly reach for his belt.

His movements were unhurried. My gaze was locked on his hands, tracking his every movement. When I peeked up, his features were settled into contentment. Like it was enough for him to watch the expression of unbridled lust that I was sure played out across my face, that locked up every muscle in my body. The anticipation of getting something I wanted buzzed through my veins like electricity. He smiled, and I heard his zipper, my eyes forced back to the movement of his hands.

The moment seemed to draw out forever until his cock sprang free. My mouth watered again at the sight of it, and I swallowed hard. It was darkened at the tip, with a vein bulging on its underside. He was so hard for me. I grew even wetter. What this man did to me was unreal. I was on my knees, begging with my eyes and my body to put my mouth on him. I was turned on so much my body took over, and I reached down to play with myself rather than reach for him. He groaned in response and took a step closer. His hand gripped the back of my head as the flared tip of his dick pressed against my lips.

I opened for him, and he pressed into the wet heat of my mouth. A shiver racked his body, and his chest rumbled. He lost control of his slow, methodical movements and shoved in the rest of the way, bumping the back of my throat. I swallowed to fight the urge to gag. I'd never felt more powerful than the moment I saw his legs tremble, before he pulled back.

The only other thought that threaded through my mind as he thrust back in with a grunt, was I might just be in love with this man. Why else would sucking his cock make me feel as if I could conquer the world, and bring me to the edge of orgasm, just watching him lose himself to me?

CHAPTER NINETEEN

Rose

Two days. I'd been without pants in this house for two days, and to be honest, being with Xander wasn't as horrible as I'd imagined it to be. It wasn't as lewd as it sounded; the borrowed sweaters and shirts were as long as dresses. Granted, I wasn't deluded enough to think that it would last forever, but for the time being, the arrangement worked well for both of us.

Like the next morning, when I got up and made breakfast. Instead of eating first, he fucked me on the kitchen counter. Then we sat and ate our mostly cold food and had a nice chat.

Despite the lack of warmth in our food, it was perfect. He was funny, made me laugh more than once, then excused himself and spent the rest of the day working on his truck. Simply put, he seemed to understand in a way that no other had before that I needed freedom, space, and time alone. He gave me a chance to think, to breathe without having to ask. I was sort of in awe. Either he was very astute, or we both needed the same thing and just fit.

It wasn't the smothering fuckfest I imagined it to be. At night, we'd have dinner and watch TV. He'd rub my feet or keep his hand on my leg throughout the program. We'd go to bed, falling asleep in each other's arms and waking up in the same position. He said that it would only be a few more days until he had all the parts "machined" and ready to reassemble. From there, it would be a day or two before he got it all put back together, depending on if he did it right.

I confess that I only partially listened to him through most of his rundown of the truck situation. His explanations of the car repairs were always rather technical, going over my head. So, I just nodded and watched him as if he were the most fascinating thing in the world, which he was—car stuff aside.

I closed the book after reading the last words in *The Queen of the Damned*. I'd finally found time to finish it with most of the cleaning done. The only thing left that hadn't been scrubbed spotless were the upstairs rooms. I was putting it off because no one went up there anymore. I'd officially moved into his room with the momentous event of relocating my purse to the top of his dresser and bringing down the items he gave me the night I arrived.

I'd also been threatening to clean out the pantry after finding a few expired items in it over the last couple of days.

I leaned back on the couch and looked out the window. I could hear the steady rhythm of his movements, between the sounds of his welding torch, alternating with the hammering of metal on metal. I'd seen mechanics work before. They ordered parts and put them in the right places. But what Xander did out there was beyond mechanic skills. I was starting to think that, given enough time, he could build a car from a heap of scrap metal.

It made me curious about his past. Did he work in an automobile factory back in Czechoslovakia? I didn't want to ask because asking questions was also an invitation to be asked. And we both knew without saying that neither of us was ready to venture down that road.

I watched the strobing lights from his blowtorch through the screen door. I vaguely recalled being told that you weren't supposed to do that—look straight at the light. You could go blind from staring at it, right?

Shaking off the stupid thoughts, I rose from the chair, thinking about the fact that I might be starting to get a bit of cabin fever.

I lived alone, but I was rarely at home. I worked more often than I did anything else. I couldn't remember a time when I wasn't working, having been on my own since I ran away from my foster home at fifteen.

I walked into the kitchen and trudged my way toward the pantry. Not exactly enthusiastic about the task at hand, I pulled open the door. It was large for a pantry, but small compared to most rooms and closets. A person could walk into it, but they couldn't do much more than spin in one spot. There were deep shelves on three walls, so it did hold a fair amount of food.

I stared at it for a moment as my mind flashed with memories of my foster father, the reason I ran away.

Aren't you turning into a beautiful woman?

Listen here, you little spic bitch…

Perhaps, this was why I didn't sit still long enough to really think. Too much time alone can dredge up things a person didn't want to remember.

My mind strayed back. He'd never had a chance to touch me because by the time he built up the balls to make a move, I was gone. Not that he would've been the first or last to try. I wanted to scream. These thoughts wouldn't stop assaulting my mind. I shook my head to clear them away and forget everything about that creepy asshole, then decided to just start pulling everything out of the pantry. Once I got it spread out all over the counters, I'd be able to sort through and organize everything better.

I found some large empty glass jars in the back of one of the lower shelves and decided to transfer all the dry goods into them. With some masking tape and a pen from a junk drawer, I labeled each one before filling it.

I was pouring a box of powdered sugar into one when I felt something cool and silky brush across my shoulder where the sweater had slipped over to one side, exposing bare skin. I jolted and shrieked, causing a cloud of white dust to explode in front of me. I knew it wasn't life-threatening, but it still startled the crap out of me. White dust coated my hair and arms. I'd squeezed my eyes shut to protect them, but I already knew the responsible party by the low snicker over my shoulder.

"Cute," Xander said.

"I'm sure it is." I frowned and attempted to peek my eyes open. "What the hell was that?"

He leaned over my shoulder and presented a yellow rose in front of me. My brows drew together.

"Where did you get that?" I asked, grabbing a hand towel off the oven handle and cleaning myself up.

"It grows out by the gate to the garden. This was the last one left, but they said it might freeze tonight, so I knew it wouldn't survive either way. I thought you might like it." He pulled me against him and kissed my shoulder. "Sweet."

"Thank you." I plucked the flower from his fingers. "It's beautiful." I turned in his embrace and offered him a smile.

"It matches your tattoo."

I snorted. "Don't remind me. I'm tryin' to forget I did that."

"Why? It is a beautiful piece of art on a beautiful work of art." His fingers traced the edge of the sweater where the art in question undoubtedly peeked out.

"You're sweet, but it was a drunken dare. I mean how unoriginal is a rose tattoo that you get because your name is Rosie?"

It wasn't even a pretty tattoo. I'd asked for a realistic sketch of a rose done only in black ink and that was what I got. The only thing unique about it was that the shading was all done in cross-hatched lines. Thin lines overlapped the others, and where they grew closer together, the shading was darker. I also knew that the artist did that to make it less painful than trying to color in a large area with varying degrees of pressure. Xander interrupted my reverie.

"I have never met another Rosie with a rose tattoo, so I would think it is very original."

I grimaced. He'd be the first. "What brings you in here this time of day?" I changed the subject and looked around the room, avoiding his stare. "I made a mess of the kitchen."

"I can see that. What are you doing?" He squeezed me a little tighter to punctuate his question.

"Organizing the pantry." I shrugged. "Your old system was horrible. But you didn't answer my question."

"I thought I would get something for lunch."

"Crap. I forgot that it was before lunch. Luckily, I opened that jar there to figure out what it is. Turns out, it's peach preserves. You wanna peanut-butter-and-jelly sandwich?"

He cringed.

I smirked. "A turkey sandwich?"

His head tipped to the side. "Better." He gave a slight nod of approval.

"Okay, then. One turkey sandwich, coming right up."

Slipping out of his arms, I stuck the rose in a smaller glass jar I half filled with water, then set about making him a plate. I put the sandwich on a plate with a couple of boiled eggs that I'd made this morning after breakfast. They were piling up, the eggs, though the cooler weather had slowed the hens down a little. I added a pickle spear and brought it to him, where he was sitting at the table.

His grin was infectious as he pulled me onto his lap after I set the plate down. The corner of my mouth tipped up in answer.

"I like this. You... here... I like you, Rosie."

My mind locked up, unable to formulate a response. "I..."

He shook his head, saving me from my floundering. "I just wanted you to know." His lips brushed over mine softly, and his arms dropped from around me, freeing me to go as I pleased.

I searched his eyes. He didn't look angry or disappointed; he just looked understanding. Anger flared from somewhere deep inside me. I didn't know where it came from or why I felt it, but it was there. I stood stiffly and returned to the kitchen to finish my task. I needed to finish this pantry job before it was time to start dinner. Fuck, I was becoming a regular June Cleaver.

CHAPTER TWENTY

Wired

Xander left after he finished eating, with a kiss to my cheek and no words. I set about finishing my task in silence as well. The goddamn silence was making me crazy. I normally languished in the quiet, loved the solitude, but now it was bothering me. Xander was bothering me. And the more I thought about it, the more I understood.

It was because my silence was giving away too much. He was reading all of it correctly. Knowing when to back down and when to push—*he* was too much. He was too close with his distance, too accurate at adjusting his actions to my moods, and it was aggravating me. It was like he knew me without permission. An invasion of my private thoughts.

I knew that feeling all that was ridiculous. You can't be angry at someone for being a good person, for fitting well into your life, for accommodating your moods and preferences. But I couldn't stop myself.

I was overreaching for flaws in his perfect facade. I'm sure that said a ton of horrible shit about me as a person, but I couldn't stop it. So, when I was clearing the shelf that was third from the top, the one at eye level, and found the hole in the wall, I was forced to investigate it. I gathered the flashlight I'd seen in the junk drawer of the kitchen and my powder compact from my purse. I held the flashlight next to the hole and used the mirror to look around inside the space.

It was just the normal space between walls in a house. Empty, save for a few wires. I was just about to call myself crazy and leave it alone when I noticed it. Just below the hole, there was a wire that had been cut and spliced into a new wire. I'd no clue what that meant, but I followed the new wire up to where it disappeared into the ceiling. It led to the room above me. And the room above was the other upstairs room—the one I hadn't been in yet.

I couldn't run up there at the moment to check it out, but I knew that was my next destination as soon as I finished this task. I'd find out what was up there. A sinking feeling took up residence in my bones. If he was really hiding something, what could I do about it? I couldn't run. I'd no way to make it back to civilization. I didn't know which direction to go; I could follow the roads, but that would be too obvious.

Why was I making plans like that anyway? Why was I even giving validity to these thoughts? I told myself I was going to stop running and give him a chance, and a fucking wire had me hatching escape routes and plans. What the hell was wrong with me? No, I just needed to let it go. This was just me self-sabotaging, again.

I shoved it to the back of my mind and finished the pantry, deciding to bake some bread when I was done. We were out of bread again after the sandwich I made. It was necessary. He'd given me the recipe a few days ago when we ran out of bread the first time. Making it was much easier than I thought it would be. I was addicted now. Nothing was better than a fresh-baked loaf of bread.

Fully distracted and hungry, my mind settled, and I let thoughts of the mystery wire go.

The next morning, I found myself at the landing at the top of the stairs. With a broom, mop, and other cleaning supplies in hand, I decided to get to work on the last bit left uncleaned. I'd thought about getting out of the house, taking the gun and the camera with me to get some pictures. I still had two and a half rolls of film left.

But of course, that morning the weather decided to get shitty. A cold front had moved in during the night, dropping the temperature and pulling all sorts of nasty sleet and hail along with it. I was surprised when Xander left to go outside after breakfast. He assured me he had a space heater in the garage, and he'd be fine. But he didn't want to put off the repairs for another day because he was close to finishing.

Part of me wondered why I didn't seem as concerned with going home as he seemed to be in getting me there. And on the other hand, the thought had crossed my mind that he was rather keen to get rid of me.

Were those the same thoughts?

I did want to get home. I needed to see if my job was salvageable. Plus, rent would be due soon, and while I'd enough savings left to cover it, I did just spend a good chunk of change on the camera. I'd have to find another job, if there was no way to keep the one I had.

Not that working at the diner was the best job on the planet, but I liked it for the most part. I'd a couple of friends there that I'd be sad to not see on a regular basis, and a few customers I enjoyed talking to. Just thinking about walking back in there sent a pang of homesickness coursing through me.

I grunted at that and set the bucket and mop down. Never thought I'd see the day I grew nostalgic for any part of my life. Pulling the feather duster from the bucket, I set about working. From the top down, that was the best way to clean a room as I'd learned at a long-ago cleaning job.

There was a stool that sat in the corner near the end of the hall next to a window. I grabbed it and pulled it away from the wall, so it was a comfortable distance from the corner. Stepping up, I knocked down the cobwebs and dust that gathered there. I almost wished that opening the window was an option as the dust kicked up, making me sneeze. But it was cold outside, and there were no heaters upstairs.

Surprisingly, it wasn't all that chilly, since the fire Xander had started before I woke seemed to be doing a great job of keeping the house well-heated. It wasn't long before I finished dusting the hall, bathroom, and guest bedroom.

The only place left was behind a closed door.

I stood there, staring at it, debating on whether I should leave it alone. Xander had never told me to stay out of it. But he also never showed me what was in there, like he'd done with the rest of the house. I walked up to the door and laid my hand on the cold wrought-iron knob.

That was perhaps the single most peculiar thing about this house. Everything in there was normal, run-of-the-mill farmhouse. Nothing fancy, just utilitarian or homemade. Those handles, though, seemed like something out of a Gothic mansion. They were the kind that required one of those ornate skeleton keys. I'd never seen anything like them in real life. I turned the knob, or tried to at least, but it was locked.

I bent at the knees and looked through the keyhole. I could see straight through into the room. It was an office. I could feel the crease between my brows deepen with my confusion. Why would someone keep, or even have, an office that they never used? He wasn't a businessman. Just a foreign mechanic who'd retired in America.

Though that was a lot of assumption on my part, because I'd never asked, and he'd never volunteered any information about his past. I hated it, but the more I thought about it, the more my curiosity grew. Coupled with the strange wire I found in the pantry the previous day, my urge to poke around grew stronger.

The only problem was, I didn't have a key and I knew nothing about picking locks. Breaking and entering was not in my bag of tricks. I sighed and stood up, going back to work.

It was about an hour later, after I'd finished dusting and polishing all the furniture. I pulled the bedding off, taking it down to wash, when I saw it. Sitting on the inside of the door to the guest room, a key head poked out beneath the doorknob. Then I remembered that it had been there from the first night. He showed it to me and explained that the door would lock from the inside.

It was smart. If I were looking for a hidden key, somewhere that obvious would be last on my list of places to look. But it wasn't that obvious either, because most of the time, that door sat open, the handle facing the wall. The only reason it wasn't open now was because I was cleaning behind it a few minutes earlier.

I balled the bedding up in my hands and transferred it under one arm. I reached out with the other and pulled the key out of the door. It was heavier than I expected it to be. Made of solid, ornately carved wrought iron, it was a beautiful piece. But it still felt so out of place. I put it back into the keyhole and twisted it. Two large bolts slid out of the door. That was a pretty secure lock for an interior door.

My mind raced with thoughts as my gaze tracked along the edge of the door. Three black strap hinges connected the door to the interior wall. It would be impossible to break down from the inside, but much easier from the outside.

That was an odd choice, since most often people locked doors to keep things out. I thought back to my trailer and all the interior doors opened to the inside, but with normal hinges that weren't decorative. These were the kind found on exterior doors. It did keep the prettier parts in the room. Maybe it was an aesthetic choice? My gaze slid past the door into the hall, and I doubted that was the answer. The door to the other room—the office—had the hinges on the outside. Which made more sense because you'd want people coming into the room to see it.

This whole situation was like a puzzle, and my mind flitted around every possible explanation. I banged my head on the door's edge. Why the fuck did I care about hinge placement? It was like I was purposely delaying getting in that room. I didn't know what I wanted. I didn't think this was me and my relationship hang-ups anymore. There was something off about the whole situation. I needed to know what was in that room.

I pressed my fingertips into my forehead, trying to think of the best way to handle this. I couldn't go snooping around without thought. If it was nothing but an ordinary office, and if I got caught, it would hurt him that I didn't trust him. If it was something more, this could be dangerous. I didn't really know Xander, and given the way we'd met, I still had good enough reasons to consider it. I wasn't being crazy or looking for excuses to run away.

I put the key back in place, then left the door open to conceal it. I'd have to come back later, when I knew the coast was clear. My feet nearly tripped over themselves in my rush down to put on the wash. Then, moving faster than I ever had in my life, I made sure the cleaning was mostly done upstairs. I knew I'd be able to hear if he came into the house, but I needed it to look like I'd spent the day up here cleaning, not snooping.

I'd almost finished; the only thing left was scrubbing out the bathtub and making the bed. The bedding was in the dryer and would be done soon. I checked the time and it was almost noon. I made my way down, fixed Xander some food for lunch, and took it out to him.

His head turned in my direction as I approached, though a welding mask hid his features. He flipped up the mask and smiled. I drooled slightly at the sight of him. He was shirtless and sweaty, wearing that heavy black apron as he used his welding torch. He was patching a hole in a radiator. I didn't know much about cars, but I knew that the radiator and carburetor were two separate things. I tried to think back to what he'd said when he'd talked about the repairs, but I only remembered tuning him out and nodding.

He stepped around the mess of car parts between us and took the plate and cup from my hands, setting it on the counter. His fingers curled around the back of my neck, his thumb pressing at the bottom of my chin to tilt my head back. I thought he was going to kiss me, but his mouth only hovered there, inches from mine.

"Will it ever stop?" His focus bounced back and forth as he searched my eyes like they held answers. "This ache for you that intensifies every time I see you, but never fully goes away."

I opened my mouth to answer. What I was going to say, I don't know. All thoughts ceased in a blink as he closed the distance between us. I kept waiting for the moment where the next kiss wouldn't compare to the last, but it never happened. Each time was better, every touch more intense. He swept away every thought, shut down every brain function aside from the ones that focused on him, in that moment. My bones liquefied, and I started to slip. He caught my elbow to steady me, but the kiss ended at that. He stepped away.

"I don't want to soil you further." He nodded toward my arm.

I looked down to find a black handprint on the sleeve of the sweater I was wearing. That was going to be a bitch to get out. He was smiling, and my breath stalled in my lungs. Even dirty and sweaty, he was mesmerizing.

"You have a little here too." He pointed to the underside of his chin and nodded in my direction. I wiped at it, and my hand came back with black smudges.

"I guess now my outsides match the inside of my brain, after being kissed like that." I gave him a saucy look and laughed.

His eyes darkened. "Later, *zvonová sklenice*."

"You've called me that before. What does it mean?"

He smirked. "I believe you call it a bell jar, some call it a cloche. It is what you bring to mind." He shrugged like he was shaking off any judgment of the name. "You build a wall between yourself and the rest of the world, but it is transparent. Every mood, every emotion, you wear on your shoulder, for all to see."

My mouth opened and closed as I struggled with a response to that. I couldn't think of anything. My lips pressed together as I jutted my chin out. "I see." I turned away. That's what he thought of me—a transparent, silly girl with issues. *Fuck him.*

"It is not a bad thing. It draws me to you, fascinates me. Can you not see that?"

Sure. I've a feeling he's more drawn to my tits and ass. I started for the door.

"Your legs are best."

I gasped and spun to face him. *Did I say that out loud? Or is he a freaky mind reader?* Probably the latter. I was going to throw a snotty retort at him, but his stare was hungry, lustful. I froze. His eyes held laughter in the way they scrunched at the corners. Like he said it to get a rise, to make me stop, and I gave him exactly what he wanted. I huffed and crossed my arms over my chest. I wasn't transparent. I had secrets. *Fuck him.*

"I'll be inside," I grumbled. "I gotta finish cleaning upstairs."

He nodded and grinned. "It was a joke, Rosie. I love all your parts best."

"Yeah, yeah." I turned and finished the walk to the door. "Keep it up and you'll *miss* all my parts."

"As if you could stay away from *my* parts," he called out just before the door shut behind me.

A reluctant smile crept across my face before I remembered my mission. My body stiffened as I was jolted back to reality. It went well; I'd successfully distracted him. He shouldn't be back inside the house for at least a few hours, so I'd have time to see what he was hiding in his secret office. I turned back one last time before I went inside. The light of his welding torch lit up the window. He'd gone back to work, not suspicious at all. Take that for transparency.

I pulled off my boots as soon as I entered the house, and practically skidded across the linoleum floor in my socks, rushing to grab the bedding from the dryer. I ran up the stairs as fast as my feet would take me and made the bed. I rehung the curtains that I'd also washed. They were dusty as all get-out. As soon as that was done, I pulled the curtains shut and bolted for the key.

Pausing in front of the office door, I took a deep breath and held it, listening for any sounds from Xander. I could hear the muffled hammering of metal from the garage and knew he hadn't followed me.

I let the breath out in a rush and stuck the key in the door. It turned with a click and the door groaned open, like it had been waiting for someone to release it. I guessed this room was rarely used.

Dust motes floated in the air, lit up by the light streaming in from the only window. The air was stale from lack of circulation, but overall, the room was clean. Cleaner than the guest bedroom had been. Like he'd only recently abandoned its use.

There were taped-up cardboard boxes stacked against every wall, and a large writing desk sat in the middle of the room. The desk chair sat opposite the window, like he liked to look outside while he worked. Though I'd no clue what kind of work he did in there. The only thing I'd seen him do is work on a truck and take care of chickens.

One side of the desk had two square-front drawers that were the size of a small filing cabinet. The other side had several smaller drawers, for supplies I supposed. There were no pictures in the space. In fact, now that I thought about it, there were no pictures in the entire house, aside from a few paintings that were all different styles. No people. I hadn't thought much of it because I didn't have a lot of pictures on display either. Just the Ansel Adams print and a picture of me with a couple of friends in my bedroom. And that picture was another gift. I'd have nothing if it weren't for people forcing me to own them. But Xander's house was more decorated and thoughtful than my bare-bones space.

I stepped farther into the room. I couldn't decide where to look first. *If I were a clue to reveal something about a very secretive man, where would I be?* That didn't help either. I sighed and walked over to the desk and pulled out the chair. It was disappointing. Everything was so clean and neat, I was scared to touch it and leave behind evidence that I'd been there.

I spun around in the chair, when it hit me. *The wire.* The wire from the pantry led to something. I got down on my hands and knees and leaned closer to the floor. It would come out somewhere around the center of the room. *Bingo.* Near the side of the desk with the filing cabinet drawers, the wire snaked out of the floor and into the bottom of the desk.

I stood up and sat back in the chair, staring at the drawer. *Please open.* I said a silent prayer as my hand hovered near the handle. I'd no way to open those boxes, so if the answers weren't in this desk, I wasn't getting any. The fact that so much hinged on it made me hesitate. I pulled on the handle, and the drawer glided open with ease. My heartbeat pounded in my ear with the sight before me—a phone.

CHAPTER TWENTY-ONE

Captive

A fucking phone. He's had another phone this whole time and never offered it up. *Fuck*. I didn't want to believe that I'd find something damning. But this was it, because if the phone worked, then he'd lied. It was a white phone, an older model that didn't have buttons or a dial. The kind you needed to speak to a switchboard operator to use. My hand shook as I reached out and grabbed it. I pulled it up to my ear, and it was there, plain as day—a dial tone. It went quiet, then all of a sudden there were a series of clicks. I'd no idea what was happening until a woman's voice, speaking in a foreign language, came over the line.

I think it was Czech, but I couldn't be sure. I'd only ever heard Xander say a few words in his native language. I slammed the phone back down on the receiver. What to do? I opened the other drawer, and there was a file—a single file folder, with some sort of form printed on the front. It wasn't helpful; everything was written in what I assume was Czech. I pulled it out and set it on the desktop.

My stomach felt as if I'd swallowed a bag of rocks. I closed my eyes and let my fingers find the edge of the folder. When I opened my eyes, what I saw took my breath away. And it wasn't breathtaking in the good way. Images flashed through my mind. Pale, waxy skin, a mouth twisted open, flies crawling in and out of the gaping, slack cavity. In front of me sat a picture of him. Though in the picture, he was very much alive. I flipped through the pages, but all were in Czech. It looked like a dossier from a spy movie, but I'd no clue. Until I found the last page, I didn't know what it meant. The last page was written in English.

We have located the man that you are looking for. He can be found in a small farm in a rural area in central Texas.

We have surveilled the residence, and he seems to live there alone. One phone line and a truck are his only connections to the outside world. You should be able to get to him and extract the information you need quietly.

Please be advised that this communication in no way grants you any permissions. You will not have diplomatic immunity and will be subject to all the rules and regulations of the United States of America and the State of Texas, as well as any local or county laws.

Please find the attached map pinpointing the location of your target. Best of luck.

It wasn't signed by anyone. It wasn't on letterhead, though the paper quality was above average. I'd no clue what any of it meant. Did it mean that someone was after Xander? Was this really Xander's house, or did the place belong to the dead man? I had more questions than answers.

The paper mentioned a map, but that was the last page. I didn't see a map anywhere in the file. I stuck the paper back in place and straightened the pages before I closed it. It was the only thing in the drawer, so I replaced it and shut it. I opened the three smaller drawers on the left side of the desk. There wasn't much, just a couple of odd pens and office supplies. But in the bottom drawer there was a map.

It was just your standard tourist map of Texas. Nothing special or fancy, but as I unfolded it, I realized it was different. Someone had printed a terrain map over the map of roads and highways. I ignored all the amoeba-shaped lines and found my hometown; then I ran my finger along the roads that I took to get here. Along the path, there was a red dot, just off the road. It had to be this house.

So why would Xander have a letter written from an anonymous source about surveillance and location of this house? There was really only one explanation. He was the killer, and this was a dead man's house. Tears welled in my eyes, and I folded the map up quickly and placed it back in the drawer the way I found it.

I bit down on my fist to muffle the sob that'd built up in my chest. I was shredded. Torn. I'd no idea how to feel—vindicated that I was right, devastated that he'd lied, scared, confused... *I was sleeping with a killer. Oh, God.*

I slipped out of the office, locking the door behind me and replacing the key in its spot in the guest-room door. I sat down in the rocking chair and stared out the window.

I was shocked out of my stupor with a jolt as the screen door cracked off the doorframe, denoting Xander's arrival back at the house. *Shit.* I couldn't let him find me like this—and he *would* find me. I wiped the tears from my cheeks and tiptoed to the bathroom. The sponge and spray bottle I'd filled with a mixture of bleach and water sat on the counter. My gaze caught on my reflection, and I froze.

In that moment, I looked like *her*—like my mama. All those things I saw in her when it came to love and life choices, they were there. Things I resented about her, things I loathed and wanted no part of. That probably should've scared me more than it did. But the first thought was that I looked older and little more unhinged than usual. There was a wildness in my eyes that intrigued me, more than the fear that I was losing myself or in any danger. Which was stupid.

I'd seen the marks on that man's body. He wasn't just killed and dumped in the woods. It wasn't some methodical kill. He was tortured. It was a level of twisted and sick beyond my comprehension. I couldn't fathom what would motivate anyone to do that to another human being. I didn't think there was a logical explanation that would excuse it. But every time my mind tried to connect that to Xander, I tacitly rejected it.

It didn't make sense. He was gentle, kind, funny, and thoughtful... it just didn't connect. I felt like I was missing something. Like I was at the butt of a grand joke but missed the punchline.

But I couldn't deny the fact that there was a subtle shift in the air. A feeling permeated around me, trying to soak into my skin. It settled over me like a thick blanket, smothering. An invisible hand, choking me. I was never a guest—I was a prisoner. And this house was my prison.

I heard the door at the bottom of the stairs open, and I turned and dropped down onto my knees. My muscles locked up. Spraying the tub with the cleaning mixture, I used the other hand to scrub at the rust-colored water stains. They lightened a little, but I'd probably need a better cleaner to get the job done right. No, this task was selected for a specific purpose. As his boots thumped onto the landing, I arched my back, letting the sweater slide off my hips, exposing myself. I don't know where I got it from—if it was learned behavior or common sense. But I knew if I wanted a man to stay out of my head, distracting him with my body was the surest way.

He paused at the open door. And though I wasn't looking, I could hear his breath hitch. I focused on the task at hand, schooling my features into a neutral mask. *Arch my back a little further, lean into the bathtub a little more.* The calcium was cleaning up well, not that it really mattered what I was doing. I was on display for him.

The first touch of his hand sent tingles rippling through my body, leaving a wake of goose bumps in its path. I leaned into his touch, pushing my hip into his palm. *God, his touch shouldn't feel so good. I should be repulsed.* But my brain and my body decided they were on opposing teams. His hand gripped the flesh of my ass cheek, exposing me further. I let out a moan and pushed back toward him. It wasn't an act. I was addicted; the sensations he brought to life in me were beyond resistance.

"I was going to take a shower and see if you wanted to join me, but I have a better idea. How about we get more dirty first?" His voice was raw and thick with unguarded lust.

I groaned and rose, pulling the sweater off in answer. I didn't turn to look at him. I didn't trust myself not to betray my emotions. Somewhere inside, I felt as if I were selling my soul to the devil. Was I doing it for survival? Did enjoying it make me evil too? His belt jingled as he undid his pants, then *thunked* to the floor. I closed my eyes. It didn't matter why. I was going to hell anyway and would gladly burn for eternity to feel this one more time. Wasn't that fucked-up, for a lifelong loner to be affected beyond the point of rational control?

His hand wrapped around my ponytail, yanking me back against his chest. He kissed my shoulder, trailing lips and nips up my neck to my ear. I sighed and melted into his expert hands. His cock brushed against my inner thigh, and I shivered, mewling.

"Oh, God. Xander," I gasped.

"Is my girl ready for me?" he whispered in my ear before tugging on my earlobe with his teeth. "I want to feel, but my hands are dirty."

The vision of him standing there with blood-soaked hands flitted through my mind. I didn't have to imagine too hard. After all, I'd seen him after he'd killed that turkey. I blinked and realized that's not what he was talking about. His hand skated across my belly to cup my breast, leaving behind black streaks and handprints across my body. My heartbeat pulsed between my legs. This shouldn't have turned me on.

I sucked in a breath. "Yes, take me."

I would've nodded my assent, but his hand was wrapped in my ponytail, twisted into it, his grip firm. I arched my back, shoving my ass toward him for a better angle. He grunted and pulled back before pressing the head of his cock against my asshole. I whimpered and flailed my arms to stop him, but it was useless. I couldn't reach him, my body twisted at an awkward angle.

"Anyone ever take you here?"

I shook my head, or tried to. His grip tightened and pulled my head back even farther. "No." My eyes rolled back in my head. I'd always loved having my hair pulled. It didn't hurt. And there was something intoxicating about the way he treated me as if he knew I wouldn't break.

"It will be mine and mine alone, yes?"

I couldn't answer him. I didn't know if that was something I'd even like.

"Do you like giving me what I want, Rosie? Have I ever failed to make it feel good?"

"Yes, it always feels good. Please fuck me, Xander."

"Please? *Zvonová sklenice*, you don't ever have to beg." He chuckled, shoving into my pussy forcefully. "It is my honor to pleasure you."

He groaned in relief as he fully seated his cock inside me and paused. I was so wet for him there was no pain, no friction. White light speckled my vision. I was already on the edge of climax. It was like the fear heightened my awareness, magnifying every point of contact. I let out a low moan and shivered violently.

He moved fast and hard, his hand still firmly wrapped in my hair, pinning me in place. Sitting back suddenly, he pulled me along with him. His hips continued to fuck up into me with my back pressed firmly to his chest.

"You want to come for me, my Rosie."

I exhaled a shaky breath. "Yes."

"Good. Touch yourself." He released my hair after laying my head on his chest. His chin pushed down on my shoulder as he leaned over my body to watch.

I wasted no time doing as he said. My fingers brushed past my clit to touch him where we were connected. He stopped, trapping my fingers between us.

"No. You do not want to do that, *zvonová sklenice*. I have a hair trigger, and I want to see you come apart first."

He pulled back, and I moved my fingers to circle my sensitive nub. But the words *hair trigger* looped in my head. Pictures flashed behind my eyelids. The gun. Shooting the cans. Waxy, pale skin. A bullet hole between vacant eyes. And God help me, I came, shouting Xander's name.

SNAPSHOT

CHAPTER TWENTY-TWO

Clarity

I opened my eyes to find it still dark outside. Looking at the clock, I noted that it was five o'clock in the morning. I blinked several times to wash away the haze of sleep. Xander's heart beat where my ear pressed against him. His chest slowly rose and fell with the deep breaths of sleep. He wasn't awake, but my mind was already preoccupied with him.

I rolled over and attempted to get out of bed, but his arm hooked my waist, pulling me back to spoon. His breathing changed. I knew I'd woken him up. Sighing, I turned in his arms to face him. Blue eyes peered at me in the darkness, looking like the glitter of two jewels in the dim light of the alarm clock.

"I want to go find my cliff and get those sunrise shots."

His dick was stiffening between our naked bodies. He grunted but didn't offer any further commentary. He trailed kisses down the side of my neck and pulled me tighter against him.

"You know if we start that, we won't be gettin' out of bed for the rest of the day."

We hadn't gotten out of bed the previous day. Well, for most of it.

He'd stepped outside to check on the chickens. They were toasty warm in their coop. I'd seen the steam rise when he opened the hatch to feed them and collect the eggs. The weather had gotten worse overnight with another cold front on the heels of the first. It was rainy and icy all day. The news had dubbed it the Ice Storm of 1989 already, like it was a grand weather event.

And in typical Texas fashion, the weather was supposed to warm up considerably. With highs in the mid-sixties, I was getting out of the house. Being cooped up had my hackles up. I was on the verge of screaming at the top of my lungs to let the pressure out. If I thought it wouldn't freak him out, I would.

As it was, I'd plans to do just that as soon as I was far enough away that he couldn't hear me. But I really just needed to think. The lack of movement only had me thinking about shit I didn't want to think about. Being near him had my thoughts dissipating and my body leading me on instinct. I hadn't had time to put my thoughts in order. And I really needed to think.

I knew I should, but it was hard to remember why with his thick cock pressed against the curve of my hip. He'd asked if the burning need for each other would ever stop. I was jaded enough to know that it would, eventually. But I wasn't stupid enough to think that it would happen anytime soon.

What would happen when it did wear off? Would that be the day he killed me? Ugh. I still didn't know how I felt about what I'd found. I still hadn't figured out the answers. And there was a part of me that doubted him—his motivations for keeping me there, his words about the necessity of fixing his truck. I couldn't discern truth from lies as long as I was in this house and near him.

He stopped kissing me, and his hold relaxed. A feeling of dread swamped me, but I didn't know its source. Why that would make me feel... off. I rolled away and got out of bed, and I borrowed clothes from him. My shorts wouldn't do in this weather. I looked a bit ridiculous swallowed in oversized clothes and a fleece-lined jean jacket of his.

"Don't forget to take the gun with you." His voice broke the silence between us like a knife, and I nearly jumped out of my skin.

I offered him a half-cocked smile, which I wasn't sure he could see with the light from the closet behind me. "I won't. And maybe when you get the truck fixed, I can take the film to get developed."

"It should be done by the end of the week."

I walked to his side of the bed and leaned down to kiss him. "Sounds good."

"Will you come back?"

"Of course. I'm just walking to the cliff to take some sunrise shots. Test out that UV filter I paid for and see if I can capture the new day."

His brows drew together. "I do not mean that. What I meant was will you come back after I take you home?"

Oh, fuck. I am a shit liar. Always was. And I agreed to be his, here. But out there—back in the real world—that was a different story. I didn't know the first thing about how to be in a relationship. I stood back up, putting distance between us. "Of course. Why wouldn't I?"

I tried to smile, but it felt forced, so I turned away quickly, shoving my feet in my boots. He didn't respond. I had to get out of there. This wasn't good, and he'd be onto me soon if I sat around being all transparent and shit. He saw too fucking much. Goddammit.

I grabbed my purse and pulled it over my head, stuck the gun in the coat pocket. "I'll be back late. The house is clean. Nothing left to do around here, so I'm just going to take some pictures."

"I never asked you to do that."

"What?"

"The cleaning. I appreciate it, but it was never required of you to do it. Enjoy yourself. I will be here when you come back."

I didn't know what to say to that. So I just nodded and let my feet carry me to the kitchen. I packed a few boiled eggs and some bread, then grabbed the thermos I found in the pantry and filled it with water. The shower turned on just before I walked out the door.

It was cold. Texas cold. The temps never dipped that low, but combined with humidity, the cold seeped into your bones. My breath puffed out like smoke in front of me as I pulled my compass out and faced a direction I thought would lead me to the cliff. With my course set, I pulled the flashlight out of my bag and set off into the woods, one hand in my pocket, resting over the gun.

The farther I walked, the more the sky lightened and my thoughts cleared. The stifling miasma of bad memories stopped assaulting my brain, without the need for physical distraction from Xander. It felt liberating. Staying in one spot for too long just didn't do it for me. I was grateful in that moment that Xander hadn't kept kissing me. I wouldn't have been able to say no. But with each step, the scream I'd planned became less and less necessary. I felt lighter than I had all week.

It was too dark to take pictures on the way, so the trip was fairly quick. My sense of direction astounded me as I arrived at the cliff, only about twenty feet away from the spot I'd lunch the first day. I stopped about three feet from the ledge, afraid to get any closer. My heartrate kicked up, but I felt at peace. The faint trickle of the stream below, the distant and nearby twitter of birds and other critters—it was all soothing.

I inhaled a deep breath and waited. The sun was nearing the horizon, turning the purple-black hues in the west a lighter shade.

I focused on taking it all in, experiencing the moment. There were no killers in that sunrise, no dead bodies or drool-worthy hot guys who may or may not be the actual killer. There was nothing but me and nature.

As the horizon started turning shades of pink and orange, I snapped a few pictures and then switched to the 35 mm lens and attached the UV filters. I'd two, and I was sure to need them since I aimed to take a picture while staring directly at the sun. I put my sunglasses on for extra measure. Then it happened, the first bright sliver of wavering light peeking up at the edge.

A buck stood at the top of the hill that formed the horizon, just where the sun came up. As the giant orb rose behind him, he was thrown into stark relief. Just a two-dimensional black shadow from the lens of the camera. But his head was held high, the large rack of antlers so clearly defined I could count the points. The rest of the hilltop was dotted with trees. It was such a pretty scene that when the sun got too bright, I stopped for a little celebration dance.

I turned and walked back into the woods to capture anything and everything that caught my eye in the dim morning light. It wasn't long before I was switching to my last roll of film. I marched back up the hill to the cliff and set out the towel I'd stuffed in my purse. Leaning back against the tree, I sighed, looking out over the hills in the bright midday sun.

I pulled out the food and nibbled on the bread and eggs separately. Sipping the water, I pulled *Midnight* out of my bag. I'd debated on whether or not to bring it. It was my last book and the only thing to entertain me outside of daytime soap operas on the local TV stations we received. But the book won because I knew what I needed was some quiet time, alone.

Away from everything. Away from Xander. Because Xander made me think. But he made me think about the wrong things. He distracted me with his presence, and that presence seemed to dredge up memories of my past.

And I knew part of the day's plans included doing exactly that— thinking. I needed to catalog every memory I'd had since arriving here, arrange my thoughts, and make a logical conclusion. I couldn't let my issues or hormones cloud my judgment. So, the longer I stayed out there, the better.

The spine creaked as I opened the book. Just a few hours of peace, then the time for thinking would begin.

The edge of the sun was brushing against the tops of the trees, casting shadows throughout the woods. I knew it was getting late. Reluctantly, I shut my book and placed it in my purse. *Xander.* His name brushed against my conscious thought like a soft breeze. I was going to have to think about him soon. I was out of time—and options—to avoid it any longer. It was getting late. I needed to start heading back.

I took a deep breath, looking out over the landscape, as if the trees held my answers. They didn't. But I knew, without a shadow of a doubt, that not all the facts lined up. There was something I was missing. It was like I had half the pieces to a thousand-piece puzzle. I could see the scattered bits and pieces, but not the entire picture.

What I did know was that the missing pieces were askew. The whole picture was off. What I did have didn't line up with the story he gave me.

And that was the other thing—he never really gave me a story. Just that he was retired and from a different country. He had a sister that he was reminded of by watching a chicken. It was pretty sad, that what I did know about him I could still tally on one hand, and I was fucking the guy. What the hell did that say about me?

Though now that I thought about it, the same could be said for every other guy I'd ever slept with too. Which had me thinking all sort of thoughts about myself. And not any of it good. I needed to derail that train of thought because the whole point of this was I needed to figure out what to do.

I needed to clear my head of all the bullshit and think. *Just fucking think.* That's why I came out here—to get distance, and with that distance regain a clarity of thought. *Clear my mind. Trees. Nature. Clean air. A soft breeze. Deep breaths.*

I tipped my head back and let it rest against the tree trunk as I watched the white fluffy clouds roll by in the clear blue sky. I swear one of the clouds looked like a hand wrapped around a thigh. My thigh. His hand. I buried my fingers in my hair and squeezed at the roots.

A thought did occur to me then. It was in the surety that Xander had when we were together. The way he knew exactly what he wanted. There was a precision to our encounters—the precision that'd be needed to torture a man for weeks, yet not kill him. The surety that would be needed to coldly put a bullet between someone's eye to take their life.

I sighed. I was being overly dramatic.

There were things he did that pointed to another conclusion, like the fact that he reminded me to take the gun before I left. Why would he do that if he was the only danger? Why would he give me the gun in the first place? He obviously believed there was a danger to me, other than him.

I hopped up, gathering my things to head back. I still had a couple of hours of walking to think it through. As I picked up my stuff, it struck me like a bolt of lightning. I needed to go back to the body. I didn't want to. There was no telling what condition it would be in. But I'd been with or near Xander since that night; he never had a chance to go back to the body. So, if it was still there, untouched, then it was likely that Xander was the killer.

Who knew what had happened to my car. That man could've been a thief or some random stranger on the road. We hadn't stuck around long enough, and I hadn't noticed if there were any other cars nearby that he could've arrived in. I was too busy trying to survive to catch the details of my surroundings.

But if the body was buried, then it was likely the killer came back but hadn't found us yet. Xander's home wasn't easy to find or conspicuous. It was well-hidden and far from the road. So the best solution was to check the body, see where that led me.

The hair on the back of my neck stood on end, and goose bumps spread over my arms. Going near there was sort of asking to run into the killer. If he'd come back today of all days, it was possible. I didn't want to do it, but I had to know what had happened to that body. I needed something else before I could make any assumptions about Xander. It seemed like the next logical place to find answers, other than sneaking back into that office. Though that was next on my to-do list—if I could find the time or another good excuse to be upstairs again without drawing suspicion that I was snooping.

With that thought, I slipped my hand into the pocket of my coat and wrapped my hand around the cold steel of the gun. Then I set one foot in front of the other, the compass in front of me guiding my way, with a steely resolve that I'd survive this. No matter what the costs.

CHAPTER TWENTY-THREE

Buried

An eerie sense of déjà vu crept up my spine. I took each step through the trees with the utmost caution, going slower than was probably necessary. But I didn't know how far I'd walked to get to the body the first time. I didn't want to make the same mistake of stumbling upon a killer again haphazardly.

The sun was getting close to the horizon, but I wasn't as worried this time. A full moon was already up in the sky behind me, so even the dark would be well-lit, and if not, I had the flashlight just in case. There was a noise just off in the distance that had a rhythmic quality to it. I slowed even further, only stepping on the balls of my toes, constantly checking to make sure I wasn't going to step on a wayward branch.

The closer I got, the louder the sound grew. *Shick... Thump... Shick... Thump.* And the smell. *Holy shit!* It was so much worse than when I was out here the first time. The body couldn't have been buried. The smell was too potent for that. But someone was definitely out there. My heart started pounding in my ears, competing with the rhythmic noise. I pressed my back against a tree and pulled the gun out of my pocket, checking to make sure the bullets were all loaded and in place. My hands shook violently as I released the latch that opened the bullet chamber. The bullets rattled and jumped in their slots. I placed my other hand over them to make it stop.

Squeezing my eyes shut, I felt the wetness clinging to my lashes. *Deep breaths. Bad idea.* I gagged and buried my nose into my shoulder. Though my stomach had other thoughts and continued to heave, I kept it down. I tried to calm myself. I could do this. I needed to see who was over there. I needed to know who the killer was. I needed it to not be Xander. Though, I wasn't really sure why. Perhaps because I felt like some piece of my soul would be redeemed with him.

Not that it was likely. I was far from a saint. But sleeping with a murderer would be icing on the shit cake of my life. And even though it wasn't the appropriate time to be considering this, it was helping.

Opening my eyes, I peered down at the gun as I removed my hand. The bullets were all there, in the appropriate place. The trembling had subsided, mostly. I clicked the gun shut and peered around the side of the tree. I couldn't see anything. I turned and looked around the other side, but there were still too many trees between me and the sound. And the smell.

I rolled up the sleeves of the oversized jacket. The cold couldn't penetrate my panic. But really, it would get in the way of the sight if I had to aim the gun. Once that was done, I steeled myself. I could do this. I turned and crouched, staying close to the tree.

I kept my body low as I crept around the tree. Sure, speed would've kept me from being out in the open for so long, but sound was a factor too. And I didn't trust myself to be both fast *and* soundless. Xander wasn't an idiot, and I doubted the killer would be either. I wasn't Chuck Norris. I couldn't put some mud under my eyes and traipse around the woods undetected.

I headed straight for another large tree, keeping my ears tuned to the area that the sound was coming from, glancing in that direction with each careful step.

Once I made it to that tree, I went to another one, then another. Another five trees later and I was able to see the clearing. I recognized the cactus that had so generously gifted me with its spines the first time

I encountered it. I still didn't have a clear view. There wasn't anyone I could see. The shovel was gone from where it was stuck in the ground that first night, and near where it had been, a rounded mound of packed dirt sat. The steady *snick... thump* was clearly someone digging. But where? Why?

The tree in front of me was an old oak. If I stood up straight, there was a Y in the branches that I could peer over. It was a dangerous move because it would put me at eye level with whoever was out there. I pulled the gun up next to my ear and placed my other hand on the trunk of the tree as I slowly rose up to my feet.

Time seemed to slow to a crawl. My heartbeat thundered in my ears as I took in the sight before me. I fought the urge to gasp. I was trying my hardest to breathe as little as possible. But before me, in the clearing, was a man. He had a bandanna over his face as he dug into the earth, most likely to block the putrid smell. He was shirtless and covered in sweat and streaks of mud, and I couldn't see his face, but I'd recognize that body anywhere.

It was Xander.

My heart stalled in my chest. The sound of my rapid heartbeat was replaced with a loud roaring echo of silence. Though he was still digging, I couldn't hear it.

The biggest shock wasn't that he was out there, it was that he was digging another human-sized hole. A grave for another victim. I didn't see the corpse of that man. I assumed it'd already been buried. But that one, the new hole, it had to be for someone else. And the only person left was me.

Xander stopped to wipe his brow with the back of his hand. He looked around, and I ducked back down. *Fuck, fuck, fuck.* I needed to get out of there. Not just away from this makeshift graveyard of a crazy serial killer and torturer, but out of his house. I needed to get home.

When the *snick... thump* started up again, I moved. I was careful to remain quiet, but with every step farther away, my pace quickened until I was flat-out running. Going back the way I came, I only slowed once

I was far enough away that I could no longer hear or smell anything from that whole scene.

I bent over, resting my hands on my knees, breathing in through my nose to calm my racing heart. I needed to get it together. I'd no clue where to go, but I needed to find my way back to civilization. And the roads were a bad idea. He'd find me. I could feel it in my gut. My stomach churned at that thought. I was sleeping with someone who was planning to kill me in a horrible, vicious way. How could I be so stupid?

Images assaulted me until I felt the bile rising in my throat, and my stomach heaved. *Fucking great.* I closed my eyes and tried to let the nauseous feeling subside. Breathing in through my nose, I felt tingles spread over my body, and my vision dimmed. I was going to pass out. I needed to think. *Think, goddammit!*

The map. I needed to go back and get that map. With it, I could chart out a course that would be the most direct path to the nearest town. From there, I needed to go straight to the police station and turn him the fuck in.

With that thought, my mind sobered a bit. I realized I was still holding the gun in a white-knuckled grip. I stuck it in my coat pocket and stared down at the imprints in my palm. I was surprised I hadn't accidentally fired it.

I shook my head. I didn't have time to ponder random shit. I needed to go back. *Get the map and the rest of my stuff. A blanket would be good, and some food.* It would take me days to walk to the nearest town out here. Food was a must. I pulled out the compass, set my course toward my best guess of the right direction, and started jogging. I wasn't going to be able to full-on run the whole way there. And Xander didn't look close to finishing.

Though he could stop at any moment, knowing that I'd return. The sun was well past the trees and would hit the horizon soon. Night would follow swiftly. My pace quickened at that thought. I wanted to be long gone before he returned.

CHAPTER TWENTY-FOUR

Mapped

I hit the door like a linebacker, and thankfully it was unlocked. It swung open and bounced off the wall. *Map, blanket, food. Map, blanket, food.* I tossed my purse on the kitchen table, kicked off my mud-caked boots, and ran straight for the laundry room, grabbing a thicker but still lightweight wool blanket and a piece of rope that was in a basket above the dryer. The blanket should be enough to keep me warm and cushion the ground a bit, while still being somewhat easy to carry. I ran back to the kitchen and dropped it on the counter, laying it out flat so I could roll the food up into it the way we'd learned to pack stuff in Girl Scouts when I was a kid. I'd use the rope to cinch it up and make a strap, so it would be easy to carry.

My breath was wheezing in and out. I could barely feel the stitch in my side from all the running. Panic and urgency narrowed my brain's depth of thought to only the necessary things for survival.

Get what I need, and get the fuck out.

I turned and flung open the pantry. I froze. In that split second, I remembered that I needed to get the map first. I didn't want to get everything together and be in such a rush that I'd forget it. That map was the only way I'd make it out of here alive. My brain was already in hyperdrive, so forgetting it was a very likely scenario. I shut the door and turned on my heels to race up the stairs. It was still light enough outside that I could see my way around the space without turning on the lights. And I was thankful. Turning on a light up here could alert him from a distance that I was somewhere I shouldn't be.

I rushed over to the guest room and grabbed the key. My hands were shaking so bad that it took several tries before I managed to pull it out. I slid on the floor in my socks in my rush to cross the hallway. My shoulder slamming into the door was the only thing that stopped me from crashing to the ground. The key bounced off the backplate several times before I managed to fit it in the hole. My hands were shaking in time with my racing heart. It sounded like a steady drumbeat pounding inside my head.

Grasping the handle, I twisted it, pushing inside. I halted in my tracks, my jaw slack, eyes blinking rapidly in disbelief. Everything was gone. All the boxes that lined the wall had vanished. The only thing left was the desk. *Did he know I came in here? Had he been planning to clear it out all along and my absence gave him the opportunity? Where did he take them to?*

I sent up a prayer that the map was still there before my feet stirred into motion and carried me across the room. I sat in the chair and pulled open the drawer where the map had been. It was there, sitting right where I left it, untouched. I grabbed it and shut the door. I started to stand, but then curiosity got the better of me. I pulled open the drawer with the file. It was still there. The phone was too.

My mind whirled with what could've been in those boxes that he felt the need to remove them, but left this stuff. The file, phone, and map had seemed pretty damning, but if he felt the need to move those boxes, that must've been worse. My breath still sawed in and out of me, but I was slowly catching my breath. I felt my brows pinch together and huffed, then shook my head. I was wasting time. Who cared what was in those boxes; I was getting out of here, come hell or high water.

I turned and left, locking the door behind me. The key went back to its hiding spot, and I looked around the room one last time. I almost felt sad to be leaving. But that was ridiculous—I couldn't stay here with a crazed killer bent on making me his next victim.

Halfway down the stairs, I heard it: a car door shutting. I did the worst thing you could do in a situation like this—I stopped in my tracks, one foot hovering over the next step. I didn't hear anything else, but I knew someone was out there, which meant I needed a new plan. I didn't know if that was Xander at his truck, in the garage, or if someone new had arrived. My heartbeat thundered loud in my ears and my vision narrowed.

The gun.

I needed to get back to my stuff and see who was out there. I stupidly left the front door open and my purse on the kitchen table. *Fuck.* I listened for a moment for signs that anyone was in the house but heard nothing. With that, I sprang into motion, rushing back to the kitchen. Sliding across the floor, I crashed hard into the table, stuffing the map in my purse and pulling out the gun. I checked the chamber for bullets. My mind slowed a bit at the comfort that they were locked and loaded.

Quickly, I turned to face the front door. It was bright enough to see outside but not enough to light the interior of the house. I could see the front porch and beyond, but I was concealed by the shadows. I walked carefully over to the windows and looked outside. There wasn't anything new from what I could see. The garage blocked the view of the driveway, so I wasn't sure if there was anything—or someone—else on the other side. The door to the garage was shut, though I couldn't remember if it was like that when I came back. The lights were off inside it.

It was getting dark fast, and if Xander was out there, he was skulking in the shadows. Then I heard him. He was softly singing a country tune in his off-kilter accent. Goose bumps burst to life across my whole body as a chill vibrated down my spine. This was it. I had one of two choices: lie in wait and hope that I could kill him before he killed me, or use sex to change his mind and give me time until he fell asleep, before I could make my escape.

Of those two, the latter seemed like my best chance at survival. He was skilled and athletic, and my most useful skill was waiting tables and cleaning. Plus, in that split second, I had to be brutally honest with myself and answer whether I was capable of pulling the trigger without forethought. The answer was no. To do that, I would've had to be absolutely sure that whomever I shot was worthy of a death sentence. If not, that hesitation would cost me my life. From what I'd seen of him in action and what I supposed he was capable of, he would use that moment of hesitation against me and I would have shown my cards.

With that thought, I slipped my gun back into my purse and crept into the laundry room to use our secret code. I hoped I was making the right choice, but I wasn't sure where my true motives lay. Maybe some demented part of my soul wanted to be with him one last time. *Even if it led to my death.*

I shook my head. Thoughts like those weren't going to help me now.

I slipped off the borrowed pants, socks, underwear, and jacket off until I was in nothing but his sweater. I took a deep breath to steel my nerves and went back into the kitchen, opening the fridge to find something for dinner. I'd just pulled out the makings for chili when the screen door cracked off its frame. I jumped, startled. My body tensed as I continued going through the motions. I knew I should look at him, greet him, but I didn't trust myself.

Would he see through me? Probably. He was very good at reading me. *This is a bad idea. Oh, God.*

I couldn't hear any movement behind me, and with each passing second, my nerves ratcheted tighter. I bent down to pull the stockpot from one of the lower cabinets when I caught sight of his boots, right behind me. I stood slowly, placing the pot on the stove. Fear thickened the blood in my veins. My heartbeat slowed, the sound rushing through my ears.

This was a dumb idea. He didn't want me; I was just a fun way to pass the time for a while. I turned to grab the meat from the counter and gasped. He was standing there between me and the counter. Water glistened off his bare chest, catching the final rays of light from the sunset, while his face was shrouded in shadow, unreadable. Before I finished drawing in that breath, his hands were firmly gripping my bare ass while his mouth swallowed any cries of shock or protest I may have uttered. His hands felt like ice, and when I placed mine on his shoulders, his skin was cool to the touch, but his mouth was warm and demanding.

He backed me up until I bumped into the island counter. When I felt the brush of wool against my lower back, I knew. I'd failed to put away the blanket. I kissed him back like my life depended on it. It probably did. I ran my hands down his chest, feeling the smooth bumps of his scars and the rigid, tense muscles. The cold beads of water gathered under my hands as they slid down his abs to his belt buckle.

I could say a lot of things about myself, but in that moment, as my heartbeat pounded in my cunt, I knew I wanted him. This. Even if it cost me my soul and my life, I would forsake it all. If he was the devil incarnate, I was well and truly Satan's whore. I couldn't have stopped myself. I didn't want to.

It felt twisted and right at the same time. Like my brain, heart, body, and soul were at war. But I couldn't decipher what was fighting for whom.

His pants were soaked and cold, but as I finished undoing them and reached in to grab him, he was hot and hard. Velvety smooth skin slid under my grip. He groaned and broke away from our kiss.

"You are just what I need at the end of every day." He rested his forehead against mine. "I see you have more than food planned for dinner."

I tried to nod and answer him, but it came out as more of a whimper as he thrusted in my hand.

"I have not done near enough in my life to deserve you," he whispered. "But I will take whatever you give me."

His hands released my ass and he pressed into me—trapping me between him and the counter—as he reached for something behind me. He pressed a kiss into my shoulder on the way back.

"Do you trust me?" His voice was graveled with unspoken emotion.

No. "Yes," I squeaked out.

He pulled the sweater over my head and I was naked before him, just like that. Then I felt it. He wrapped the length of rope that I was going to tie up the blanket with around my wrists, binding them together in front of me. My jaw went slack as my heart raced. Fear and shock struck me silent. I felt like a deer in headlights as the few seconds it took him to expertly bind my wrists stretched out into an eternity.

I didn't know what to do with this. Stop him and risk my life? Put faith in him that it was a purely erotic move? I didn't think I had a choice, which was both arousing and terrifying. I'd no clue what he was doing as he pushed a finger in between the rope and my wrist which increased the pressure, but it wasn't tight. He grunted and turned me to face the island counter. His now-hot palm pressed in between my shoulder blades, pushing me to bend over the counter.

His movements were controlled and slow. I stared at the knife block at the end of the counter and stretched my hands up to be near it as I pressed my chest into the wool blanket. At least I could try for a weapon if this went sideways. I turned my face, pressing my lips into my shoulder and feeling the rapid breaths escape my nose and tickle my skin. It was like every nerve ending in my body became hyperaware of every hint of stimulation. His palm trailed over my back, my ass, and down my thigh, like he was mapping every curve on my body.

I felt myself growing wetter with every drawn-out moment, like this was his plan all along. His hand hooked behind the knee of my right leg, coaxing it up over the edge of the counter until my thigh pressed into my ribs. The toes of my left leg were left to dangle, barely brushing the floor. I was so exposed and helpless in this position.

His hands disappeared. I waited, completely still, listening to the heavy silence. The whisper of cool air from the still-open front door teased my skin, and goosebumps sprung to life. His cedar smell carrying on the breeze seemed to calm me a bit.

Then his hot breath puffed over my most vulnerable flesh. I could feel my arousal drip down my leg. He hummed appreciatively. He wasn't close enough to touch, but close enough that I could feel the vibrations of that hum. It ricocheted up my spine, making me raise my head and gasp for breath.

"Xander," I moaned, my voice a plea.

"*Zvonová sklenice*, I knew from the moment I laid eyes on you that you were something special." His tongue trailed up my thigh, lapping up my juices. "But you are so much more than I ever imagined."

His face dove into my pussy, and he moaned as if basking in the most delicious food. I cried out at the assault of sensations from the vibrations and strokes of his tongue. From this angle, the rough whiskers of his five-o'clock shadow scraped against my most sensitive parts, only heightening the pleasure. *Holy fuck.* His hands gripped my hips, pinning them in place against the counter's edge. I couldn't move, though that was the last thought on my mind.

Until his tongue strayed up and circled my asshole.

I squealed and squirmed to get away. It felt beyond good, but Holy God, no one had ever done that to me before. It was no use anyway. I couldn't overpower him, and he had a firm grip and I was in a position with no leverage. He bit my ass cheek and chuckled at the way my body clenched.

"Stay still."

His fingers pumped in and out of my soaked cunt, his thumb toying with my sensitive bundle of nerves until he had me on the precipice of release. Then he pulled out and his mouth was back. He bit down on my clit and sucked hard. I came on his tongue, screaming his name. Off in the distance, the chickens cackled, startled by the noise. I lay my head back down and breathed into my shoulder. I heard his pants hit the floor.

"I have never seen a more perfect picture, my love." He smoothed his hand over my ass cheek. "I will have this soon enough. But I want you to roll over to your back and sit up."

I did as he asked. He helped me with the sitting-up part as I struggled to find a way to leverage my bound hands. I arched my back to counteract the forward momentum as I teetered on the edge. He looped my hands behind his neck and put each of his arms under my knees.

"Look down," he said.

I watched every inch of him as he lined up and disappeared inside of me. His movements were measured, slow. The controlled drag, every twitch of his dick, felt exaggerated and real. It lit a fire inside me, felt more substantial because I could see it.

"This is the way we are joined as one. You are a part of me. You see the monster in me and instead of tremble in fear, you tremble with need. I will worship you until the day that I die."

My release came as a trickle, like molten lava dripping from the base of my skull, sliding along my spine until it reached my core and burned through me. It utterly consumed me, and I clenched around him in heavy spasms, arching my back. My head snapped up with the movement; his too. He trapped me in his gaze, watching me while we came together, as he said the words that would mark my soul forever.

"I love you, Rosie. And I won't let you run away from that."

My heart slowed to a crawl, thudding beats in my head and clouding my hearing.

Thuuump.

Thuuump.

Thuuump.

And I remembered that I needed to breathe.

CHAPTER TWENTY-FIVE

Run

Those words echoed in my head hours later. *I love you, Rosie. And I won't let you run away from that.* He knew. He had to know I was planning to leave, and that show with the rope and fucking me on the blanket I was prepared to run with was a message. But the real question was... how would he stop me? If you really love something, you can't kill it, right? And I felt truth in those words. Or at least I thought I did. Though I couldn't decipher which part was the truth.

But the simple truth was that it wouldn't last. Xander and I had no future, and he was bound to see it eventually. I was about as fucked-up as they came, carrying enough baggage for an entire roomful of people. And he was dangerous in more than just the figurative sense. I needed to run as fast as I could, as far as I could, at the first opportunity. My survival depended on it.

After the sex earlier, Xander had carried me to the bathroom and bathed me, and then he'd reheated leftover turkey to feed me in bed. I couldn't have walked after if I wanted to. But it was all the care and attentiveness after he fucked me senseless that always rocked me to the core. It didn't line up. He'd knocked me off balance this entire time, until I couldn't see the situation for what it was.

And then there was the other shit he'd said. *You see the monster in me, and instead of tremble in fear, you tremble with need.* As fucked-up as it was, it was true. The thought didn't fill me with butterflies and have me picking out flowers for our wedding. It had me scared shitless. Not so much of him, though parts of me were for a multitude of reasons, but of what I was becoming: dependent on a guy and even worse, one with murderous tendencies. Feeling whatever it was I was feeling toward him wasn't good. It went against everything I'd fought so hard for. It had me twisted around backward, trying to reconcile the depths I'd fallen.

I would not become my mother. I would not become one of the vast majority of the women in my backwoods hellhole of a home.

Fuck. I lay in the bed, listening to his breaths even out. I needed to make sure he was asleep, then I'd find the first opportunity to get the fuck out of here. I'd sacrificed myself, and now it was time to collect the bounty. I could tell he was tired when we lay down. He would be dead asleep soon, after a hard day of digging graves and fucking.

The tick of the clock on the living room wall was loud in the dead of night. It echoed in my ears, a hollow, empty taunt from the inanimate, telling me that the world still spun on its axis even if it felt out of control from my point of view.

Minutes passed.

Hours.

He slept.

I made my move in slow, measured increments. The hare never won the race. I'd make it out of here with my life, even if my soul was a lost cause. He rolled in his sleep, moving from his side to his back and edging closer to me. I took that as my cue and made my move rolling in the same direction until I was at the edge of the mattress. I waited to make sure my movements didn't wake him.

When I was sure I hadn't, I slid out until my knees touched the floor, and I let my body follow. Silently, I crouched next to the bed, listening for signs of movement. Nothing. I crept out of the room on my hands and knees. Once I was well past the door, I stood. I tiptoed through the kitchen and into the laundry room, dressing as quickly and as silently as I could in the clothes I'd abandoned.

Back out in the kitchen, I pulled the sweater over my head. Xander had moved it to the counter, where it sat folded neatly next to his clothes. He was probably the cleanest man I'd ever met. Even his garage was spotless, organized, and tidy. I'd never seen anything like it before. Which made the fact that parts of the interior of the house were in such disarray—just another thing about him and this house—this whole situation—that didn't add up.

I grabbed my purse off the table and started throwing random food items in without thought to anything other than not making a sound. Once my purse was heavy enough to start digging into my shoulder, I stopped. I'd forgotten the coat, so I grabbed that and the blanket as I raced for the door, scooping up my boots from the floor along the way. I twisted the lock and the doorknob so slowly that a hundred heartbeats pounded in my ear in the time it took to open each one. I pushed the normally squeaky screen door open just enough to slip through and pull the door shut behind me.

Once outside, I shoved my feet in my boots, threw the blanket around my shoulders, and hit the ground running. My breath puffed out in front of me in the cold night air like smoke. It trailed around my body as I pushed through it with each reaching stride. My purse thumped heavily against my thigh with near-bruising force. I didn't have time to stop and adjust it. I didn't have time to study the map. I needed to get away as fast as I could. So I took off in a direction I knew I'd find on the map—the cliff.

I was well past the tree line, and in the thick of the woods, when I heard it. The screen door cracked off its frame, followed shortly by an animalistic roar.

"Rosie!" Xander's angry voice ripped through the night, echoing off the trees.

Distantly, coyotes howled in response. This was it. I passed the point of no return. I was on my own now because surely if he caught me, he was going to kill me. And I had no intention of letting either happen.

CHAPTER TWENTY-SIX

Shelter

Off in the distance, a storm was rolling in. Lightning streaked the sky, lighting up the world like the day, brief flashes before the night took over again. I could see the edge of the clouds creeping closer to the full moon, and I knew my time was running out. Soon that guiding light would disappear. After that, my current state of dry warmth would vanish.

My feet slowed, and I took big gulps of air as the surroundings became familiar. I knew I was getting close. My mind slowed, too, as my breath caught up. I looked around but didn't see anything out of the ordinary. I didn't think he followed me. If he did, he wouldn't have gotten far before he had to turn back and get dressed. The cold was bitter.

I found my spot next to the tree and set the blanket down long enough to remove my purse and put the jacket on. Shuffling through the contents of the purse, I searched for the gun. Once my hand found the cool metal, something inside me clicked into place. My heart rate calmed, and my thoughts felt more steady. I placed it in the pocket of the coat.

Shelter. I needed to find somewhere where the rain wouldn't get to me. Walking to the edge of the cliff, I waited for the world to light up again to see if I could spot something helpful. I scanned the rolling hills that lay before me in the brief flashes. I was about to give up and try walking farther when I caught a brief glimpse of it. At the bottom of the cliff, on the opposite side of the creek, there was a dark spot. I couldn't be sure what it was, so I turned and fished the flashlight out.

I crouched down and scooted on my knees, closer to the cliff. I wanted to hang the flashlight over the edge so when I turned it on, it couldn't be seen from behind me. I'd no idea if he was close enough to see the light, but I was going to be as careful as I could be. I scanned the woods behind me, slowly, but I didn't see any movement beyond the normal sway of the trees in the gusts of chilly night air.

Leaning over, I flicked the switch on and scanned the area I'd seen in the darkness. It was an alcove in the cliff side. I moved the light to shine on the ground below and trailed it up the cliff side off to my right, looking for a way to get down there. About a hundred feet away, there was a spot where the cliff broke with a jagged edge that sloped downward toward the creek. There were roots from trees that grew at the top and poked out in random places. It would have to do. And from here, it only looked to be about thirty feet from the top of the cliff to the creek bed below. I turned the flashlight off and grabbed my purse, cramming the blanket inside as I quickly walked in that direction.

Once I got there, I took a deep breath to steel my nerves. I couldn't believe I was actually doing this. I wasn't afraid of heights, but I didn't go actively looking to get myself in dangerous situations either. I scanned the area surrounding me, but there were no signs that Xander had followed me.

I arranged my purse across my body, so it hung in the back, and crouched down, lowering my feet to the sloping edge below. The outcropping was only about six inches wide, so I kept my weight on my toes and inched sideways searching for the next root in front of me.

It was a slow process because I'd have to wait for the lightning to streak the sky and reveal the next root to grab hold of. I tried not to think of the distance between me and the ground below, but every time my foot would slip, or the width of the ledge narrowed, I'd look down and be reminded that falling was not an option. *I will survive this.* I had to. I had a future. Not a particularly bright one. I was never going to change the world, but I had to believe that my existence had enough meaning that there was a purpose to fulfill. And I don't think dying at the hands of a crazed killer, or at the foot of a cliff, was the point.

You are meant for great things, baby girl.

My mother's voice invaded my thoughts. At any other time, that would've been unwelcome, but I needed a distraction. So, I let the thoughts flow.

My sole purpose in this world is you. I was put here to make you. And I've done my job well.

Tears welled up, and I stopped and brushed them aside with the sleeve of my coat. I could still remember the warmth of her soft lips as they pressed against my forehead. I didn't know what hurt worse: remembering what she did, or remembering when she was just being my mom.

Though there was no way I'd let myself think of that night. Not in a million years.

My foot slipped again, but this time I heard rock break away from the cliff and tumble down its side until it plunked into the water. I gripped the root in my hand until my knuckles were white, pressed myself against the stone face of the cliff side, and waited for my heart rate to slow back to normal speed.

I had to have been more than halfway down—past the point of dying if I fell, but it was no less scary knowing that fact. I took in a deep breath and counted to ten. I'd move again when I was done. I couldn't stay here all night. With that thought, the first raindrop landed in my hair. The icy-cold water soaked through to my scalp, causing goose bumps to scatter across my flesh. It wasn't technically raining yet, more like warning drops from the outer perimeter of the storm. But it did add some urgency to my progress. I didn't know how well the roots would help stabilize me once they were wet, and I wasn't keen on testing it. It was too damn cold to come back from being soaked, and I didn't need to die from hypothermia either.

As I got closer to the bottom, the roots became shorter, more sparse, and harder to hold on to. I had to switch to finding spaces in the rock to grip. The lightning seemed to be getting brighter and the thunder louder as more raindrops thumped against my coat.

The next step, my foot found solid ground, and I had no time to stop and think or contemplate what I'd just done. I turned around, sprinting in the direction of the alcove, and pulled out the flashlight to find a spot to cross the creek. The creek wasn't very deep, and the bed was uneven, forming tiny islands in one part that were just close enough. I hopped across, skipping from dry spot to dry spot until I reached the other side.

When I finally reached the alcove, only seconds had passed before the sky opened up and a deluge poured down from above.

Off in the distance, I heard screaming, but as I sat and listened through the harsh pounding of the rain, I realized it wasn't screaming, but the cries of a mountain lion. The ceiling of the alcove was low, low enough that if I stood on my knees, I could reach up and touch the ceiling. I crawled toward the back as far as I could until I was forced to lie down, then scooted until my back pressed against the cool stone wall. I prayed to whoever might listen that nothing called this space home.

CHAPTER TWENTY-SEVEN

Breathe

I pushed the peas around on the plate, willing them to disappear. Why we don't have the ability to make bad things vanish with our thoughts is something I question quite often. If I'd a superpower, that would be it. I didn't need a lasso of truth like Wonder Woman; I saw the world quite clearly already.

My fork clanked against the plate, causing Mama to look up. She was thinking again, with a frown squishing her pretty features. She did that a lot. It never meant anything good. And Fred wasn't home. The combination of those two factors already made it feel like we were standing on the edge of a cliff, waiting to be pushed over.

"If you're not going to eat, go scrape your plate and leave it in the sink," Mama said, sounding tired.

I frowned and forced myself to eat one more forkful of the mushy green balls. Yuck. Then I couldn't take it anymore. She went back to staring at the wall, and I quietly pushed my chair back and walked into the kitchen.

After I was finished, I paused at the door. She didn't look up or acknowledge any movement, so I walked past her to the living room and went back to the spot I'd left my coloring book and markers. I wanted to watch a show on the TV, but I'd learned long ago that quiet activities were best when I was home. Drawing too much attention to oneself was never a good thing.

My stuff was right where I'd left it, and as I picked up the purple marker, I gasped. When Mama had called me for dinner, I'd rushed to the table so she wouldn't have to call me twice, but I forgot to put the cap back on the marker. And while I ate, the purple ink had bled into the carpet fibers.

I spit on the spot and leaned over using the edge of my shirt to try and scrub away the stain. To my horror, the spot only doubled in size and I now had a bright purple spot on my T-shirt. I panicked when I heard Mama get up from the table. I scooted my coloring book over to cover the spot and watched her carry the two uneaten plates into the kitchen. She scraped them into the trash with a low groan and turned her back to me as she washed off the plates in the sink.

I left the coloring book and ran down the hallway of our trailer to get a soapy washcloth. Except there were no washcloths in my bathroom, so I had to go to the master bath to find one. I was just about to turn the corner back into the hallway when I heard the front door slam shut. The whole trailer rocked. I knew what had happened without even looking. My stepfather, Fred, was home.

Oh, God. I froze, not knowing how to react. I wasn't allowed in their room when Fred was home. I really wasn't allowed in there ever, unless it was an emergency. I took a step back into the bedroom, shutting the door without a sound. My heartbeat raced like the flap of a bird's wings as it took off into flight, becoming more rapid as the reality of my situation set in.

I didn't know how I was going to get out of this.

The yelling started immediately.

"Why isn't dinner on the table?" Fred demanded.

I heard the slur in his words and the waver in his voice and I knew. My heart sank. I couldn't hear my mother's response; it was muffled by the door. But I imagined the tired drone of her voice as she let him know just how late he'd been.

"I just had a couple of drinks with the guys after work. It's a Friday night. What do you expect?"

More muffled response from my mama.

More shouting from Fred.

When I heard the plates crash to the floor, I wanted to be in my room. I needed to find my safe space, but I was stuck inside my parents' room. And the only way out would be putting myself in the line of fire. I tuned them out as I scanned the room for an exit. I could try to go out a window, but it was December and rainy. I was wearing cotton Snoopy pajamas, hardly fit for the current chilly weather. My indecision cost me, because by the time I built up the nerve to crack the door open, I heard the next words out of Fred's mouth.

"Fuck... why is your little brat always leaving her shit on the floor?" I heard the thud as what I could only assume was my coloring book was kicked across the room. "What the fuck is that shit? Did you see this? I've had enough of that fucking brat. It's time someone taught her some discipline."

The heavy thump of steel-toed boots thundered toward the hall.

"Don't you dare lay a hand on her. She's my daughter!" Mama screamed, her voice growing closer with every syllable.

I shut the door and backed away as I heard a smack and a thump, which could only have come from Mama being hit hard enough to send her crashing into a wall. Then came another crash. I looked around for somewhere to hide, but there weren't a lot of options.

"You'll have to kill me before I let you lay a hand on her."

"Where is that little bitch?" Fred asked, ignoring Mama. I could hear him in my room, the slam of doors, the struggle of my mother to stop him. "She's not here!" he roared.

"Fred, stop." I could hear the tears in my mama's pleas. "I'll clean it up. She only has washable markers—it can be fixed."

Their voices were growing closer to the door, and I stopped thinking.

I dove onto the floor and rolled under the bed as I heard him crash into the bathroom I usually used.

"I don't give a fuck—you don't discipline that bitch. She's never going to learn. She'll grow up to be a worthless piece of shit just like her mother."

The door to the room flung open, banging against the wall with such force that I was sure it had to have left a hole. Not that that was uncommon. There were patches everywhere. Mama was actually becoming quite good at repairing them. I saw Mama's bare feet facing toward the hall like she was standing in the doorway.

"Here, kitty, kitty," Fred taunted.

I cringed and squeezed my eyes shut. That superpower would come in handy now. Make it go away. Make it go away. Make him go away, *I chanted in my mind, trying to ignore the smack of flesh on flesh.*

"Get out of my way."

"No."

"Why do you make me do this?" Smack.

"Please, Fred. Just stop. Leave her alone. I'll take care of this."

Smack.

"Come out here, kitty. I've got something to say to you."

"Leave her alone." Smack.

My mother's voice became more garbled the longer she stood there taking blow after blow. I couldn't open my eyes until it got quiet all of a sudden. I peeked my eyes open, but they were no longer at the door. I was just about to let out a breath of relief when I felt it.

His hand gripped around my ankle like a steel vise. I screamed and kicked at his hand with my other foot, trying to make him let go. My fingers dug into the carpet and ripped painfully as I lost the battle. He pulled me out.

When I was clear of the bed, he swung me by my ankle until I hit the wall. All the breath whooshed out of me and I struggled to catch my next breath. When he bent down in front of me and his hand wrapped around my neck, I thought for sure I'd never breathe again.

I couldn't scream. Tears poured down my face as he lifted me by my neck, dragging me up the wall. The rough texture scraped against my skin through the thin pajamas. My eyes widened as I clawed at his hands and kicked at his stomach.

His eyes were glassy and bloodshot. He smelled like he'd bathed in rum, and when he opened his mouth, my eyes burned.

"You're gonna learn, little bitch. One way or another."

Then I heard it. The shriek of my mama. The weird wet crunching sound. I didn't realize my eyes had closed until I heard her next words.

"Keep your eyes closed, baby," she cooed in a soothing voice.

Flesh smacked against flesh as he hit her again. Then her cries became garbled and choked. Tears streamed down my face as I thought for sure he was going to kill her this time.

The odd thumping, crunching sound continued as my mama sobbed and released a strangled scream. I both felt and heard the moment they both hit the ground. I gasped for air and clutched at my throat, still feeling his hand there, but trying to reassure myself that I could breathe.

I cried out, "Mama!"

"Never touch her. You don't get to touch her..."

I curled against the wall, hoping that Mama would make it stop. That everything would get better. That this time she'd finally leave him. Hoping this would be enough to push her over the edge.

When I felt a hand on my back, I screamed. My mama sobbed and pleaded with me. "Keep your eyes closed, baby. Keep 'em closed. Promise?"

I nodded and kept them closed as she gathered me up and led me from the room. She sat me on my bed, and as soon as I felt the soft fuzz of my stuffed animals, I opened my eyes to watch her. She was covered in red spots from tiny little specks, to the big splotch over her tummy. She pulled *out my suitcase, packing it with clothes and pictures and other stuff. I kept quiet, not knowing when Fred would come back and stop her.*

But soon she was zipping up the case, putting on my coat, and ushering me to the car. We got in and drove. I wasn't surprised when we arrived at the police station. We'd done this every time we needed to stay in the women's shelter. But this time was different. The drive to the station was silent. This time, she turned off the car and got out, taking me and my suitcase with her.

The waiting room was cold and bare as we walked in. Mama sat me in a chair. The lady working the front desk dropped her pen and her jaw and picked up a walkie-talkie on her desk, mumbling something into it.

A lady police officer walked out next to a man in a mismatched suit. The man stopped to talk to Mama as the lady officer approached me and asked me if I wanted hot chocolate. I nodded and followed her to a room in the back. She told me that her name was Sheila and that she had two boys, but they were older than me. She talked and talked, about everything and nothing, until the lady from the front desk came in with a camera in her hand. She whispered to Sheila, and Sheila nodded.

"Sweetheart, I need to take some pictures of you. Your mommy said it was okay. Can you show me everything that hurts?" Sheila said, taking the camera from the other lady.

I stared at her, unblinking, not knowing what to do. I wanted my mama there to tell me it was okay. At twelve years old, I was old enough to know letting a stranger take pictures wasn't okay, but not old enough to know how to politely state that.

"It's okay. I know you're scared. I would be if I were in your shoes, but this'll help your mom. I promise."

I nodded and pulled off my jacket, tugging the collar of my pajamas down to show her where my neck hurt. The lady from the front desk gasped and covered her mouth with a shaky hand. Tears welled in both their eyes, but mine had dried up long ago.

When she was done with those, I showed her my ankle and my back.

When I pulled up my shirt, the lady from the front desk made a strange noise and left the room.

"Thank you, sweetie. Is that all of it?"

I nodded.

She wrote stuff down on a clipboard I didn't notice she had. She gave me another cup of hot chocolate. It wasn't until later that a man in a sweater, khaki pants, and loafers showed up, looking so much like Mr. Rogers that I swore it was a purposeful decision.

"This is Mr. Tilde," Sheila said. "He's going to be taking you to a place where you can stay tonight."

"What? No." I shook my head, not even bothering to look at the new guy. "I'm not leaving here without Mama."

Sheila's eyes grew wide, like she couldn't believe I had a voice. Or maybe it was that my voice was all faint and raspy. It did hurt to talk. She looked up at the man and back to me.

"Sweetie, your mom's not leaving here tonight. She might not be leaving for some time. But you can't stay here. Mr. Tilde will keep you informed and bring you back to talk to her when that's possible."

"No." I folded my arms over my chest, pulling my coat closed over my Snoopy pajamas.

"You can't stay here," she tried again.

A big scary-looking man in handcuffs entered ahead of an officer. I looked to him, and at Mr. Tilde and Sheila.

"Mama!" I yelled. It scratched and burned my throat, but I continued anyway. "Mama!"

The man in the mismatched suit stuck his head out of a room. His eyes found me, and he ducked back inside. Moments later, Mama appeared in the same doorway. Tears ran down her face, streaking black from her mascara across her cheeks.

Only once I broke free did I realize I'd been struggling against the hold Sheila had on my arm. I ran to Mama and wrapped my arms around *her. She didn't hug me back. Then I felt the cold metal cuffs binding her hands behind her back.*

She sobbed. "Baby, you have to go with these people. They'll take care of you."

"No, Mama. I'm not..." Mr. Tilde's arm came around my waist, and he picked me up. "No, Mama. Don't let them take me. I need you."

Sheila stepped into my view of Mama, and I screamed. I kicked and bucked to get out of Mr. Tilde's hold. He didn't budge. I screamed as loud and as long as my voice would let me.

I woke up, screaming and kicking, only to find that no one was holding me. Lightning flashed across the sky, but the storm had passed. Raindrops still trickled from the cliff face to the leaf-covered creek bed below. I had to get up. I had to get moving. Daylight would be coming soon, and so would Xander. My screams would've helped him find me. *Fuck.*

CHAPTER TWENTY-EIGHT

Direction

I'm not becoming my mother. I will not fall in love with a violent man the way she did. It's for the best. No use in letting history repeat itself. Those words had been stuck in my head on repeat since I'd woken up. It was surprising how many times you could repeat that in a few short moments.

It wasn't the first time I wished my dad had been around at some point in my life. Had he been, things would've been different. Fred would still be alive at least. Not that Fred was a great loss to humanity, but I'd still have my mother. But even before then, the nights I'd spent in my closet were usually filled with vivid visions of him coming to get me and take me away from the madness.

Sadly, he was just another statistic, another name on the big black wall they built in Washington a few years before. My mom's high school sweetheart. He didn't know when he voluntarily joined the Army during Vietnam that my mama was pregnant. Another part of her life that puzzled me—her first love was a hero; how could she ever have claimed to love a man like Fred?

I shook my head to clear away thoughts better left to ponder when I wasn't on the run from a crazed killer. I needed to move, and the sooner the better.

After pulling out the map and the flashlight, I tried to lay it flat. The map was awkward and large, catching the wind. It didn't help that I was trying to simultaneously peel a boiled egg I'd found in the bottom of my purse, while using my leg to hold down one side of the map. The light of the flashlight illuminated the map as held it next to my face and bit into the egg.

It could use some salt and pepper.

I let my gaze trace over the area surrounding the red dot, looking at the terrain outline until I found the creek and what I thought was two cliffs.

I could've been totally wrong on this. I hadn't read a map since I was, like, ten. Once I finished the egg, I rested my finger over the likely spot that marked where I was. It seemed awfully close to the house, compared to the surrounding cities. It would take several days for me to reach civilization.

The thought oddly gave me some respect for the original settlers here in Texas. The journey they must've had to reach here. *Crazy.*

I dug out my compass and adjusted the map for north, then found the nearest town I wanted to go to was roughly east-northeast. It was doubtful that walking a straight line was an option. I knew I'd have to stop and adjust my course along the way.

Quickly, I packed everything up, folding the blanket so it fit in my purse with the rest of my stuff. I put the flashlight and compass in my left jacket pocket, the gun in the right for easy access, and I was set.

The bed of leaves at the foot of the alcove was spongy beneath my feet as I crawled out of the alcove. The smell of rain and damp earth was potent, but the faint traces of cedar on the wind had my eyes darting around in paranoia. Breathing deep, I tried to calm myself. The scent vanished as quickly as it had appeared. There were cedar trees out here. *It wasn't him.*

My hand wrapped around the cold metal handle of the gun,

calming me a bit as I set off in search of a place to climb up the cliff and head in the direction I wanted to go. The moon was back, but it was low on the horizon, casting eerie shadows while lighting the way. Thunder still rumbled in the distance, as lightning flashed across the sky. I couldn't believe I'd slept through that so completely.

I also couldn't believe I'd dreamed about her, and that night. But now that I thought about it, that was probably where my fascination with the dead body came from. I never saw what happened to Fred. I'd always wondered what it had looked like. Not that I ever wished I'd looked. I'd struggled through what had happened as it was; seeing his body would've made it that much harder.

But when I'd watch movies and TV shows, I'd wonder if that produced death came close to real life. I had my answer now; it wasn't even close. Which made me more thankful that I was an obedient child and listened to my mother.

The cliff to the east gave way to a steep sloping hillside, and I was just about to attempt to scale it when I heard the snap of wood. I whipped around, bringing the gun up in front of me in the position Xander had taught me.

I didn't see anything immediately, so I pulled out the flashlight. Pressing it to the side of the gun, I flicked it on. I swung the gun around, sweeping over the visible area around me. The trees grew thick in this part of the creek bed, so much so I couldn't see the other cliff, just glimpses of it through the trees. It was unsettling.

Seeing nothing, I turned off the flashlight and spun around to scale the hillside and get the fuck out of this gorge.

"Rosie." Xander's voice drifted on the cool breeze.

It was soft like a whisper, yet loud at the same time. My heavy breaths puffed out like smoke in front of me as I scanned the area. I didn't know which direction it came from. It seemed to come from everywhere and nowhere. Just when I was starting to believe that it was all in my head, I saw him.

He was soaked to the bone. That much was obvious from a distance, but he was shrouded in shadows, unmoving. A ball of emotion lodged in my throat as I raised the gun with shaky hands in his direction.

"Why did you come after me?" Tears welled in my eyes. "Just let me go. I won't tell anyone about you. I only want to go home."

It was a lie because I'd every intention of going straight to the police, but I really didn't think honesty would improve my odds of survival.

He didn't answer; instead he started toward me. My heartbeat thundered in my ears as fear took over. Survival instincts as old as time had me reacting before my brain caught up.

I squeezed the trigger.

CHAPTER TWENTY-NINE

Catch

I wasn't aiming directly for him, but rather a few inches to the left of his head. The bullet had to have flown right by his ear. It had the intended effect. He stopped his advance, dropped to a crouch, and darted behind a tree.

"*Do prdele*! *Zvonová sklenice*, are you trying to kill me?"

I shrugged slightly, tipping my head to the side as I watched for him to come out. "If I wanted to kill you, I would've aimed further to the right."

"*Hovno*!" He paused. "Why are you running away from me?"

"Does it matter?"

"Yes."

"Because I know you did it. You killed that man."

"It's not what you think, Rosie."

I snorted. "I think it was murder. Can you tell me anything different?"

He didn't speak immediately, and I knew every assumption I'd made about him was right. I didn't feel vindicated. The knowledge sank to the bottom of my stomach like a hot stone, uncomfortable and suffocating. I drew in a shaky breath.

"I finished the car." He peeked around the side of the tree. "I finished fixing it the day before yesterday. I was going to tell you… I just couldn't bring myself to let you go. If you come back to the house, I will give you the keys and you can go home."

My laugh was hoarse and full of darkness. "Go back so you can murder me? Fucking unlikely."

"I would never hurt you, Rosie." He started to step around the tree, but I fired another shot.

"I don't believe you. You already lied once."

I only had four more bullets loaded. We couldn't keep this up all night. I was sure he knew that fact as well as I did.

"I meant it when I said I love you. I never lied to you."

"You did. Telling me that you didn't have a working phone when you clearly had one in your office is a fucking lie."

"Did you use it?" His head poked out from around the tree, watching me with narrowed eyes. "This is important, Rosie. Did you get on that phone?"

"What does it matter!"

His nostrils flared as he stepped out from around the tree, looking like the Terminator on a mission to destroy. I fired again, but he didn't flinch, didn't cower. I had to make a decision: run or shoot him. Running won out. Unfortunately, I wasn't a killer.

I turned and bolted back toward the alcove. It was the only option, really; I wouldn't have made it up the hill quickly enough, and the other directions led me toward him or a cliff. Only ten steps into my sprint, and I felt his body crash into mine.

Time seemed to slow. My body prepared itself for impact as the ground rushed toward me, but at the last second, with his hand braced behind my neck, he flipped us. When we landed, he took the brunt of the fall. The gun fell from my grip and skittered across the wet leaves.

The chilling, cold wetness of his clothes seeped into mine. It shocked me into inaction for a second before my mind caught up to the fact that his hold had loosened with the impact.

I rolled off to the side and started to scramble to my feet before he caught my ankle. My breath sawed in and out of me as visions of past and present collided. I wanted to scream, but my voice wouldn't work. He was going to kill me. Xander would finally finish what Fred had started all those years ago.

My vision dimmed as I kicked at his hand with my other foot and clawed at the wet ground. *Do not pass out. Do not pass out. Fuck. Fuck. Fuck. Fuck. Fuckity-fuck. Fuck.*

He dragged me toward him before I felt his weight pressing into my back. Ragged breaths puffed near my ear, stirring my hair. I pushed up from the ground only to have my hands ripped out from under me and pinned behind my back. He sat up, still squeezing my thighs together with his knees. His ankles held my calves to the ground, rendering me immobile.

"I want you to listen to me, Rosie." He barely sounded winded.

I was still struggling for breath, wheezing out wispy breaths like I was incapable of breathing in. I didn't want to acknowledge him as much as I couldn't, and he must've noted that because he kept talking.

"I did not lie to you. I would not ever lie to you. You have to believe that. I love you." He used a free hand to push the hair out of my face as he leaned down to look at me. "But I need to know if you used that phone."

He stared at me, expecting an answer.

I nodded.

"*Do háje*! What did you say?" His face was a mixture of panic and anger. It scared the shit out of me. "Tell me, Rosie."

"Nothing." I spluttered and spit as a leaf tickled my lips. "I didn't say anything. She just answered, and I hung up."

He leaned his forehead against the space between my shoulder blades. I didn't know if he was going to say anything else, he sat there so long, silently. There was a low, quiet groan that left him and vibrated against my back so quickly that I could've imagined it. But it sounded pained, and then he spoke.

"You need to leave."

"That's what I was doing—"

"I do not want to let you go. Can you not see that?" He sat up, but he was out of my range of vision. "No," he mumbled and rocked in place, not letting me up. "You are right. I have no right to keep you. I did kill that man. And I would do it again and again. Because it was necessary."

I closed my eyes and squeezed them shut, holding tears at bay. Not tears for the mystery guy, but because I knew this was it. The killer can't let you go once you know the truth. They can't risk the loose end.

"You remember the man on the TV, the night of your Thanksgiving dinner?"

I nodded.

"The man buried in these woods was his private secretary. The only person on earth that knew the location of the minister's family. My job was to get that information from him and deliver it to the right people. It was to stop a war that was inevitable... up to that point. That was all we needed to get him to keep the army from attacking our own people. To ensure a peaceful transition of power."

I opened my eyes and tried to look at him, but I still couldn't see him.

"I will not say what I did was right. I am a monster. A highly-trained and skilled monster. I work for an agency much like your country's CIA. I have done many, many horrible things. But I did that—I killed that man—to save lives. My mother and my sister would have suffered otherwise. And I already lost my father to that corrupt government.

That was how they recruited me for this job—the people who needed that information. It was a trade. One life for thousands, possibly more. And you have to understand that you can never tell anyone about this. It makes you a threat to those people, but also your own country's involvement in any of this cannot be known. Promise me you won't tell."

My head spun with what he was telling me. The implications... whoa. That's not something I ever thought to be in the vicinity of. Xander had changed the course of history, and some nobody from Texas was the one flaw in his plan. A stupid girl wandering in the woods she never belonged in.

"Please, promise me, *zvonová sklenice*."

"Who would believe me?" I tried to shrug. But I knew I needed to give him the answer he was looking for. Doubtful he'd leave me alive if I didn't. The stakes were way too high for loose ends. "Xander, I won't tell a soul. You can trust me. I don't even have a cat to tell."

His forehead was back between my shoulders as he slumped over. Hopefully in relief. His body pressed into mine, and somewhere on the other side of the press of cold, wet fabric, I felt the heat of him. He must've felt it too because he groaned.

"I want you to promise me one more thing."

"What's that?" I breathed out.

"That you will come back to the house and take the truck. You don't have a car anymore. It will be my gift to you."

I nodded, unable to find the words or truly comprehend what was happening.

He leaned back, releasing his hold on my wrists and pulling my purse strap over my head. The sun was nearing the horizon; the sky to the east was navy blue. It wasn't much, but it was enough light to see by, now that the moon had set. He dumped the contents of my purse onto the ground, shaking it out. He jumped up off me, snatching two items—the blanket and something... I only caught a flash of silver.

Pushing up on my hands and knees, I gave myself a moment to

adjust after being held in that position for so long. But when I moved to stand up, Xander was there, helping me.

His hands settled on my hips, but I didn't move. "I need you. One last time. I need to mark you. I want to burn part of me into you so you will never forget me."

"I don't think that's possible."

"No?"

I shook my head. His fingers curled around the back of my neck, and he tipped my chin up with his thumb. Lips that were chilled at first touch warmed quickly as they gently pressed to mine. It was a slow caress that matched the pace of his other hand that slid under my jacket and pulled my body flush against his. I trembled against him, but not from the cold. It was this overwhelming urge to touch, to kiss… to connect. I felt like a can of Coke that had been shaken too hard for too long, ready to burst.

He growled deep in his throat and lifted me off my feet, walking us to where the blanket was at. I wrapped my legs around him and held on tight. He fell to his knees, then pushed and pulled off my jacket. My shirt was next. It was like something inside of him snapped. Some measure of control was lost. He ripped and pulled at my clothes and his, until I only had my underwear left and he was fully naked. Goose bumps pebbled his flesh in the purple light of the early morning. Adrenaline pumped through my veins, numbing me to the cold. He paused and looked me over.

One.

Two.

Three heartbeats, and he pulled me toward him by my ponytail, until I lost balance and fell against his chest. His mouth crashed into mine, his lips insistent and demanding. I opened my mouth on a sigh, something like relief consuming my whole body at being back in his arms. His entire body shuddered in response. Our tongues danced and fought for dominance as he lowered me to my back. Once he settled between my legs, he ground his hips into me with near-painful force.

A quiet groan that was half pain and half pleasure sounded deep in his throat. He broke the kiss, panting.

"I cannot be gentle with you right now." He pulled the sides of my panties away from me until the fabric tore, the sound loud against the quiet gurgle of the creek nearby and the utter silence of the early-morning woods.

Throwing the tatters over his shoulder, he watched me, one side of his mouth tipping up in a smirk. The smile was somewhere between sinister and playful. It had me on edge. Then he reached for me and roughly flipped me on my stomach without so much as a warning.

"What are you doing?" My whole body tensed.

"What I promised I would do. I am going to mark you. You will remember me forever after this."

"What does that mean?" I tried to flip over, but he held me down with a hand to the center of my back.

I heard a grating sound and the clink of something metal. Then I smelled it.

Peaches.

"What is that?"

He chuckled. "You don't know?"

"I wouldn't be asking if I did."

When I felt the brush of his fingertips against my ass cheek, I tensed even further, but nothing could've prepared me... I yipped as something cold and wet touched my skin. He made a noise, half heavy breath and half laughter, as if he found my discomfort amusing.

His hand was gone from my back for only seconds before I felt it on my pussy, teasing my folds and prodding my entrance.

He hummed in appreciation. "So wet for me."

The other hand slid the cold, wet stuff down the crack of my ass.

Peaches.

It took a couple of seconds more for it to fully sink in. I must've grabbed the jar of peach preserves in my mad dash to escape. And now he was smearing it all over my ass. But as he massaged it against my skin it began to warm, and as the fingers of one hand fucked my cunt, the other circled the tight ring of muscles. I relaxed into it and let him have his way.

When the first digit pressed against my asshole, I froze. I didn't know how to handle it. *Was it going to hurt?*

"Relax," he cooed. "Breathe in through your nose and out of your mouth. I promise this will feel good."

I did as he instructed, trusting that he was right. He leaned down until I could feel his breath tickling the shell of my ear.

"You are so beautiful right now. Such a good girl." His finger slid inside of me.

I gasped, my eyes widening. A low moan bubbled up from within my chest.

"You like that, do you not? Does it feel good?"

"Yes," I rasped out on a gasp.

"Just wait until you feel my cock inside you."

I could feel the release building inside of me. "Please, Xander. Fuck me."

"Not yet, *zvonová sklenice*. I have to get you ready for me. You will remember this. This ass will always be mine." I felt a second finger at my back entrance at the same time as his fingers curled inside, hitting just the right spot. My body jolted from the added stimulation and the fullness of further penetration. "Any other man who touches you here will have your thoughts coming back to me. Though, if I had my way, you would be chained to my bed for eternity and no one would ever touch you but me."

"Oh God, yes. Yours. Only yours."

He scissored those fingers in my ass, stretching me open. "You can't keep that promise, Rosie. Because you are leaving me."

I didn't know how to respond, but I wouldn't have to. A third finger joined the other two and a mewl gurgled out of my mouth. It was almost too much and yet somehow not enough.

The hand at my pussy disappeared, and I heard the telltale *tink* of the metal lid to the jar of preserves.

"*Ježíšmarja*! It is cold."

I couldn't stop the laugh that bubbled out of me if I wanted. The smell of peaches permeated in the frigid air surrounding us. I turned my head to see him, and my breath stalled at the sight of him, stroking his cock, in combination with his fingers that pushed and pulled, stretching me for him. It may have been cold, but it didn't look to affect him in the least. The heat in his eyes had me lifting my hips for him to get a better angle.

He leaned over. I could feel the heat of his chest against my back, even though he was holding himself above me. His fingers pulled out of me, but I didn't have time to think, to process, as the flared tip of his dick pushed into me. I screamed through gritted teeth, and Xander bit down on the back of my neck, pulling my focus from the pain.

A buck with a huge rack, at least sixteen point, stumbled out of the tree line, made eye contact with me, and froze. Xander grunted and thrusted in farther. How this became my reality, I'd never fully understand. I was being fucked in the ass with peach preserves by a European spy, out in the woods in the dead of winter, while a deer watched. The same spy that had recently killed a man to stop a civil war in his country.

It felt so surreal and vulgar, like we were spoiling this peaceful piece of nature. Xander wasn't mine; he was larger than that. He belonged to history, to the world. And I was a nobody. This must have been what Eve felt like when she bit into that apple and discovered the wicked ways of the world—the sinful pleasures that could exist—but also knowing that it was only within reach for a fleeting moment before it would all vanish. That the cruel world was just around the corner.

As Xander's hand snaked under my belly, reaching for my clit, I groaned and my body clenched. Xander grunted in response and intensified his thrusts, his skin slapping against mine, punctuating the silence of the serene countryside.

All thoughts fled my mind, and I surrendered to the sensations. When his fingers entered me and moved in tandem with his cock, his thumb rolling over my clit, the buildup was fast. The pressure started low in my belly and climbed up my spine. It had me panting and mewling. I pressed my face into the blanket to muffle my sounds until I was gasping for air.

"Please, Xander."

I didn't know what I was asking for. It ceased to matter in the next second as his fingers pinched my nipple, and that in tandem with his other hand and his cock… it was all too much and just right. My sight narrowed and sparks of light filled my vision. I screamed as my body jerked and spasmed in his hold. The orgasm went on and on, like nothing I'd ever felt before.

He quickened his pace for a few more thrusts and stilled. A sound ripped through his throat that could only be described as a roar. He held himself still as his release poured out of him. It was so animalistic, so masculine.

The flap of wings echoed through the trees as birds scattered.

And that's when I knew. He did it. He ruined me. Because any other man would never measure up to this kind of perfection. The only thought left in my head when I came down from the high was that I was well and truly fucked. Because now I had to leave.

CHAPTER THIRTY

Release

I stood beside the truck as it idled. My gaze strayed over the house, the barn, and lingered on the chicken coop as I opened the door to get in. I would've hesitated more if I hadn't come back to the house, showered, and put my own clothes back on, which were hardly fit for this weather. Luckily, Xander had started the truck and turned the heat on so it was nice and toasty warm.

As I slid into the seat, the strange sensation was a reminder of what we'd done. My fingers curled around the slim steering wheel. Xander shut the door behind me. I closed my eyes, fighting the urge to get out and ask him to hold me one more time.

All I wanted the entire time I'd been here was to leave, but now that I was, everything felt wrong.

I opened my eyes and released the emergency brake. Pressing down on the clutch, I shifted into gear as the passenger door opened.

Xander climbed inside. He reached over, pulling my face to his. Everything faded to the background outside the point of contact. My lips tingled as if he were weaving a magical spell and my body was absorbing every bit of the magic. The world seemed to get brighter at that moment. Though it wasn't until he pulled back, pressing his forehead to mine, that I realized we'd rolled out of the garage.

I pressed the brake to halt our movement.

"It is so hard to let you go."

I tried to smile, but it was weak.

"I wish that things were different for us. But you need to know that you have changed me. I am not the same man I was when I met you. I will never forget you. You will be on my mind with my dying breath."

I inhaled, not knowing what to say. What was there to say? All we could ever be was a snapshot. A moment frozen in time. Something that would live imprinted on our memories but couldn't exist in reality. It was too fleeting for that. He was meant for bigger things, and I was meant to live out my days in my small, meaningless corner of existence.

Unbidden tears welled in my eyes, and I breathed deep to banish them. I pressed my lips to his again to hide the emotion bubbling up. When I pulled back, I searched for something to say to distract from the moment.

"You never told me how you knew... what to do... all the work you did on this truck." I struggled to put my thoughts into words.

He huffed an amused breath from his nose before speaking. "When I joined the military as a young boy, I was a mechanic. It wasn't until my commanding officer noticed that I had a gift for languages that I was moved to Intelligence."

I tipped my head back, staring at the ceiling of the truck cabin. "How does a mechanic become a spy?"

He made a quiet, low hum, like he was searching his memory for the answer. "I never really gave it a thought. It was a series of events in my life that built off of the next. But now... I think it was no less than fate. It brought me here—to you."

I smiled, but I couldn't look at him. "I should get going." I choked out through the ball of emotions lodged in my throat.

He sighed before he pulled me toward him for one last kiss—to my lips, my forehead—and then he was gone. The door to the truck shut, and I put it in gear. I tried to fight the urge to look, but it was too much. I watched him grow smaller in the rearview mirror until the driveway turned and he disappeared from view.

The quiet hum of the truck's engine and the clank of rocks kicking up from the tires felt heavy, oppressive. Solid reminders that I was once again alone. I reached over and flicked the radio on. It was on a local country music station, playing Merle Haggard and Willie Nelson's story about Pancho and Lefty.

Letting it play, I listened to that song, and the next and the next. Almost as if I got to keep a piece of him through his horrible taste in music.

Sleep had eluded me since the brief nap in the alcove. The heat and the soothing voices started getting to me. I rolled down the window a smidge, letting the cold whip through the top of my hair, and pulled my sunglasses over my eyes.

I didn't know it was possible, but the farther I drove down the desolate country road, the more jaded and hardened I felt. It leached into my bones, a sort of numbing apathy. My time with him had forever marked me, though not in the way he'd meant it.

Reaching in my purse, I felt the cool metal of the gun he let me keep. I was definitely not the same girl who'd tripped over that body in the woods. I was something more. But if that more was something good, only time would tell.

CHAPTER THIRTY-ONE

Home

When I pulled into the driveway in front of my trailer, Joanne and Billy were out on their front porch, screaming and yelling as usual. But at the sound of my truck tires crunching the gravel driveway, they both stopped, staring as I got out.

I ducked my head to hide from their watchful eyes as I darted to my door. Pulling the spare key out from its hiding spot, taped to the bottom of the deck boards on my front porch, I took a moment to peek over at them. Their eyes strayed back and forth from the truck to me. When my hands found the key, I nearly cried in relief.

I'll have to find a new place to hide a spare key.

When I closed the door behind me, I could hear their murmurs. They weren't low-volume people, so I knew the chatter was about me. But I guess after being gone for more than a month and showing up in a new vehicle, I was something of interest in their small, monotonous world. It would pass.

I rubbed my hands up and down my goose bump-prickled arms. When I'd last been here it wasn't cold outside, so the AC was still on. Not that it was actually running at that moment with near-freezing temps outside. It really did make it feel like I'd been gone longer. We'd officially moved from fall, which felt more like summer in Texas, to winter. Not that winter was dramatic or long-lived. But it was a shock to the system when you were used to the year-round heat.

I sighed into the quiet stillness, watching dust motes glitter in the early-afternoon light. Home. It was exactly the way I'd left it, but it didn't feel quite the same. It felt off. I just couldn't put my finger on what that was.

A yawn cracked my jaw as I crossed the room to the short hall where the thermostat was. Once the heat kicked on, and that odd smell of burning dust filled the room, followed by warm air rising from the vents in the floor, I walked into my bedroom and pulled up the comforter that rested at the foot of the bed until it covered the whole bed, then stripped out of all my clothes and dove in. My mind had shut down the second I entered my house. Now, I was coasting on autopilot.

I shivered under the covers, rubbing my feet together to stifle the chill. As heat filled the room and my body warmed the space under the blankets, I drifted into a dreamless, restless sleep.

When I gave up and let my eyes stay open, the sun was setting. I lay in bed watching the shadows grow longer across the ceiling. My mind was drifting—a thoughtless, listless pool of nothing. The heater cut off, and the silence thrummed in my ears, growing louder with each passing second. It was the kind of loud that only exists in silence, screaming at me.

Something was off. Nothing felt right. I was happy to be home, sleeping in my own bed, surrounded by my meager belongings, though I wasn't quite sure what it was that was bothering me. My thoughts felt disjointed, disconnected.

I knew what I needed to do, as much as I dreaded the thought. I needed to go to the diner. I needed to see if my job was salvageable.

Oscar, the owner, was a grumpy, irritable sort on a good day. I doubt he'd be pleasant about my disappearance. Which also brought me to the thought that I needed a good story. I couldn't tell the truth.

No one would believe it. It would likely just cause more anger at my thoughtless vanishing act.

I could always say my car broke down and caught fire in the middle of the countryside, and it took well over a month to hike back. No. I would've starved to death.

What the fuck was even a believable excuse for disappearing for more than a month and then expecting to resume life as it was before, like nothing even happened?

Bending the truth was always an option. I went hiking, my car was stolen, and a nice man let me stay with him until he fixed his truck and gave it to me.

And why did he do that? I hadn't questioned it because I really didn't know how I was going to get by without a vehicle. Everything was too spread out not to have a car. Though I supposed if I tried, I could walk to work, and it would only take a few hours. But he was now stuck out there, with no option to leave. Maybe he could call the people on that phone for a ride. Or maybe he was expecting them. Would he be in danger?

Ugh. Why am I even thinking about that? Xander is not my... I didn't even know what. But I knew I needed to forget everything about that place, for my own safety.

He was just a nice man, with a few broken-down cars, who'd fixed one for me, but it had taken a month. He didn't have a phone, so I couldn't call.

Ugggh. I pulled at my hair.

Nothing about what happened was even remotely believable as a good excuse. Trying to save my job was most likely an exercise in futility. Oscar would probably laugh at me as he booted my ass out the door. There just weren't a lot of options, other than to try and explain and beg for forgiveness.

With that as decided as it would ever be, I crawled out from the bed and darted into the bathroom. Turning on the shower, I hopped back and forth between each foot, rubbing my hands on my arms to fight off the cold. The second steam started curling into the air, I jumped into the shower, nearly slipping, to get into the hot stream of water.

Steam curled into the air as I leaned back into the water, letting the soothing heat penetrate my skin and relax my muscles. I was slightly sore from climbing down a cliff and sleeping on a rock less than twenty-four hours ago. Without looking, I reached down to the corner of the tub, picking up the bottle of shampoo. I flipped open the cap to squirt some into my hand but drew up short when the smell invaded my senses.

Peaches.

Holding the bottle out at arm's length, I glared at it. The scent was so strong. How had I forgotten that I owned peach-scented shampoo and conditioner? But it wasn't exactly peach. It was a fruity essence, but the peaches were overwhelming the whole scent. I looked around, which was silly because I already knew that I didn't have an alternative set of shampoo and conditioner. Just the one. I was going to have to suck it up and spend what was left of the day smelling like the one thing that would be a constant reminder of him.

I hurried through the rest of my shower and stepped out with one foot, grabbing the towel off the hook. When I moved back into the shower to avoid dripping water everywhere, I slipped, lost my balance, and crashed to the tub floor. One foot still hung over the tub's edge, and I found myself staring up at the ceiling with an ache in the back of my head.

"Son of a bitch." I hauled myself up out of the tub and finished drying off. "It's not like I'm clumsy."

I meant it. I'd never done that before. And then it hit me that I was talking to myself. I shook my head at myself and was suddenly dizzy. I braced my hand on the wall and closed my eyes. My stomach roiled, and a pressure built just under my throat.

I turned back into the bathroom and collapsed to my knees in front of the toilet. Fumbling to open the lid, I heaved several times before it finally bubbled up. Yellow bile. Nothing else. I dry heaved for several seconds more before my stomach settled. I rubbed the tender spot at the back of my head.

Shit. I must've hit my head harder than I thought. I glared at the offending bathtub. Going to a hospital was out of the question; I'd no insurance and no money. How had I made it through a really dangerous situation unscathed, only to injure myself taking a damn shower? I probably just needed to eat something. The last thing I ate was that egg while sitting in the alcove. It had been well over twelve hours.

I was sure that any food in the house had spoiled. I pulled myself up from the floor. Just another reason to go to the diner. I needed to eat... and hopefully, save my job.

SNAPSHOT

CHAPTER THIRTY-TWO

Battleship

I pulled into the nearly empty parking lot at half past five. It was too early for the dinner rush, too late for lunch patrons. Out of habit, I drove around to park in the back, turned off the engine, and listened to the steady *tick tick* of the cooling metal as I breathed deep, trying to steel myself.

I wasn't a liar. I didn't like being put into the position to have to do it. But I wasn't stupid enough to not see the necessity of it in this case. Even then it didn't sit well. My stomach was twisted into knots. Though, that could've been a side effect from the bump on my head.

Threading my fingertips into my hair, I felt the lump. I took a breath. I could smell him everywhere. That combination of cedar, engine grease, and male, haunting me. And even if my rational brain knew it was the truck his scent clung to, I could still close my eyes and see that strong jaw laced with evening stubble. His denim-blue eyes, watching me...

Suck it up. Let's get this show on the road.

The door creaked as I swung it open. Walking around to the front of the strip center, I stopped in front of the frame shop. There was a different Ansel Adams print hanging in the window display. It didn't bring me the same joy as it used to. It was still a pretty landscape from a distant yet beautiful place, the dark, almost black sky framing the cliff face filled with so many shades of detailed lines. The man made black-and-white photos look like they contained more colors than the rainbow.

But the darkness in his photos is what drew me to photography in the first place. The stormy skies and monotones made me feel less alone. The solitude of the viewer looking at a photo of simple untouched nature—it felt comfortable, like he understood me. Even his predominantly white works held a moodiness that most people wouldn't understand. They'd see the snow and not the shadows.

I'd spent countless hours at the library looking up his work after the first print appeared in the frame shop's window. It was that ability to convey emotion, to say more than words with just nature and a spectrum of grays—from black to white—that's what I'd wanted to do.

As impressive as it still was, and even though I'd been eying this one since the girls had bought me *Vernal Fall*, I couldn't see myself wanting it anymore. I really didn't know why. It wasn't any less impressive. The darkness and emotions were still there. The black-and-white photo of the giant cliff made me think of my own encounters with a much smaller cliff that wasn't quite so anonymous, and then my mind drifted back to him.

Wendy, the frame shop's owner, looked up from behind the counter when she spotted me and waved with a warm smile. I tried to smile back, but my mind was off in a dark place and the effort fell flat.

My tennis shoes scuffed the pavement as I turned quickly on my heel and hurried away, trying to ignore the way her face fell at the look on mine. *Maybe I shouldn't have done this today.* I should've waited a day or two. Got my bearings back before attempting to greet people and be social.

Just to the left of the diner's entrance hung a "Help Wanted" sign. I sucked in a breath and tried to suppress the hope that Oscar would let me have my job back. My head was filled with visions of him laughing in my face, even if I'd never actually seen the man laugh in all the years I'd known him. It just felt like something someone would do to a girl who disappeared for a month and attempted to get her job back with a shoddy excuse.

To tell the truth, I really didn't know what to expect as I opened the glass door, greeted by the tinkle of the doorbells and the familiar smell of greasy foods.

"Holy shit." Tia gasped, her jaw dropping as her emerald eyes pinned me in place by the door. "I quit," she hollered over her shoulder. "You hear that, Oscar?" She tugged hastily at her apron.

Oscar looked up from the papers spread before him in a booth, and when his gaze landed on me, his eyebrows rose a fraction.

"You are *not* quitting on me. What's going on?" Rachel said, as she walked out of the hallway leading to the kitchen access and halted in her tracks.

Her jaw went slack as she paused for a moment that felt like hours before she mumbled, "You're alive?" At the sound of her own voice, she unfroze and shoved past Tia, nearly knocking her friend over as Tia grappled to remove her apron. "You're alive!"

All five feet two inches of the way-too-perky blonde crashed into me. My breath rushed out involuntarily as she squeezed with a strength that belied her petite frame. She let go and leaned back, clasping my cheeks in her hands, her hazel eyes glassy with unshed tears as she searched over my face and my body. Then she tugged me back into a hug, burying her face in my neck.

"Where the fuck have you been? You had me worried sick." Her voice was muffled by my hair, and it made me huff a laugh. She drew back, glaring. "I'm not kidding. I went to the sheriff. Course they couldn't do nothin' about it, useless bastards."

A throat cleared next to us. "Don't I deserve a hug too? I mean, I'm the one who's been working in this hellhole since you left. Antonio told me last night that I smelled like a *mannaggia* hamburger. That is so gross. Your job should never overpower your Chanel." Tia's gorgeous face wrinkled into a frown, marring her smooth olive-toned skin.

Rachel and I held an arm out and she wrapped her arms around both of us. We stood there like that for a few moments—a few too long moments, and it began to feel awkward. I didn't know what to do with it. Stay and continue a hug that had passed its prime, or break away and risk offending one or both of them?

Tia pulled back first and wiped at her eyes, turning away to stare out the window. "I'm glad you're all right. We both worried about you."

I tilted my head and watched her. She wasn't being dramatic. Neither was Rachel. They both seemed genuine. It almost felt like a punch to the gut—the realization that they'd cared if I disappeared. I'd felt like we'd drifted so far apart since they both married and had kids. They had families, and all I had was them. I was the loner and always felt like the fifth wheel, on the outside. Like they tolerated me, but I wasn't important. A feeling that could only be described as guilty relief coursed through me. Guilt because I had discounted their feelings so much, but relief that my life wasn't as dismal as I thought.

I didn't realize I was crying until Rachel leaned forward and wiped the tears off my face. Taking my hand, she led me toward a booth. It was the one right next to Oscar's usual spot, though he had gone back to whatever he was working on, paying no attention to us.

There were no customers in the place, aside from Ethel and June, two older ladies that came in with various games and drank hot tea, while chatting and playing. This time, it looked to be Battleship. But with the teapot between them and a container of tea bags, they wouldn't need anything anytime soon.

Why am I even thinking about that? I didn't work here anymore. I didn't need to worry about when the customers would need something and if I'd enough time to sit before I was needed again.

"Sit." Rachel shoved me toward the seat and slid in across from me. Tia pushed her in farther as she sat next to Rachel. "Tell us where you've been. What happened? You're obviously upset, but you seem healthy enough, other than the fact that you look like you haven't slept in a week."

I bit my lip, frowning. I didn't know where to start. "I... I went hiking. On my day off. I bought a camera and drove out to the country to take some pictures."

Rachel nodded. "Little John told us that you bought the camera. He was convinced that you ran off to Hollywood to become a photographer." She shook her head. "I tried telling him that you go to Hollywood to become an actress; photographers don't need to go anywhere."

"*Idiota*," Tia mumbled under her breath, massaging her forehead with her fingers.

"Then my car—"

"I told you to get rid of that thing. Did it explode?" Rachel leaned in. "They're all the time talkin' on the news about how those damn Fieros keep catchin' on fire. That thing is a death trap."

I was shaking my head no before I thought to agree with her. I only noticed my mistake when her brows drew together.

"It was stolen." Ugh, this wasn't going well. The way both of their lips twisted into a frown was enough to tell me that I was crashing. "I don't know who it was. Some old dude in a camo hat. I saw him take it, but I didn't stop him because he was big and scary-looking, and I was alone in the middle of nowhere." I closed my eyes and hoped they accepted that. It was the truth, for the most part.

"What happened after that?" Tia asked, reaching across the table to lay her hand on mine.

"I tried walking. But there was nothing around. I'd gone out west toward Kendall county. On FM473. Then I took some road. It wasn't marked. I just wanted to get some good pictures on the new camera... I just didn't think it would be a big deal. Nothing ever happens around here." I took a breath, mentally preparing myself for talking about him. "There was a farm, but the guy didn't have a phone. He only had a broken-down truck. He let me stay there while he worked on it." I slid the keys onto the table. "He gave it to me, so I could get home."

"Was he hot?" Tia asked. Rachel jabbed her elbow into Tia's side. "Ouch."

Rachel frowned. "He worked on his truck for a month while you just hung out at his place? Really? I mean, I can tell by lookin' at you that you're not seriously hurt. But nothing else happened?"

"No," I said, probably too quickly. I needed to not act like I was hiding something. "No, he was nice. I just cleaned his house and read books while he worked on the truck." I shrugged and looked over at Ethel and June, both deep in concentration. "It was uneventful."

Neither of them stopped frowning as their eyes roamed over me, dissecting every subtle line and expression in my face. Or maybe that was my imagination. I closed my eyes and rubbed the heel of my palm.

"He was a nice guy. We got along well, but he fixed the truck and it was time for me to go home." I shrugged and laid my hands on the table in front of me, palms up.

Tia gasped. "You like him… He was hot. I'd lay money on that."

"No. More than like. I've seen her like guys and this is different. She's all subdued." Rachel smirked. "Not that you're usually chipper, but you've always had a certain air about you. That's what had me worried that he had hurt you, but I see it now. You're upset you had to leave."

"What?" I drew my hands back to me. "No. It wasn't like that. We hardly even talked." I shrugged.

"Nope. She fucked him." Tia tapped her long, manicured nails on the table. "You totally did."

I held my breath, trying not to react, but I could feel my face heat up. Which was weird because I talked with these girls about my sex life all the time. They liked to live vicariously through me. Why was I getting embarrassed now?

"Oh, my God. She did," Rachel gasped, reaching her hand across the table.

Mine were still under the table, twisting my fingers into knots. I didn't move. She rested her hand flat on the tabletop between us.

Rachel's head cocked to the side. "That's what this is about? You're not coming back?"

I blinked, trying to figure out how she jumped to that conclusion. "No." I cleared my throat. "No, I am coming back. It's not... I never left. I just couldn't get back. And no, the guy was..." I shook my head, searching for the right words. "...nothing. I'm back home now. I really just came to see if there was an ice cube's chance in hell that I could get my job back." The moment their faces fell, I knew I said the wrong thing. "And to see you guys, of course."

A grunt sounded from the next booth over. As the girls turned their heads to look behind them, my eyes met Oscar's across the distance. His lips were turned down at the corner, and one eyebrow raised. *Fuck.* That was his pissed-off face. Really, the man had very few expressions and most looked unfriendly, but I'd learned over the last seven years of working for him to spot the subtleties. I'd no idea how to even start.

I slid out of my booth and sat across from him. "I'm sorry, Oscar, I am. I would've called if I could. You know that. I've never been late or missed work before this."

He was nodding, but his expression didn't change. "I know, but I'm trying to run a business here. And I can't set an example like this for others to follow. I already had enough trouble when Tracey and Ronnie quit, and I still hadn't found replacements for them when you pulled this. I'm just lucky that Tia was willing to work. I was down to running this restaurant with three servers. And Rachel was willing to work, but did you know she had to bring her kid here and keep him occupied during those shifts?"

"No," I uttered, defeated.

I knew my disappearing act would have consequences, but I honestly hadn't given it much thought with all that had happened. This ugly feeling coiled tight in my belly and sank. I felt awful.

At the time, the urgency of survival felt larger than concerns of what anyone back home would think. But having made it out to the other side, unscathed, just put a different, more selfish, color to my actions. And I couldn't stop it. I couldn't tell them the truth—how scary it was—or even explain why my effort or excuses seemed lackluster.

My vision wavered with the buildup of tears. "I'm sorry, Oscar. I wish I'd a better excuse. I wish there was something I could have done to change what happened. But I need a job. There aren't many options in this town, and I thought that maybe... I don't know. I'm sorry. I'm sorry for wasting your time."

I started to get up, but he raised a hand to stop me.

"Hold on, now. I didn't say no. I just want you to know what's at stake. Up until this, you were my best worker. The only one willing to work holidays and late hours. And I'm still short-staffed. Not to mention that sales have slowed without you here. Your friend isn't all that good—"

"Hey!" Tia leaned over the back of my seat. "I already told you I quit."

"You're not quittin' 'cause she's back," Rachel interjected. "We still need you."

Oscar ignored the girls and continued to watch me, one eyebrow still raised but his lips slightly less pinched.

"I could use the break on having to pay to train another. But this can't happen again. I need you to know if you're so much as one minute late, even once, that's it. You hear me?"

"Yes, sir." I tried to fight back the grin, but couldn't.

His frown deepened. "Now get out of my hair and go back to your girl talk, away from me. I have checks to write and a schedule to fix. I'll let you know when you need to come in, but you're starting tomorrow."

I jumped from the booth and hugged the man. He grumbled but didn't move, which was the Oscar equivalent of a welcome home party. "You won't regret this. I promise. You can count on me. Thank you, Oscar."

He shoved me off him with a grunt, and I stepped back. The girls wore matching grins as they got up to move to a different booth.

"I ain't paying you girls to chat either. Polish silver and refill the ketchup, salt, and pepper while you talk about whatever."

"Sure thing, Oscar." Rachel saluted, winked at me, then turned on her heel to do exactly that.

CHAPTER THIRTY-THREE

Jack

"What sides would you like with that?" I asked.

"Ummm… french fries and…" I sighed, waiting for this customer to make up her damn mind. "What did you get?" she asked the man sitting across from her.

He answered her, but I tuned them out. My mind had not returned to running full steam and it had been days. Long, tiring days, as my body remembered what it was like to work again. Nothing eventful happened in that time. I never heard from Xander or saw anyone suspicious hanging around. Life was normal again, like it had never happened.

Except it had. And I remembered everything in vivid detail. My dreams alone were proof of that. Daydreams too.

"Can I get a salad?"

"Yeah, sure." I scribbled that down on the order check. "Dressing?"

"Ummm…"

Oh, my fucking God, lady! And that happened too. Things were the same and they weren't. From the outside, all appeared as it was before, but I'd changed. And now I'd no patience for dimwits who couldn't make a simple fucking decision. How hard was it to pick a dressing? We only had four options.

She finally settled on ranch. Big surprise to all. And I made my way behind the counter to put the order in. I clipped it to the wheel and spun it until the check faced the kitchen.

"Order up," I shouted and then took a step back, leaning against the counter.

I sighed and tucked the order pad in my apron, fighting the urge to rub my eyes. Not only would it destroy my makeup, but my hands were coated in grease. I'd learned long ago exactly how bad that was. I could feel a headache building, though, so I closed my eyes.

"Sleeping on the job?" Rachel asked.

I peeked one eye open to glare at her. "Hardly."

"Still pining for the mystery man?"

I opened the other eye, still glaring.

"One of these days, I'll wear you down enough that you'll talk about him. In fact…"—she bent down and rummaged under the counter, pulling out a bottle—"I have just the thing to ensure that."

She turned the bottle around until the label was facing me. Jack Daniels. Except it wasn't her. I could see him clear as day, holding out the bottle for my inspection. Blinking until the scene faded from my mind, I frowned.

"Not your drink of choice? S'okay. We'll make do. You have off tomorrow. I don't have to work until two. Gary took the kid to his parents' place. And we close early tonight. Gotta love Sundays." Her face lit up with a slightly sinister smile. "This is so happening."

I didn't have it in me to argue with her, so I shrugged, grabbed a towel, and went to bus a few tables. The rest of the evening flew by as the dinner rush started. Before I knew it, I was busing the last table of the night while Rachel checked them out at the register. I dropped the tub of dishes at the dishwasher station for Hector and went back out into the dining room. We'd already wiped everything down and finished all the other closing duties. The only thing left was to stack the chairs on the table and sweep.

When the bells above the door jingled, I was so ready for the night to be over.

I didn't bother to look up. "We're closed."

"I didn't know I was one of the rabble," Tia said, cocking her hip and resting her hand at the top of her acid-washed miniskirt. Her full red lips were pursed into a frown as she watched me sweep.

A smirk grew on my face as I continued my task. What was even funnier was watching *her* sweep. I didn't think the woman ever did a chore in her life before working here. But I couldn't give her too much guff for it; she did take this job to help me and Rachel. And I was grateful because things were a little less hectic since I'd been back. We were still short one waitress, but I wasn't working doubles for thirteen days straight.

The door jingled again as Rachel escorted the customers out and locked the door behind them.

"Let's get this show on the road." Rachel clapped her hands together and skipped, literally skipped, in our direction. "I needs to get my drink on. This is my first day to celebrate having our girl back, and our first chance to get the skinny on the mystery man. And we *will* be finding out."

"Rachel…" I sighed. "I don't want to talk about it."

"You say that now, but I have to know. You've been moody and depressed since you came back. Not to mention you watch the parkin' lot like a hawk, *every shift*, like you're expectin' someone to show up. My money's on the fact that you're hung up on this guy. Which begs the question: why aren't you goin' back to see him?"

"Why won't you talk about him?" Tia added, leaning against a table and crossing her arms.

"Because there's nothing to say that I haven't already said." I shrugged.

Rachel bent down into my line of vision. "Bullshit."

"Okay, she doesn't want to talk about it." Tia raised her hands in surrender. "I'm ready to get this show on the road." Her head swiveled back and forth as she inspected the rest of the restaurant. "I think we're done here. Besides, I'm the one opening tomorrow morning. I'll deal with it then."

Tia pulled the broom out of my hand and replaced it with a bag. My brows drew together in question.

"Change. You look cute as-is, but I'm sure those clothes are coated with grease. Not to mention the smell." She wrinkled her nose. "And hurry. Gruene Hall waits for no woman."

"Wait. We're going to Gruene?"

Rachel folded her arms across her chest. "You won't talk about mystery man, you won't stop moping either. So best thing to do is saddle you up with another hot cowboy."

"Now go." Tia grasped my shoulders and turned me to face the bathrooms. "This is my first night out since before I was pregnant. I'm going to enjoy the hell out of this."

She was right. That was the main reason why I'd felt so isolated from them before. They had family barbecues and kid birthday parties where we once spent time together. And yeah, they always included me, but I just didn't know how to do family stuff. It felt awkward.

I sighed and dropped my head. "Fine."

Even then, I wasn't sure why I agreed to it. I was definitely not in the right state of mind for dancing. But I'd nothing better to do. I would just end up at home, lying in bed, and staring at the wall until I fell asleep to the tune of Joanne and Billy's fighting. Whatever the girls had in store for me couldn't possibly be any worse than that. And this was what I wanted before...him.

I pulled out items from the bag, realizing at some point she must've gotten my keys and gone to my house. Rachel had to have given them to her from my cubby hole behind the counter. Inside the plastic grocery bag was a white layered kerchief dress and my boots. The dress had an empire waist with layers of triangular crochet and lace panels that hung loose like flower petals. It was beautiful, but I never wore it because it was so short. I constantly feared a brisk wind would bare all.

My head fell back against the stall as I clutched the dress in my hand. Did I really want to do this? Could I? I didn't know if I was ready to get back out there. Was this what a breakup felt like? I'd never felt this level of uncertainty about anything. But it was ridiculous. We never had a relationship, so there couldn't have been a breakup. Therefore, I was being weird about nothing.

I was pulling the dress over my head when Rachel burst into the bathroom. She had my purse in her hand and paused to watch me pull on my boots.

"I brought your purse, so you could freshen your makeup. Do you still have that lipstick?"

She set the purse down on the counter and started rummaging through it. When she froze, my mind took a few moments to catch up to what was happening before she spoke.

"Is that...? Why d'you have this?" She took a deep breath and stepped back from the purse, eying it like it held a poisonous snake. Her eyes found me in the mirror, and her brows drew together. "What are you not tellin' me? You said nothin' happened, but now you're carryin' that? Do you even know how to use it?"

The gun. I nodded slowly. "I do. And I told you everything. But that guy that took my car... that was scary. I thought it would be a good idea." I shrugged.

I watched her in the mirror. The way her shoulders relaxed at that answer, the slight, almost imperceptive nod, indicating she accepted it. The world spun around me. I was going to hell because this lying shtick was getting easier and easier. But the dizziness didn't subside, and I turned, bolting into a stall just before my dinner made a reappearance.

Rachel pulled back my hair and rubbed my back. "You feelin' okay? Or was that something related to what happened to you? You started talkin' 'bout the guy who stole your car and your face went white as a sheet."

"I'm fine. It seems to have passed," I said, rising to my feet.

I went straight to the sink to rinse my mouth out. I frowned and felt the back of my head. The lump was gone. I'd no clue why I was still getting dizzy spells. But I was absolutely fine. Luckily, I had a toothbrush in my purse. I pulled it out and brushed my teeth, touched up my makeup. Rachel watched me the whole time, a frown pulling down the corners of her mouth as she studied me.

"You sure you're okay?"

"Yeah, it's nothing. I slipped in the shower a few days ago and hit my head. I've had a few dizzy spells since then, but other than that, I'm totally A-Okay." I smiled at her, and her face softened, but she still looked skeptical.

After a moment, she moved. Crossing the floor, she grabbed my shoulders and pulled me into a hug. "I just worry about you. You live in that shitty trailer park alone. I guess... I'm glad you got the gun—one less thing for me to worry about with you."

I pulled back and met her gaze. "I'm surprisingly good at it. I'm like Ellen Ripley in *Aliens*, total badass." I grinned.

Her answering smile was reluctant but grew to match mine.

I nudged her shoulder. "Let's get out of here."

"Let's." She nodded.

I shoved my uniform and work shoes into the plastic bag and grabbed my purse from the counter. She threaded her arm through my elbow and turned out the lights as we passed through each door on our way out.

The parking lot was deserted, and the whole strip mall was dark, everything closed for the night. Clouds hung low in the sky, blocking out the moon. So, the only light was from the headlights of Gary's car. Tia and Antonio stood, wrapped in each other, leaning on the bumper, while Gary, Rachel's husband, sat on the hood, smoking a cigarette.

Gary was a handsome man; a mechanic by trade, he had muscles for days, broad shoulders, and a barrel chest that led down to a trim waist. He was one of my favorite people on the planet. Gave the best hugs.

"There she is." Gary tossed the cigarette and stood, holding his arms open wide. He grinned as I walked into his hug. "You drove my old lady crazy, you know. I've gotta think of a good revenge."

"Old lady?" Rachel scoffed. "I'd be careful threatening her—she knows how to use a gun now."

Gary grunted as he let me go. "Really?"

I let a smirk tug one side of my mouth up in answer.

"This mean you'll go out to the deer lease with me now?"

"Ugh, no." My smile dropped. "I may know how to use a gun, but I'm not killing poor defenseless Bambi."

He crossed his bulky arms over his chest and glared at me. "It's not like that at all. Hunting is manly."

I rolled my eyes. "Yes, I know. You're all man, Gare Bear. But next time, to make it fair, maybe you should try killing the deer with a knife. I'd definitely go with you to see that."

Patting his chest, I laughed and walked past him to get in the car. I thought I heard him mumble something that sounded a lot like "no one hunts deer with a knife," which only made me laugh harder. I slid into the back seat, and Tia joined me, Antonio, her husband, on her other side.

Just as we were pulling out of the parking spot, I swear I saw movement on the side of the building. Like someone was standing at the edge of the strip center, watching from the entrance to the back parking lot where my truck was. I craned my neck as we passed it, but there was nothing there. Weird.

The drive to Gruene wasn't short; it was several towns away, but it didn't feel long. We laughed and joked, listening to music. Gary was a huge fan of Metallica, which was a big reason why I liked him. In a town full of same, I loved that my friends were the ones who were different.

Rachel passed me the bottle of Jack. I groaned internally before I put it to my lips and tipped my head back. It burned going down my throat, warming my belly. It wasn't going to take much to get me drunk, now that I had no food in there. I handed it off to Tia and Antonio, and it made it back to me several times before we arrived.

We all piled out in front of the fake white wall with its asymmetrical windows and doors. The oldest dance hall in Texas was a study in odd design concepts and wood. Everything was made of wood: the floors, the walls, the bar, the long bench-seating tables. All wooden. Surprisingly, the band that was playing that night wasn't a country band, which was rare. They were this weird mix of rock that landed somewhere between metal and sock-hop.

"It's rockabilly," Gary explained, leaning over the bar to signal for drinks. "They're called the Reverend Horton Heat."

It wasn't bad. It was different. I liked it. Gary pulled Rachel to his side and kissed her. I looked down at the scruffy bar top. Tia leaned over in front of me.

"Don't look now, but there's a guy behind you, checking out your legs. I'm surprised there aren't holes in them."

"You know there's a mirrored wall in front of me. Can I look at that?"

"Oh, yeah." She looked over at the wall in question and back over my shoulder. "Go for it. I doubt he'd notice if you didn't move."

I looked up, searching the mass of people behind me, but I didn't have to search long. Because I knew exactly who she was talking about the second I laid eyes on him. My heart started racing, and the old butterflies in the belly started dancing in time to the fast-paced music.

Tia yelled over the music. "It's him, isn't it?"

"Who?" Rachel asked.

"Mystery man," Tia replied.

"Where?"

"There."

"Holy... he is hot."

"Who is?" Gary asked.

Tia huffed. "The mystery guy."

Their voices faded to the background as I turned around. His gaze connected with mine. We sat like that, staring at each other from across the distance, neither of us moving for a long moment. Pushing off the bar, I took large strides to erase the distance, my mouth already opening to form words, questions.

Then, like a record screeching to a halt, a brunette, with large tits and pants so tight I wondered how she could breathe, stepped in between us, plastering herself to his body.

Shock slowed my reaction time, and I couldn't stop my momentum, colliding with her back. Blood rushed to my head, warming my face. The woman turned around, obviously a fan of Tammy Faye Bakker; she had eyeshadow so blue and vivid on her pale skin, framed with mascara-caked lashes, and bloodred lipstick.

"Watch it, you wetback slut. Why don't you go find one of your own kind?"

My lips flattened as I fought back a chuckle. *Why are all racists so unoriginal?* I normally didn't react, but seeing her plastered all over Xander made something in me snap. I was just about to open my mouth and say something when I heard his voice.

"Si eres de mi propia clase, quiero cambiar."

The sound melted my anger a bit, but the shock on her face wasn't lost on me. I'd no clue what he was saying, but I did know the why. This guy with pale, lightly-freckled skin, light brown hair, and the bluest eyes was trying to pass himself off as Mexican. My hand flew to my mouth to smother the laugh that wanted to burst out of me.

He winked at me and looked back at her with a serious expression.

"¿Qué? Usted no habla español?"

"Ugh, seriously? Don't y'all have a cantina you can go to?" She huffed and turned off in a storm of bad makeup and cheap perfume.

I let the laugh loose in her wake. Xander joined me. His smile was wide, showing off his white teeth. Those nearly perfect teeth where the front two overlapped a bit, making them slightly crooked. He was beautiful. I thought I'd never see him again, and here he was. I was lost, taking him all in. But when the joke died and the tension of his appearance at this bar returned, the questions came crawling out.

"What are you doing here?"

The smile on his face died. "I am leaving on Tuesday. I wanted to see you again before I go. I hope that is all right."

"How did you know where to find me? I don't normally come here."

He flipped his palms up in front of his chest and shrugged. "Skills?"

I nodded, but I'd no idea why I was nodding. That didn't exactly explain anything.

"Can I kiss you?"

My head stayed in motion, nodding again.

His lips curled up at the corners. "Good."

He tugged me into his arms, bracing my neck with his hand as he tilted my head back. His lips brushed against mine, ever so gently, sending tingles racing throughout my body. The smell of cedar trees and engine grease enveloped me. My mind felt like a skipping stone, soaring between brief bits of contact with reality. My mouth parted, and he deepened the kiss, pulling me closer with his arm around my waist. My knees went weak. I never wanted to stop. But I was forgetting something. *Breathe.* I broke away, sucking in air and meeting the electric gaze of those denim-blue eyes.

"Mmmmmm... peaches," he mumbled.

My heart rate somehow increased more, and I fought down the urge to climb up his body. But my face heated at the mention of our last time together.

"So, you gonna introduce us?" came a voice over my left shoulder.

I swiveled my head in that direction with a wry look. "Yes, Gary, I will. Xander, this is Gary. Gary, meet Xander."

Antonio joined Gary as Gary shook Xander's hand. All of the men quietly assessed each other, until Gary nodded and then slapped Antonio on the back, introducing him as well. I let out a breath of relief just before I was jerked to the side.

"Well, I know why you've been moping," Rachel said, craning her neck to get a good look at Xander's ass.

I nudged her. "Cut it out."

"Pssh," Tia scoffed. "Don't tell me you never checked out Antonio. We can look. We always have, but you're tetchy over this one. That's a good sign."

"This is so exciting!" Rachel bounced on her toes.

Xander's gaze strayed back to me.

"Xander, this is Tia and Rachel." I pointed to each, and he shook their hands.

"You ladies mind if I steal Peaches for the rest of the night?"

I raised my brows in question. The slight quirk of his kiss-swollen lips as answer made my pussy clench. The way his eyes hooded was enough for me to read—clear as day—what he had in mind.

Rachel's jaw went slack, and Tia was speechless for once in her life. It was the accent, I knew, or maybe it was that he just called me a fruit. Antonio was an oddity as far as foreigners went in these parts, but no one had ever given me a pet name either. Tia shook her head and elbowed Rachel.

"No, not at all. You and *Peaches* go and do whatever it is that you want to do." Rachel looked to me with a huge grin. "You want to give me your keys? I'll drive your truck to your place after my shift."

Oh, God. I wanted to get out of this place before they asked about the name. I scrambled to open my purse.

"Sounds good." I dug my keys out and handed them to her. "Oh, wait." I grabbed them back. "I need the house key."

I handed her back the keys after pulling the one to my house off. She smiled softly. "I'm so happy for you."

I nodded and smiled back. I didn't have the heart to tell her he was leaving. That this wasn't permanent. It didn't matter what we felt or wanted. We lived in different worlds that had only collided for a brief moment. But that time was almost up. I would make the most of it, but I wasn't deluding myself that it could be more than this.

Xander grabbed my hand, saying bye, telling everyone it was nice to meet them, and then he pulled me behind him to the parking lot. It wasn't until I felt the gravel crunch under my boots that my brain finally caught up with the moment.

"Wait. How did you get here?"

CHAPTER THIRTY-FOUR

Two Wheels

His mouth descended on mine before I could utter another word. My mind ceased its questions. I could only feel. His body heat warmed my front as the cool December air chilled my back. It was still cold for Texas but had warmed significantly since I'd last seen him.

I stumbled backward as he walked me toward the cars. Eventually he picked me up, and my legs wrapped his waist. He groaned at the feel of my bare ass in his hands. Picking up the pace, he navigated the mess of vehicles. My eyes were closed, my thoughts lost in him.

When I felt our bodies tilt and lower, I opened my eyes just before my bare thighs met cold leather. I sucked in a breath as my eyes widened. We were sitting on a motorcycle.

"I hope you won't hate me if I confess that I had this the whole time." He brushed the hair away from my face.

My brows drew together. "How?"

He shrugged. "It was in the barn. You never went in there."

"But…"

"I wanted to know you. You intrigued me. But I also needed to make sure you would be safe. And you are now."

"Okay," I whispered, nodding. I didn't fully understand, but I knew enough not to ask. "I don't hate you."

His answering smile lit up the dark corner of the parking lot. I honestly didn't care anymore. I didn't care what lies he had told or how we'd met. I was just glad to have known him, to have more time with him, even if it was fleeting. Goose bumps sprung up over my skin, and I rubbed my arms to stave off the chill. He leaned back, removing his leather jacket, and draped it around my shoulders. *Cedar. Engine grease. Man.* It felt like home. And even if home had never been a welcome place for me, with him, that word took on a new meaning.

He was still leaning close, adjusting the jacket around me, so I turned my head and kissed the corner of his mouth. He stilled. I needed him. Right here. Right now. Time was running out, and I wanted to fit a lifetime with him into one night.

Dropping my purse to the ground, I trailed kisses down his neck and nibbled on his ear, as my hands made quick work of undoing his belt and jeans. The feel of his hard length was hot in my cold hand, velvety smooth. He groaned and lifted me up. My feet scrabbled to find a foothold on the sides of the bike. I managed to push my panties to the side just before I sank down onto him.

My nerve endings lit up with the contact. Strangely, it was like I could feel more. My mind wasn't filled with fear or questions. It just felt right. This was where I belonged. I pushed up off the bike and his shoulders. He pulled me back down. I gasped and moaned into his mouth as we built a cadence of desperate movement.

We were starved for each other. We both knew that this was it. My body shuddered its agreement. I was hypersensitive to each pulse of him. It ricocheted throughout me, consuming me with pleasure.

The feel of his shoulders flexing under my hands. The softness of his lips as they caressed mine. Our tongues danced to the languid rhythm of our bodies. And I didn't care about where we were. If anyone saw us, we looked like any other couple making out on a bike, fully clothed. I just needed to feel him. To be one with him.

"I love you, *zvonová sklenice*."

I nodded, unable to speak. I was lost in the sensations overwhelming me.

When I came, I exploded into a sea of stars, floating up to join the heavens. And I remembered. Every moment, every smile, every look, every touch, since the moment we met. And it wasn't the same. The memories weren't clouded by confusion or fear of suspicion.

There was this man, and he saw me, understood me like no one had before. With the chickens that weren't his, yet he named them and cared for them. His infectious laugh and smile. The carefree way he danced with me when he was happy, celebrating his secret victory. He didn't do it for the glory, to be called a hero—no one would ever know his name. Deep down, he was a good man, and I would always see that. I would know. And the way he owned my body... he knew how to please me in ways I'd never dreamed.

His release quickly followed mine, and I collapsed into his arms. Fully sated and relaxed, I breathed in the cool night air.

That was the moment I knew I loved him. I'd fallen in love with him. I couldn't run away from it because it was stamped onto my soul, written into my blood, carved into my memory. We were just destined to be like two wheels on a bike—always working in tandem, but forever separated by time and space.

He reached into his saddle bag and pulled out a piece of cloth. I couldn't see it in the darkness, but he made quick work of righting me.

I moved to the back of the bike and clung to him, still huddled in his jacket, near freezing as he drove back to my place without any direction. He knew where to find me. And though parts of my rational brain knew that should scare me, given who he was and what he did for a living, it felt comforting nonetheless.

When he pulled into my driveway and cut the engine, I sent up a silent prayer of thanks that Billy and Joanne were nowhere to be found.

I didn't know what he had planned, so I stood from the bike, pulling off the helmet he had given me and handing it back to him. He attached it to the handlebar, and the moment he was done, I kissed him.

"Stay with me," I whispered. "Stay the night, please."

He stared off into the woods behind my house, a silent battle taking place in his eyes. "I will stay as long as I can."

I let out a silent breath of relief and held his hand as I led him to the door.

"This is your home?" he asked as I shut the door behind him.

He removed his boots by the door and stepped farther into the living room. His gaze roamed over the space, taking in my meager furnishings and lack of decoration. The only thing to look at was the Ansel Adams print, so I wasn't surprised when he stepped closer to it.

"Yup, the one and only." I set my keys and purse on the counter, watching him. "I'd give you a tour, but there's not much to see. Just an empty bedroom, a bathroom, and the room I sleep in. You want something to drink?"

I turned and walked into the kitchen, opening the fridge. I didn't have much. I stood up, but he was no longer in the living room. I frowned and shut the fridge.

"No."

I yelped and spun around to face him. His ability to move silently was both amazing and startling. He stalked forward until I was pinned between him and the fridge.

"I only want you."

I let out a shaky breath. "Same."

"So we will not waste our time being polite. We both know what we want."

I nodded. He made quick work of undressing me, and we fucked. Again, and again, on every surface in my tiny trailer. In the kitchen, the living room floor, the shower, my bed, until the sun was just below the horizon and I was both physically and mentally exhausted.

Curling up into his side, I stared at him, trying to commit him to memory: every line of his strong jaw, the various shades of golden-brown stubble that graced his cheeks, his long dark lashes, the way the dip at the center of his top lip sloped out to create a defined ridge, the tiny crease in his bottom lip...

I tried hard to stay awake, not wanting to miss a moment I had left. Losing that battle, my eyes starting to drift shut, I uttered the words that I never thought I would say to another human being again.

"I love you too, Xander."

"I know, Rosie. I have known it since the first time you tried to run away from those feelings and came back."

I wanted to argue. I wanted to say more, but I was spent. Sleep pulled me under. And with that last conscious breath, I took in the smell of him, felt the warmth of his body pressed against mine, and drifted off to dreams of the future we would never have.

210

CHAPTER THIRTY-FIVE

Complicated

I woke up to the bright sun leaking through slats in the blinds of my window, directly into my eyes. The first thing I noticed was that Xander was gone. But that wasn't what woke me up. It was the incessant pounding on my door. The walls of my tiny trailer shook, rattling the only picture on the bedroom wall—the one of me, Rachel, and Tia.

I pulled my ass out of the bed with a groan as the pounding continued. It sounded like they were using a battering ram. *Boom. Boom. Boom.* I checked the time on the alarm clock as I pulled on my robe. It was nearly five in the evening. Walking down the hall, I could hear Billy and Joanne's voices outside.

My clothes from last night that I'd tossed on the floor were neatly folded and stacked on the kitchen counter. Next to it sat an envelope with my name on it. *Boom. Boom. Boom.* I didn't have time to check it out. I needed to answer the door while I still had one.

I went to yank it open, but the dead bolt was locked. I blinked and rubbed my sleep-weary eyes, then unlocked it and tried again.

"It's about fuckin' time." Rachel shoved my keys in my hand and shouldered past me. "I swear if I'd to listen to those two bicker and toss accusations for ten more seconds… I don't know. You need to move out of this place. Those people are too much. You know the place next door to me is up for rent?"

"I do know this because you've mentioned it to me no less than ten times a day since I've been back. But it's a three-bedroom and two hundred dollars more a month than this place. I don't need the space." I motioned around to the sparse furnishings. "And I can't afford it. Not after missing a month of work and spending all my savings."

"I know, I know. I've heard all that. I just wish you were closer. Tia lives down the street, but it would be amazing if you were next door and we were all within walking distance. We could carpool?" She grinned.

I sighed and went to make some tea. "You want some?"

"Sure, but I'd an ulterior motive to comin' over, other than to bring you your truck. Which is a nice truck, by the way. Classic. I had to pry Gary away from it." She hopped up on the counter. "Gary's not coming to get me for a couple of hours, so we have time. But I wanted to bring you this."

She dug around in her purse and pulled out a box. Waving it around in the air, she watched me with an expressionless face as I put the kettle on the stove. I grabbed it and read the box. *Virtually 100% accurate…*

"You bought me a pregnancy test?"

"Uh, yeah. You did say that you'd been getting sick and throwing up lately. And that was how I knew when I was pregnant. Mornin' sickness is a bitch."

"I also told you that I'd hit my head pretty hard. I'm not pregnant."

Her hands went to her hips as she pinned me with a glare. "Have you ever been pregnant?"

"No. You know that." I gave her a deadpan look.

"Exactly. Leave the know-it-all to us experts." She tapped her fingernail on the bottom of the box. "So where is Xander?"

I set the box on the counter. "I don't know."

"You don't know?"

I threw up my hands, palms up. "Are you impersonating a parrot now?"

"No. It's just that he took you home last night. I assume you got your freak on. Figured you'd know where he was going when he left." She shrugged.

I huffed out a breath. "Look, I would assume he went home, but he left while I was asleep, so I don't have confirmation of his whereabouts."

"Wow, testy much?"

"Sorry, I just woke up."

"No, it's something else. I've known you since we were kids; you've never gotten short with me. *This* is something else. So what's bothering you?"

Tears welled up in my eyes, and I fought them back.

"Nothing. So, you think I might be pregnant?" I waved the box in the air. "How am I supposed to work this thing?"

"You pee on the stick. It's not rocket science." Rachel shrugged.

I took in a deep, ragged breath. "Fine, I'll go do that."

"Fine. Then you'll tell me what crawled up your ass when you get back."

I glared at her and flipped her off.

"No thanks, honey. You're not my type. I've got Gary's cock for that."

"Must be satisfying." I held up my hand, displaying my thumb and index finger an inch apart.

"Go pee on the fuckin' stick, bitch. Stop trying to piss me off to avoid it, or I'll tell Gary you said that."

She probably could have used any threat in the world and I would have stayed out of stubbornness, but I loved Gary like a brother, I didn't want him getting angry with me. And he wouldn't understand my mood swings the way Rachel did. I knew Rachel back before my mom got sent away. And every time I ran away from a foster home, she was who I'd run to. Tia, we met when we went to high school, where the district was wide enough to span from our side of town to the rich people's side.

"Fine," I huffed and stormed back to the bathroom.

I did need to go pee anyway, having just rolled out of bed. And I'd do it if only just to prove her wrong. I ripped open the box, narrowly avoiding spilling its contents all over the floor. I set all the pieces on the counter and pulled open the instructions. It really was pretty much just peeing on the stick. So I sat down, positioned the stick where it needed to be, and let loose. I decided to do the second one too, in case I screwed it up. I wasn't going to be able to make myself pee again anytime soon.

Setting the tests on the counter, I finished up and washed my hands, because yep, I peed on them too. I was just about to sit on the tub's edge to wait when I heard the kettle. I rushed back to the kitchen, pulling the kettle off the stove. Two mugs and the honey were sitting out. Rachel knew how I liked my tea. It brought a little smile to my face.

I peeked back at her as I poured the steaming water into the mugs. "I'm sorry. I shouldn't take all this shit out on you."

"I'm not sure what shit you're referring to, but I'll take the apology."

"How are things with you?" I called back to her over my shoulder. "We haven't had much time to really talk since I've been back."

"It's great. Gary's great."

"And the kiddo?" I smiled thinking about him.

"Just like his dad, it's almost scary. Like I brought another Gary into the world."

I smirked. They did have the cutest little boy. He even called me aunt. I finished making our tea and stirred in the honey.

"You wanna see the verdict?" She rubbed her hands together.

CHAPTER THIRTY-FIVE

I handed her the mug of tea. "Can you make it sound less… criminal?"

"It's a life sentence, no matter which way you look at it." She took the cup with a shrug.

"You look." I nodded toward the bathroom.

She grinned. "Really?"

"Yes, hurry. The suspense is killing me." I made a shooing motion with my hands.

She walked around the corner into the hall. I listened for a reaction, but I heard nothing. Just silence. I tapped my fingers on the side of the mug as I blew on the tea to cool it down. Then the toilet flushed. *Really? I'm waiting to find out if I'm having Xander's baby, and she decides to use the bathroom.*

Rachel finally came walking out, looking as normal as she would any day of the week. She was giving nothing away, and I wanted to strangle her.

"So, what is it?"

"You, my friend—" She picked up her tea and took a long sip.

My eyes were shooting death rays at her.

"—are sentenced to life with child." She grinned and set the mug down, then bounced on her toes. "You are so pregnant. That's two positive tests on the counter."

The mug of tea in my hands crashed to the ground. The room spun around me. Pregnant. I was pregnant. With Xander's kid. And he would never know.

"Holy shit!" Rachel dashed across the kitchen and threw a towel down on the tea as she reached out and grabbed me.

She wasn't strong enough to stop me, and my ass hit the floor with a thump.

"Okay, now. Now's the time to tell me what really happened when you disappeared."

I felt dizzy, confused. "He's gone."

"Yeah, I noticed. But why are you—"

"No, I don't mean he's gone from my house. I mean that he's not from around here."

"I caught that, too. The accent sort of gave it away."

I needed to tell her. I needed to tell someone the truth about it all, and she made the most sense. My oldest friend could keep a secret. She had kept many for me throughout the years. So I did it. I told her everything. Though I left out the part about the motorcycle. I think love was the only thing that made me overlook that, and I didn't want to make her angry at him for not bringing me back sooner.

"So he's a Czechoslovakian spy that just diverted a war. That's some crazy shit. And you're right. If I hadn't known you my whole life, I wouldn't believe you. But I know you're not creative enough to make up something like that."

My jaw went slack. "Hey!"

"Can't run from the truth." She shook her head and sagged until her back hit the kitchen cabinet.

I sighed, moving on. "You can't tell anyone. Not even Gary."

"Your secret's safe with me... What're you gonna do?"

"Huh?"

"About Xander and the baby?"

"Oh... I don't know. I'm keeping it. It's a piece of him that I get to have forever."

She shook her head. "I didn't think you would get rid of it. That's just not you. But are you going to tell him?"

I shrugged. "He's leaving tomorrow. I don't even know what time."

"Then you should go now." She leaned forward, propping her chin on her fists. "He deserves to know."

"I'm not supposed to go back there."

"I don't think he'd be running around town with you if some secret spy group dropped in because you picked up a phone."

She had a point. I tilted my head as I considered it. But then I remembered the note. I stood up, swiping it off the counter. It wasn't just a note. It was a standard mailing envelope, but it was thick. I opened it and pulled out the contents. There was a large stack of hundred-dollar bills—there had to be ten thousand dollars here—and a note. A key slipped out too and clattered to the floor.

"Holy shit!" Rachel gasped, staring at the money.

She yanked it out of my hand and started counting. The note was written in slightly legible handwriting.

Rosie,

I can never give you the life you deserve, but I wish I could. I know you missed out on work while you were with me, and I wanted to make up for anything you lost in that time. Please accept this and know that no matter where I am, you are in my heart. And don't leave a key under your potted plant anymore.

Eternally and forever yours,

Xander

Nope. Hell to the fuck no. I took care of myself, and I needed no one's money to get by. I was on the fence about going to see him, but I would do it, if only to give this back. I didn't have much, but I was nobody's charity case. And yes, I could see that he was just trying to be sweet; he loved me, and I loved him more for trying, but this was a hard line for me.

Rachel grabbed the note out of my hands and read it.

"You're so movin' in next door now." She smiled wide. "In fact, I'll call the realtor while you're gone and get the application."

I shook my head. "I'm not keeping it. I'll give it back to him when I go talk to him."

"That's bullshit." She huffed. "You'll need this, just for the baby and medical bills alone."

"I don't need it."

"You do." Her brows drew together. "Don't be stubborn about this."

I crossed my arms over my chest. "I'm not bein' stubborn"

"Are too."

"Fine." I flipped one hand into the air. "What the fuck ever. I'm stubborn. So sue me. I'm not taking money from the man. Not now, not ever." I stood up. "I'm going. I'm going to tell him about the baby. I'm going to give him back the money, and that will be that."

"Fine. Hopefully he can talk sense into you. It's obvious you won't listen to me. But I can tell you now. You say the words 'baby' or 'pregnant,' and he's not taking it back. Not if he's half the man I think he is. So, I'm still callin' the realtor. And I will leave the application on the counter." She swiped the key off the floor and shoved it into her pocket. "You'll want to be near me, because I'm going to help you raise that baby. I'm going to answer all your questions, and babysit, and love the shit out of that kid like it was my own. Got me?" She stood up, red-faced.

I stood there quietly and stared at her. I don't think I'd ever seen her get *that* mad at me before. I didn't dare say a word back. She used the words *got me*. That's the signal that makes code-red sirens go off. I watched her as she paced the floor and huffed. I slowly shoved the money back into the envelope, stuffing it into my purse. I grabbed my key and slid the house key back on the key ring.

"What I don't get is why did he call—"

"I'm going now. It's getting late and I want to catch him before he leaves."

I knew what she was going to ask, and I didn't have time to explain it. He could be leaving early to stay the night somewhere closer to an airport. I didn't know. But I wanted to tell him—I needed to. If only to give the child a chance to know him.

CHAPTER THIRTY-SIX

Return

I pulled out of my driveway in a hurry. The sun was already dipping low on the horizon, and I knew that I had to make it there before sunset. I didn't think I would be able to find it any other way. The driveway was pretty nondescript and easy to miss on a sunny day. Finding it at night would be impossible.

The farther I drove, the better I felt about this decision. I was still nervous. How did you tell a guy you were pregnant with his kid? Other than the obvious. I knew the words *I'm pregnant* were involved, but did you just dive off into that phrase, or did you need a warm-up?

I was so full of nervous jitters, I turned off the radio. The music was only ratcheting up my nerves even more. Though I was more worried about how I was going to tell him than how he would react. I didn't know what being a father would mean to him, but I knew he valued family. He would treasure this little pea, even if he couldn't be around full-time.

The sun had set by the time I pulled into the driveway of the farmhouse. But the sky was still a royal-blue stain above. Only a few brave stars had peeked out. Rocks clanked against the truck as it tossed up bits of the gravel drive. I'd forgotten how long this driveway was. It seemed to stretch out forever.

Eventually I saw the back of the garage, then turned the corner around to its front. The motorcycle sat in the front yard, near the house. Lights were on inside. I killed the engine and let out a breath of relief. He was here.

I gave myself a few moments as I gathered the courage to do what I needed to. And when I finally opened the door and stepped out, I believed I was ready for what happened next. The tiny rocks crunched beneath my boots as I made my way toward the front door.

The door was open, but the screen door still covered the entrance. The evening news played on the TV in the living room, but I didn't see him anywhere.

I knocked and heard shuffling coming from the kitchen area, but still couldn't see him. I turned and looked out over the yard, waiting for him to answer the door. I considered walking in, but given the news I had to deliver, bursting in his front door and announcing I was pregnant seemed rude. Right?

I was just about to knock again when I heard the voice. A deep, raspy, accented voice.

"You are looking well, for a dead girl."

I turned in what felt like slow motion. It seemed like hours passed before my eyes landed on his face, and when it did, it felt like I couldn't breathe. It was the guy from the car. My car. It was the guy who stole my car. No, that was the story I told the girls. I wanted to say it was the killer, but that wasn't right either—Xander was the killer.

I didn't know who he was, but I knew he was dangerous. It fell off him in waves. He was younger than I initially thought, but still much older than Xander.

I stepped back.

Another step.

I still had my keys in my hand, and I gauged the distance to the truck in my mind. I decided to go for it. I turned, and promptly miscalculated. I was too close to the edge of the porch and tumbled down the three steps to the dirt yard below. Scrambling to my feet, I got one whole step before I felt the firm grip in my hair.

"Where are you going? You didn't even come inside."

I started to scream, but his sweaty palm clapped over my mouth.

"Now, now. Don't go ruining the fun for me yet."

SNAPSHOT

CHAPTER THIRTY-SEVEN

Survival

"I find it infinitely humorous that you showed up here, all bright-eyed, for him. I am going to love taking this back to the home office. Our most ruthless, efficient agent has gone soft, leaving loose ends. We can't have that."

Time seemed to slow to a crawl. Every heartbeat felt like the reverberation of a thunderclap played on one-tenth speed. I pulled my head back as hard as I could, but his grip was solid. Dread sunk to the bottom of my stomach like a hot stone. He grabbed hold of my wrist and twisted it behind my back. I crumpled from the pain.

Pressing his chest to my back, he picked me up, trapping that arm in place. He was so much taller than me that my feet dangled helplessly, searching for the ground. I was so screwed. My only hope was that Xander would save me, but he had warned me. I knew coming back here was a bad idea, yet I allowed other things to cloud rational thinking.

This wasn't a safe place. There were no truly good memories, and Xander wasn't a good man. He was just good to me in a moment of weakness.

The man started moving. I kicked and screamed into his hand.

It was useless. He was too strong and had me locked in his arms, one around my waist, the other over my mouth, pressing my head back onto his shoulder. I tried biting him, but he just laughed and kept a steady course. I was looking up at the stars, spinning as he shifted.

It took a few moments for me to gather where we were moving. *The barn.* I struggled harder, knowing the one time that I was in there, the place was covered in blood. Turkey blood. But that wasn't comforting enough. They had tortured a guy here, and the barn seemed a likely spot.

He removed the hand from my mouth to open the barn door, and I seized the opportunity. I screamed as loud and as long as my lungs would allow. Sucking in a deep breath, I did it again.

The man laughed. "Do that all you want. There is no one around to hear you."

My heart raced. My chest felt like it was in a vise as tears welled up in my eyes. Xander wasn't here. I tried to grab on the doorframe as we passed through it, but he kept moving like it was nothing more than a minor annoyance. This was so stupid. I was so stupid. All this time spent trying to survive, to play it smart and keep safe, and I did the dumbest thing I could do.

I closed my eyes, but it didn't block the pain or reality. He let go. It was unexpected, and I collapsed to the floor like a rag doll before I knew what was happening. My head hit the floor with a thump, and I groaned. But I think the hit knocked some sense into me because I wasn't panicked anymore. I remembered.

I had a gun.

The purse was still strapped over my torso. I curled my body around it to hide my hand as it slid into the purse, fishing for my weapon. But I didn't see it coming when his steel-toed boot connected with the left side of my back, just under my ribs. The force was enough to throw me across the space and into one of the half walls that partitioned the stalls. The corner edge of the wall hit just under my shoulder blades, and as momentum carried me farther away, the rough wood tore through my sweater, scraping my back up to my shoulders and knocking the air from my lungs.

I took a moment to find the ability to breathe, but that moment was a moment too long. He pulled the purse over my head and tossed it to the other side of the room. My eyes locked on it, and I cried out internally for its loss. That was my last best chance at surviving this.

Protect the baby. Live for the baby.

Those words skipped through my head on repeat as I stood. Still gasping for air, I took the chance and ran for it. And that's when he hit me. I don't know if it was his hand or an object, but pain raced through my skull like lightning. The force sent me stumbling forward. It wasn't far enough. I collapsed to the ground, and my vision began to dim. I reached for my purse, but it was still a foot away or more.

Darkness.

I didn't know if I was dead or merely unconscious. I didn't know how long that moment lasted. There was a sound. It was loud and high-pitched, like a snap.

Plink.

Plink.

Plink.

Water.

Drops.

Rain.

It was raining. My heart did a little flip at that. If it was raining, then I was alive. The first thing I did was reach up to feel the part of my head that was pounding its own heartbeat. My pulse raced at the feel of the swollen, matted, soggy mess of hair. I blinked rapidly as my vision slowly came back. It was dark, but strips of filtered moonlight leaked in with the light rain through gaps in the barn's weathered siding.

Cold.

The temperature had dropped again. I raised my hand in front of my eyes, trying to see if the wetness in my hair was from the rain or blood. The shadows were too deep, and the bottom of my hand only looked like more darkness.

I heard another sound. Something shuffling from the other side of the room. I froze, putting my hand back where it was when I was unconscious. I listened. He didn't kill me while I was down, which meant he wanted me awake for whatever he had planned. I could use a few moments to come up with a plan.

Xander had to be back. Unless he was gone for good.

I couldn't see my purse from the direction my head was tilted. I only knew one of two things: either he was smart enough to look there and found the gun, or he thought it wasn't necessary because he had control. He might assume I had hair spray or something a woman would likely carry. So, it could still be there.

The right side of my body was numb. Possibly because I'd been in the same position for too long. I needed to move. The shuffling sounds continued, punctuated by a few thumps. He was far enough away that I should be able to make it to my purse if it was still there.

Move.

As fast as my brain wanted me to go, my body was still sluggish. I didn't move quite as fast as I hoped. Then the light flickered on.

Ever heard the expression *deer in headlights*? It's possibly the stupidest thing a deer does. It costs them their life more often than not. So when I found myself in the face of a bright light, I stopped. And I wanted to kick my own ass for doing it.

"She is awake."

At the sound of the stranger's voice, my synapses fired again, and I set into motion too late. I only had enough time to get to my hands and knees. I spotted a loose board nearby just as his body crashed into me. But I got it. I grabbed the board, and when he flipped me over to my back, I swung.

I put every ounce of strength into that swing.

Protect the baby. Live for the baby.

It cracked against the side of his head. The force reverberating up to my arm made me lose my grip, and the wood clattered to the floor.

"*Piča*," he muttered as he shook his head.

There was an angry gash on his cheek, oozing blood, but it wasn't enough to make him lose consciousness. *Fuck*. I reached for the board again, but he grabbed it, yanking it from my hand and tossing it across the room. His hands fumbled at my waist, and when I felt my jeans loosen, I knew what he had in store for me.

I only had one last option. I opened my mouth and screamed.

CHAPTER THIRTY-EIGHT

Welcome

My head was pounding, and my throat was dry from screaming. I fought against him, to the point that my muscles were shaking from the strain.

"No," I croaked.

I found an opening and brought my knee up to his groin with as much force as I could muster. He groaned. His face changed, the deep lines creasing even further with anger. He reared back, raising his arm. I braced myself. I knew it was coming. He was going to hit me, and I didn't know if I would survive it or even remain conscious.

But that's not what happened. One second, his fist was barreling toward me, the next, he was gone, and the only evidence that he had been on top of me were my gasps for air in the absence of that weight. I heard them shouting in Czech to each other as they grappled on the floor, a few feet from my head.

Xander.

Relief swept through me so sharply, tears streamed from my eyes. He came back. He was here. But that relief was short-lived as I watched the stranger get the upper hand, punching Xander over and over again. I had to react fast. I was too weak to stand, so I crawled the short distance.

It was there. The gun was still in my purse, fully loaded. I flipped off the safety and struggled to stand. Using the last of my strength, I squared off my feet, and raised the gun. Xander was too close to him to get a decent shot.

"Hey!" I shouted.

Xander glanced in my direction and gave a slight, barely perceptive nod. He did some move that was too fast for my eyes to track, pushing the man up and away from him. The man glanced over, and I stared into his eyes as they widened with realization.

"Welcome to Texas, bitch." I pulled the trigger.

Blood, brain matter, and bone arced out from the back of his head as the bullet hit its mark. Sort of. I was aiming for his forehead and hit his right eye instead. It took a moment before his body slumped over, falling on top of Xander. Longer than you'd think it would take for death to fully sink in.

Xander rolled the body off him, and everything hit me all at once. My legs folded underneath me like a marionette, and I dropped the gun.

I killed someone. I just killed someone, my brain repeated on an endless loop. Xander was in front of me, inspecting me for damage. Words were coming from his mouth, but I couldn't hear them. They were muffled by the endless ringing in my ears and the repetitive thought running through my head.

He kissed me, pulling me into his arms. I lay there, limp. Every part of me felt like Jell-O shaking in a loose mold.

"I killed him," I mumbled. "I killed someone."

"I know, Rosie. I am so sorry." Xander squeezed me a little tighter, and I winced.

He loosened his hold and wiped the tears from my face. I didn't know I was crying. No, I was sobbing. I fought to catch my breath. Reaching out a shaky hand, I traced my fingertips over the deep-purple bruises blooming on Xander's cheek and chin. The split in his lip was still bleeding. Yet I didn't care as I pulled his head down and ghosted my lips over his. When I moved away, his lips turned down at the corners.

"What are you doing here?" he asked.

"I had to tell you. I needed to tell you before you leave…" My throat was dry, and the words caught, choking me. I coughed a few times, feeling the ache throughout my body. "I'm pregnant."

Xander's face played out a myriad of emotions, from shock to happiness, then anger as he looked over at the other man. When his gaze returned back to me, the smile in his eyes would have taken over his face if not for the injuries. He kissed me again, not being careful of his injuries. And when he pulled back, tears filled his eyes.

I looked over to the dead body, trying to wrap my mind around all of this. "Who was he?"

"Čeněk Prochazka. He was my partner on this mission."

"You know, the first thing he said to me was: *you look well for a dead girl.*"

Xander closed his eyes and didn't respond. I was beginning to think that I needed to phrase it as a question, when his eyes opened and he pinned me with a serious look.

"I was to kill you. The day we met." He nodded once before his eyes took on a distant, faraway look. "We heard you in the forest. Čeněk decided that he would dispose of your car and report the information we gathered back to home. I was to destroy all the evidence. That moment when I first laid eyes on you, it was not only that you were beautiful. You didn't react like anyone else would. I have been surrounded by death most of my life. I have seen many people discover bodies. No one had ever been made curious by it. Until you. You leaned in and took a picture. You studied it. You intrigued me for what you did. I wanted to know more about you. And I have never felt that urge before."

I didn't know what to say to that, so I stayed silent. My morbid curiosity saved my life from the man I loved. I felt detached from it. Like I couldn't reconcile the fact that he was supposed to kill me.

Perhaps because I'd spent so much time thinking exactly that, only to work through those feelings to realize that I loved him. It just didn't matter to me anymore. None of it did. Only him, me, and the baby were important. And we were alive.

"Everything you did from that day drew me in further. Until I realized that I love you and there was no going back. I could never hurt you. You, this baby, mean more to me than you will ever understand. I did not know that I needed it until you said those words. My heart feels so full, and I thought that I could never have that. I told myself that I was not built for it."

Can a heart break out of joy? Because it felt like mine did in that moment. This broken, lonely man, whose path in life separated him from everyone he loved, met a girl who separated herself from life because of things that were beyond her control. And in each other, they found someone who could accept the weight of who they were.

He spared my life and saved me instead, and I saved him back.

"I love you," I said, stroking his cheek.

He sighed and cupped his hand to the back of mine, pressing it to his face. "I love you too, *zvonová sklenice*."

"So... what do we do now?"

CHAPTER THIRTY-NINE

Relief

"Order up," I shouted into the kitchen.

It'd been one week to the day since the incident at the farmhouse. Xander insisted I go to a doctor; I got several stitches and a nice bald spot shaved on the side of my head for the trouble. He stayed with me that night, making sure I survived the concussion. But after that, he went back to the farmhouse to "clean up the evidence." Then he was going back home, to Czechoslovakia.

He promised to return, but he didn't know when he would be able to.

"Before the baby is born," he whispered in my ear, kissing my neck. *"I would have come back for you alone, but I will not miss meeting my child for the world."*

Today was day seven. Christmas Eve.

The restaurant was slow. Not many came in on holidays, which is why it was me and one cook manning the place. We had a few early diners, those who didn't want to cook. But it was past eight o'clock now, and the only ones left were the lonely souls, like me, who had no better place to be.

I worried to no end what would happen. What he would say to make it all better. You didn't kill someone without consequence, and I 'd taken a life. A member of his organization, no less. He was scared that I picked up the phone—what would they do when they found out I killed one of their own?

"Do not worry about it," he cooed. "I will take care of it, and you will be safe."

"It's not just me. I'm worried about you too."

"Nothing will happen to me. You have no reason to worry." He stroked my hair and kissed me.

Then the next morning, he was gone.

I didn't care how many times he said it, I'd never fully believe it until he was back in my arms. It'd been seven long days that felt more like seven months. I'd chewed every fingernail on my hands down to the quick.

Rachel nearly shit a brick when she saw me at work the next day. If Xander had been there, and she had Gary's shotgun, he would've been a dead man. It took hours for her to calm down and fully comprehend that it wasn't Xander who put the bruises on my arms. When she finally understood, she shoved the application for the house next door in my face and told me she didn't care, she wanted me close by. Somehow, I'd managed to skirt the issue this long. I wasn't entirely sure what Xander and I would do when he did return.

I sighed, looking out over the restaurant. There were only three customers in the joint. Franny and Jack, an older couple whose kids had grown up and moved away, and Benny.

Benny was a regular who sat at the counter every night. He was a widower in his late fifties. His wife died about five years back. Cancer. He didn't cook and didn't like being at home alone, so he was here after he got off work until we closed.

"Need some more coffee, Benny?"

He looked up from reading the newspaper and smiled. "Can't say no to an offer like that."

I pulled the carafe from the coffee machine and walked over to him.

"I never got the chance to tell you before, but I'm really glad you're back. You make the best coffee in three counties. The boys and I stopped coming here in protest when you were gone. Told Oscar if he didn't get you back…" He shook his head, scratching his thinning hair. "It was tough. Had to eat at McDonald's. And their coffee is terrible."

"You didn't have to do that, Benny." I filled his cup and set the carafe aside, leaning my elbows on the counter and looking him in the eyes. "Oscar didn't fire me. It was my fault."

"We all make mistakes, dear. But don't go doin' somethin' like that again. Y'hear?"

I smiled. "Sure thing, Benny. You need anything else?"

He shook his head and went back to his paper. I busied myself, working on closing duties for the rest of the night. With only one more hour 'til close, time seemed to fly by.

"Merry Christmas," I called to Benny as he finally shuffled out the door.

I was wiping down the counter where he'd sat when I heard the bells jingle above the door. My heart quickened with hope. My head couldn't turn fast enough. But my shoulders dropped as Gary strolled in.

"I didn't think I'd have to tell you that we're closed, Gare."

He pulled off his hat and twisted it in his hands. "I'm here on Rachel's orders to make sure you get home without any trouble."

"You don't have to do that." I sighed. "She's just bein' paranoid. And I told her it was fine. I've made it home all week without incident."

He shrugged. "Don't need you gettin' lost again."

I rolled my eyes to the heavens. "Let me just wash out this mug and we can go. Pete already closed the kitchen. I've done everything else."

Gary nodded and sat at the counter to wait. I hurried back to the dish station, making quick work of the mug. Gary stood and followed me out the door, waiting as I locked the place up tight. When I turned, I noticed his car wasn't here. My lips twisted into a frown.

"Tony dropped me off," Gary said, reading my confusion.

"So you need a ride home?"

He smiled. "You could say that."

He put his arm over my shoulder, leading me to my truck in the back parking lot. The drive to his and Rachel's house was quick. They lived closer to the diner.

As I pulled into their driveway, I noticed the trailer next to theirs had all the lights on. A fully-decorated Christmas tree sat in the window. My heart sank. I know I told Rachel no a hundred times and avoided it, but part of me thought that maybe Xander would come back and we'd make the decision to move there together.

I hesitated as Gary got out of the truck. "Someone moved in next door?"

"Yep, today of all days, if you can imagine that." He looked over his shoulder at the house and back to me.

I snorted. "Who moves on Christmas Eve?"

Gary shrugged. "You wanna meet the new neighbor?"

"What? No." I cringed. "I'm not bothering a strange family on Christmas Eve."

"Suit yourself."

Gary shut the door and was walking across the yard to the neighbor's front door before I could blink. I scrambled to kill the engine and chase him down before he got there. But the door opened. Tia stood in the doorway. *What the hell is going on?* Gary walked in past her, and she watched me, waiting.

I blinked a few times and marched up the steps to the door. "Why would you move down the street?"

"I didn't." She tilted her head to the side with a grin. "You gonna come in? Or you want to stand out there all night?"

She stepped aside, and I walked in.

The first thing I noticed was that the person who lived here had the same Ansel Adams print that I owned. And the same pillows on the couch that I had on the makeshift twin bed I called a couch. *Weird.* There were other items I'd seen before but couldn't recall where. It took a couple of minutes for it to fully sink in, but when I saw him, I knew. This was some of the furniture from the farmhouse.

Xander.

He was framed by the opening to the hallway behind him as he leaned against the wall. Though parts of his face were still yellow from the fading bruises, he was still the most beautiful man I'd ever laid eyes on. Rachel, Gary, and their little boy were on the couch. Antonio sat on an armchair with his boy in his lap. But my eyes tracked back to him. Every muscle in my body seemed to relax with his soft smile.

"You're back?"

He nodded.

"For good?"

He shrugged, pushing off the wall and walking toward me. "That depends on some things."

There was a look of apprehension that crossed his face before he schooled his features. He was damn good at hiding things from people, but the longer I knew him, the more those brief flashes told me everything I needed to know. Something was off. I'd no clue what, and now wasn't the time to ask. I was too overwhelmed with relief that he made it back alive and whole.

I looked around, and everyone was watching me. I began to get self-conscious a bit, as tears of relief welled in my eyes, but this was my family. I didn't need to feel embarrassed in front of them.

Xander stopped in front of me and held out a tiny box. It was a wooden box, a little worn but intricately carved. A shiny gold ribbon was tied around it.

"Merry Christmas," Xander said.

I pulled on the end of the bow and the ribbon fell away, fluttering to the floor. Opening the box, I found a set of three gold rings, one large one and two smaller ones, all of them carved with detailed engravings. I looked up, but Xander wasn't there. Instead, he was down on one knee.

He cleared his throat as his cheeks pinked. "Those rings belonged to my grandparents. My mother gave them to me when I went back home and told her about you. She wants to meet you one day. I had to promise to bring you to my country soon to get those. And I will. If you allow me. I want to spend every day for the rest of my life, making you feel loved. You will never feel alone again. If you will have me as your husband."

I couldn't speak, holding back the sob that had lodged itself in my throat, but my head was already nodding. I never thought I would, but I wanted that, more than anything. I pulled his face to mine, kissing him with everything I couldn't say. His arms wrapped around me, and I was lost. His smell, his warmth, the feel of his strong arms... all of it.

Then a cork popped, bouncing off the ceiling. I broke away and turned to find Tia pouring glasses of champagne into mismatched cups.

"Oh, my God. I'm so fudging happy for you." Rachel bounced over to us, wiping tears from her eyes and wrapping her arms around us. "Congratulations. And Merry Christmas."

"Merry Christmas," I mumbled and hugged her back. "And thank you."

"Congrats and Merry Christmas. We normally open presents on Christmas Day," Tia said, handing Xander and me cups of champagne. "But we all have a big day tomorrow, so we let the kids wait up. They're dying to open their gifts. But—"

"We want you to open yours first," Rachel said, moving to the Christmas tree and pulling out a box and a card from a large pile of gifts. She walked back to me, holding out the card. "You can open Tia and Antonio's gift first."

I took the proffered card. "You guys really didn't have to. I didn't buy anything—"

"Not the point." Tia held a finger up in the air. "Just open it."

I opened the card slowly and carefully, trying to give respect to it. It was the first Christmas gift I'd received since I was a kid. Rachel groaned, and Tia lurched forward but then stopped.

"Just open it," Gary sighed.

I laughed. "I'm sorry. It just feels like a big deal."

I pulled the card out and opened it. A mass of papers fluttered to the ground. Xander helped me gather them up. Looking through them, I frowned.

"You bought me eight tickets to Las Vegas?" I looked to Tia and Antonio, my brows drawn in confusion.

"There are eight of us in this room," Antonio said.

Rachel hopped on her toes and shook the box in her hands. "We're goin' to Vegas!"

I was so confused. It seemed so random. "Why?"

"Oh." Rachel held out the box for me. "This should answer that. This is from me and Gare."

I handed the card and tickets to Xander, then ripped into the box, curious about what it meant that this present explained the trip. Once the wrapping paper was cleared, I pulled off the lid and shuffled the tissue paper aside. White. That was all I could see, so I pulled it out. It was a white dress. A wedding dress.

It was simple, plain, classic lines. Not flashy or garish with beads and ruffles. It was perfect. But it was too much. It was all too much. They'd moved me into a new home and planned my wedding that was happening the next day. I didn't deserve this. I would never deserve this. I wouldn't insult them by shoving it back in their face, so I did the only thing I could do.

I let the tears fall.

"I'm afraid you're going to be disappointed for the rest of your life when it comes to Christmas." Rachel hugged me to her side.

I wiped at my face and set the dress back in the box. "Why's that?"

Tia squeezed me from the other side. "It's not every day that you get the chance to give a friend who truly deserves it a family for Christmas."

More tears fell. And my heart felt so full.

CHAPTER FORTY

Truths

We stepped out of the limo. Yeah, a fucking limousine. Apparently, Tia had a few connections in this town. A man in a suit that probably cost more than my monthly rent held the door open for me. The other one, who was actually driving, stepped out of the Little White Wedding Chapel with a nod to his friend.

Rachel was the last one out. The man in the suit shut the car door behind her. Xander had been eying the two men since they picked us up, which gave me pause. Like he was wary. Or maybe that was just me being paranoid. He'd assured me repeatedly that he made a clean cut with the organization he worked for—that there was nothing to worry about. Antonio shook these guys hand, laughing and joking with them like old friends. They maybe were old friends of his.

I was so lost in my thoughts, I didn't realize I was the only one who hadn't moved until Xander stepped back and grabbed my hand, pulling me toward the building.

The roof of the carport to this place was painted blue with stars, a moon, and angels. It was tacky, but in a sort of endearing way. The sign as we drove in called this the Tunnel of Love. I did giggle at that as we drove the stretch limo into its entrance.

When we stepped into the lobby, the walls covered in all the pictures of people who had been married there, famous and not. That's when it hit me. I was really doing this. The shock wasn't about Xander. I knew he was it for me. But my feet halted all the same.

Xander felt the tug on his hand and looked back at me. Seeing the look on my face, he frowned.

"What is wrong. Do you not want to do this?"

"No… I mean, yes. I do. It's just… she's not here."

He tilted his head in confusion.

"My mama. This is one of those moments she should be here for, but she never will. She'll never meet you or the baby. And none of that stuff mattered when I got the call, but now it does." I watched cars drive by on the street outside the window, blinking back tears. "I know none of that makes sense. It's been five years since she died."

His brows rose. And shit. I knew that was news to him. I was about to marry this man, and he knew so little about me.

"She died in a prison fight. Some gang attacked her. I can't imagine what life had to be like for her. And I never thought of it that way until now. Like knowing we are going to have this baby. I want to protect it. I killed for this baby. And that's no different than what she did. But I have spent so many years hating her for what I went through because she wasn't there." The tears started rolling down my cheeks. "I don't know what I'm saying or why. I'm sorry."

"Do not be sorry, Rosie. I want this. You. All your thoughts and worries. Never apologize for trusting me."

"That's about the fifth time I've heard him call you that," Rachel called from the other side of the room. "Are you seriously going to marry the man and never tell him your real name?"

Xander smiled. He smiled so big that it turned into a laugh. A laugh so contagious that even though I was confused by it, and I think everyone else was too, eventually we were all laughing. And I needed that. I didn't know how bad I needed that, but it felt like the room shifted. The world became brighter. I knew at that moment this was the best decision I would ever make in my life.

"I love you," I said.

His smile shrank a fraction but didn't go away. "I have a confession."

"You do?" My smile grew wider. "What kind of confession?"

"The kind where you do not know my real name either."

My shoulders shook in a silent chuckle. "Oh really?"

"You two are so weird." Tia shook her head. "Definitely meant for each other. I can't think of a single other person who would find this situation as cute and amusing as you two seem to."

I shrugged. "The best stories are made from the things you did that were different." I pressed a finger to his lips. "Don't tell me now. I think we should wait for the ceremony."

He kissed my forehead and nodded behind me. "We should go, Peaches. I think we have a schedule we are ignoring."

I blushed at the name and followed his gaze back over my shoulder to where the chapel employee waited with a tapping foot.

"Right. I will see a lot more of you soon enough." I winked.

He was ushered off in the opposite direction. I was taken to a dressing room where Tia and Rachel primped and preened over me with the resident makeup artist, but I shooed them all away after a few moments. I still wanted to look like myself.

A few more minutes went by and a woman strolled in with a rolling cart, allowing us a choice between two sets of flower bouquets: a mixture of flowers dominated by white roses or calla lilies. I loved the simplicity of the calla lilies. A grouping of three long-stemmed lilies for me, and a single stem each for Tia and Rachel, each bouquet wrapped with a white satin ribbon.

Then there was a knock at the door. It was Gary. His face was red, and he did not look happy. Rachel said something to him in a hushed tone.

"I can't believe that you want our son to be a flower girl," Gary huffed.

Rachel's lips pinched. "He's the flower boy. Nicky's already the ring bearer. And I didn't want to leave him out."

"He's not doing a girl's job. That's final."

That's when I saw the little cherub face and the wide hazel eyes peeking out from behind Gary. The toddler looked adorable in his tiny suit.

I tried to hold back my laughter, but it was pretty damn funny. "I have a better idea." I walked over to Gary and bent down, eye level with the little boy. "I don't have anyone to walk me down the aisle. You think you could do that?"

The little guy looked a little lost as to what the big deal was, but he nodded and smiled. I pulled the basket of flower petals from his hands and set it on the ground behind me. I looked up to Gary.

"Better?"

Gary nodded, looking a bit abashed. "Sorry."

I shrugged and patted his shoulder. "We all have our limits."

"We're ready," Rachel announced and stepped into the hall.

"I'll go tell the guys." Gary hurried off.

We waited, and Rachel coached her little boy on what to say and when to say it. It was going to be the cutest thing. I felt like I blinked and then the doors opened. Music was playing, and Tia disappeared inside. Rachel followed her. And then it was my turn. I felt the tiny hand take mine, and we turned the corner into the chapel.

My eyes locked on him first. It wasn't Xander. No, it was Elvis. He was shifting his hips back and forth and striking poses, singing "I Can't Help Falling in Love With You" as I walked down the aisle. It was so fucking ridiculous, I laughed out loud. I absolutely loved it.

Everything about this was so perfect. It was tacky, all the way down to the disco ball hanging above the altar.

Then I locked eyes with him. He was watching me, smiling at my laughter. He looked at peace. Something I hadn't realized until now was so different from the man I'd first met.

When I got to the end, Elvis wrapped the song up. "Who gives this bride to marry this man, uh-huh."

"We all do," Rachel's little boy announced.

Tears filled my eyes quickly as I looked around the room. God, I loved these people. I was so wrong about my life. Before I met Xander, I'd looked at everything through a filter. I isolated myself out of fear and refused to see what was truly there. But I saw it now. This was my family, and I was as important to them as they were to me.

Elvis read the words of a standard civil service, asking us to fill in and repeat as necessary.

"Do you Catherine Rosita Dominguez, take Alexander Josef Dobransky as your lawfully wedded husband?"

Dobransky? It could work. I raised a teasing brow at Xander, and he mouthed *Catherine* at me, wrinkling his nose.

I tried to smother a laugh. "I do."

"Do you Alexander Josef Dobransky, take Catherine Rosita Dominguez as your lawfully wedded wife?"

"I do."

When he asked if we'd anything more to say, Xander had something else in store.

"We did not meet under the best of circumstances, but you still managed to captivate me. I had never seen anything else quite like you in all my life. You asked for nothing from me but honesty and truth, and in return you gave me your trust and *your* truths. Even though I could not give it to you then, I can now. I promise to love and protect you. To never lie and to trust you with my truths. I am not a rich man.

I will never be able to give you everything you deserve in this life. But I can give you everything that I am, for as long as our souls exist, in this life and the next. I hope that is enough to keep you by my side."

"It's more than enough," I choked out in a whisper through the tears clogging my throat. "All I want is you."

"Mmmmmhmm… I'm all shook up," Elvis replied.

I couldn't help but laugh as the tears rolled down my face.

"Did you have any words you would like to say, darlin'?"

I shook my head, unable to speak. I was still torn between laughing and crying.

"Then I now pronounce you… husband… and wife, uh-huh. You may now kiss your bride."

Xander's lips pressed to mine, and I felt whole. Everything would forever be right in my world with him by my side. I never thought I would have this; I couldn't imagine anything this perfect before. But it was mine. This future was mine. And I would enjoy every minute of it—in this life and the next.

CHAPTER FORTY-ONE

Love

"I fucking hate you, you..." I gasped. "Motherfucker. Howdareyoudothistome?" I screamed through clenched teeth.

I squeezed Xander's hand with every drop of strength I had in me. The point was to hurt him. He didn't blink. He didn't react. A little smile played on his lips as he watched me.

"I'm going to rip your dick off if you don't stop looking at me like— oooooohhhhhhhhh."

Breathe. Breathe. I needed to breathe. Everything in me was clenched so tight I couldn't utter words. *Fuck. This hurts.* My muscles relaxed again, and I wanted to thank the heavens. *No. Not again.*

"Okay, I need you to push with this one," the doctor said, as she rolled farther between my legs, inspecting my vagina.

I felt her fingers probing down there, just before everything squeezed the life out of me.

"Aaaaaahhhhhhhhhhhhhhhhhh." I pushed and pushed until it felt like I was going to break something.

The doctor nodded. "You can relax."

You *can relax, dick-faced bitch*.

"God, you are so beautiful. So amazing. You're doing great," Xander cooed, stroking my head.

My eyes cut to him in a glare. He was enemy number one at the moment. This was all his fault. Everything was his fault. I was not taking to motherhood well. I sucked at this. I hated everyone. Thank God I didn't have laser-beam eyes, or I would have murdered everyone in this room. Including Rachel.

Snotty bitch was standing on my other side, her shoulders shaking in silent laughter as she smirked at me.

"You're doing great. You got this." She leaned over and peeked at my cooch. "I can see the head!"

"What does that fucking mean? Is it...? Is—Ohmygod."

"Push," the doctor commanded. "Keep pushing, keep pushing, keep pushing..."

I wanted to push a broomstick up her ass, is what I wanted to do. But I also wanted this baby to get the fuck out of my body.

"You're doing great." The doctor smiled. "One more push, and the shoulders will be out. You can do this."

Why do people keep saying that? You're doing great? What would I be doing if I was doing bad?

My scream came out as a high-pitched gurgle. "Holyfuckgoddammit! What? Whydoesithurt... ahhhhhhhh."

"Keep pushing. It's just the shoulders. You're going to feel more pressure." The doctor nodded. "And we're out."

Relief. A tiny cry filled the space. Just over thirteen hours of labor.

"It's a girl. Congratulations, Mom and Dad, you have a baby girl."

They plopped the tiny, filthy human on my stomach. The nurse wiped her down as she screamed and cried until her tiny little face turned purple. *Tell me about it, little one. I feel the same.* I reached out and touched her skin. She was so ugly and beautiful at the same time. I couldn't understand it.

Xander just stared at her with this awestruck look, like they had laid the secret to life on my lap.

"So, Mr. Dobransky, what shall we name our girl?"

"We already talked about this, Catherine."

"I think it's cute that y'all still get a kick out of the name thing," Rachel said. "But seriously, what're you callin' this cherub?"

"Madison Rose—" I replied.

"Lane Rose—" Xander said at the same time.

She rocked back with a belly laugh. "Well, sounds like you got at least one part figured out. What is it with you guys and names?"

I knew he wanted to name the baby after his sister, but it just didn't feel right to me. And naming a kid was a big deal. I'd have to say that name a million times at least. It should feel right.

"Nurse Keenan will be taking the baby back for her tests and measurements now," the doctor interrupted. "Dad, you can go with the baby. Mom, we still have work to do. I'm going to need you to push again."

"Again?"

"This one'll be easy. It's just the afterbirth. Ready? And push…"

After we were done, I dozed off. Giving birth was exhausting work. Rachel shuffled around helping the nurses put the place back in order for visitors, and Xander had left with the baby. I couldn't keep my eyes open for another second.

When I woke, a nurse was nudging me awake. I couldn't have really fallen asleep; it felt like I'd just closed my eyes. But almost everyone was gone from the room.

Rachel still sat in a chair, flipping through channels on the TV with the sound on mute.

Xander stood behind the nurse, holding a grunting baby. His face was the picture of fatherly joy.

"She's ready for her first meal, Mama," the nurse whispered.

I nodded and adjusted, welcoming the baby in my arms. The nurse showed me how to get her to latch on, and once everything was situated, she left the room.

Rachel turned from the TV. "How about you combine them, Cat?"

"Combine what?" I asked.

Rachel shifted in her chair, facing us. "The names. Madison and Lane. You could name her Madelaine?"

My eyebrows climbed in surprise. I looked over to Xander with a shrug. He nodded.

"I like it." Xander stroked the baby's fuzzy head.

I smiled at the little chubby-cheeked angel. "Me too. Do *you* like it, Madelaine Rose Dobransky?"

Looking at that face, I knew I would do anything for this tiny human. I would kill for her. I would die for her. I would do anything to protect her and to give her the life I never had. And it was funny how that worked. That little bit of DNA in common would make you go so far, would change your perspective of the entire world. But it did. All it took was finding out she existed and everything changed for me: my past, my present, and my future. I would never be the same.

And I owed it all to the man standing next to me. The man who changed my world. The man I loved. And it all started with a camera and a dead body.

EPILOGUE

I set the pen down on the legal pad and stretch my hand. The spaces in between each tiny bone seem to ache from the effort of writing everything down. Of course, I left out the sexy parts, but I couldn't help but let my mind wander. They were great memories.

The house has been quiet as I write my thoughts on paper. Xander took Maddie outside to the garage with him while he worked on his car. They do that every time he goes out there. She is a daddy's girl to the core. She'll climb in there with him, handing him the correct tools when he asks for them. It's unbelievably cute.

Looking out the window, I realize how late it has gotten. People will be arriving soon, and I haven't done a thing to prepare for it. But this had to be done. I don't know everything, or anything really. I just know that time is a finite resource. That it can slip from your grasp before you even realize it.

I tuck the card under my legal pad as I hear the doorknob turn. A little head of mahogany waves peeks in the gap between the door and the frame, and the second those big brown eyes find mine, she smiles.

"Mommy!" Maddie streaks across the room, diving into my arms and knocking me back on the bed. "Daddy wanted me to tell you that Aunt Rachel and Tia Tia are here."

"They are?" I smile.

I can't help it. She makes me smile every day.

"Uh-huh. So are Lucky and Dusty. We're gonna go play in the woods."

"Okay, don't get too dirty." I kiss her forehead and wipe a smudge of grease off her chin. "Or go so far that you can't hear us when we call. You have a party tonight."

"Are we having chocolate cake?"

I chuckle. "Yes, we are. I'm going to go make it as soon as I finish this up."

"What ya doin'?" She leans over, looking at the folded sheaf of papers on top of the notepad.

I smile and set her back on the floor. "I'm writing a letter."

Her face twists into a frown. "To who?"

"To you. But you don't get to read it until you get bigger." I wink at her.

"I *am* older." She stands taller, thumping her chest with a fist. "I'm five now." She splays her hand, holding it up in demonstration.

"I know, baby girl. But this is for when you get to be my age."

Her brows lower, and she chews on her bottom lip. "So I have to be twenty-eight to read it?"

"Something like that." I smile and hug her, smoothing my hand over her head.

"Maddie, come on." Evan's voice calls down the hall, just before he appears in the doorway. "Oh, hi, Aunt Kitty."

"Hey there, Ev. You two be good. And take care of my girl."

"Always." He stands a little taller with a wide smile on his face.

"Come on, Dusty." Maddie grabs his hand. "I'll race you. Last one to the clubhouse is a rotten egg."

He nudges her side with his elbow. "You know that'll be Nic."

"Hey, I heard that!" Nic yells from the living room. "Just for that, I'm getting a head start. Eat my dust, Dusty."

The door slams behind them as they leave. I can still hear their screams of joy and laughter as they race off into the woods, taunting each other. And it seems so perfect, like nothing bad could ever happen. I almost believe it, but then this showed up this morning.

I pull the greeting card out from under the notepad.

I saw Xander's face as he was opening the mail with Maddie. The second he laid eyes on it, an expression of panic filled his features. It was fleeting, only lasting for a few fractions of a second before he schooled his features. I asked him about it, and he looked at me, confused, before shaking it off.

"Oh, yeah. Everything's fine." He smiled and kissed me.

I knew right then that he was lying. And it wasn't the first time he had lied to me. But it had been years since that. We'd moved past that, or so I thought.

I didn't know what to make of it, but something about it seemed familiar. I cross the room and open my closet door, flicking on the light. There's a file box at the top labeled Maddie's Memories. I pull it down and walk back to the bed. Tossing the lid to the side, I search through the contents, looking for one specific item.

When I find it, I take a deep breath and open it. It's a greeting card from the day she was born. And like the one on my nightstand, it has an image of a hummingbird on the front, and inside, it's signed with a large, sloppy *X* with a little hook on the end, over a smaller circle. I didn't think anything of it back then. I never saw his face when he first looked at it.

I don't know what it means or if it means anything. But I know my husband. He will protect us at all costs. Even if it means hiding the truth from us. So I want Maddie to know. I want her to know everything that I do, because a day may come where she needs it. And who knows if I will be around to tell her. My mama sure wasn't.

I set the other card on the notepad and return Maddie's box to the closet. Grabbing a shoe box, I put the items inside: my letter to her, along with the two cards. Then I hide it. I bury it under my shoes. It'll be there if she ever needs it.

Everyone has to pay for their sins sooner or later. I never paid for mine. Xander hasn't paid for his. But I can't help the gnawing feeling inside that she may have to pay that price for us.

*If you enjoyed Snapshot, you won't want to miss
Maddie Dobransky's epic tale, The Falling Small Duet.
Check it out at rebelfarris.com/fallingsmall*

FALSE START

(FALLING SMALL DUET, #1)

Sometimes bad decisions... are made for the right reasons.

I lost everything with the death of my bandmate—my privacy, my reputation, my career, and the love of my life.

I'm nothing but the living ghost of Madelaine Dobransky. Still, I've managed to make a new life for myself and build a successful business from the ashes. And even though my world is filled with guilt, secrets, and suspicion... it lies buried beneath the surface.

All I wanted was a tattoo. I didn't know that it would bring *him*—the one who watches—back into my life. Nor did I expect the tempting tattoo artist, Dexter McClellan, to lay claim on a place in my world. Dex wants to know me, to know the truth.

But I can't let that happen. Because the truth is buried for a reason.

The truth will destroy me.

256

PIVOT LINE

(FALLING SMALL DUET, #2)

Sometimes the worst lies... are the ones we tell ourselves.

His death left me broken—destroyed.

It wasn't the incident alone. I was already damaged beyond repair by the events leading to that moment. But seeing his lifeless body only sealed my fate. So many mistakes. So much regret.

Dex wants to know what happened that night. He wants to catch a killer and put my demons to rest. I'm just not sure I can trust him after the lies he told to get close. I'm wary... guarded. Still, I'll welcome him to my world and lead him into the darkness.

He'll see me for what I truly am. But I'm not the only one keeping secrets. And maybe...

The truth will set us all free.

https://rebelfarris.com/series/falling-small-duet/

257

258

BACK OF BOOK SHIT

Welcome to the Back of Book Shit, aka the BoBS. This is the part of the book where I blather on about shit that relates to the story and the thought process behind developing it. If you are new to my books, like this is the first of my books you have ever read, you're probably wondering about that ending. Well, there's good news for you. Little Maddie Dobransky has her own series, the Falling Small Duet, and you can totally go one-click that bitch now.

The whole concept for this book was born out of a conversation with my editor about just how complex the Seven Hummingbirds storyline is. I told her that it was ridiculously massive and had this whole complicated backstory behind everything. And setting out to write the Seven Hummingbirds, I knew I had to stop and give a peek at what is to come.

Every character of mine is like a real person. I'm sure most authors feel that way, but for me, these people feel real. I know all their histories, their ancestors, and to be honest, I think I know them better than I know myself. So when Sandra asked if I actually knew where the Seven Hummingbirds series was heading, I was like "Hell yeah. Hold for a moment, I got this."

But even then, there are things this backstory in my head is missing.

I knew that Rosie was a photographer that never followed through with that dream. It's how Maddie got her photography knowledge when she compared Dex's art to a famous photograph at the beginning of False Start. I knew Xander was a Czech spy. But I didn't know how they met until I was scrolling through stock photos one day and came across a woman crouched down in the middle of a field taking a picture of the landscape. The area she was standing looked an awful lot like central Texas. But I didn't see her car. I was looking at it, wondering how she got there. How did she arrive at that exact spot? What would she do if someone nefarious was out there with her? What would happen if she stumbled upon a killer? What if she fell in love with that killer?

The rest, they say, is history.

Also, the fact that Rosie is Mexican and Xander is Czech comes from my own genetic makeup. I am a Czech Mex. I've never known quite where I fit in with the whole politically correct racial identity thing. I just consider myself American and a Texan. And I tend to write characters that just don't identify with racial stereotypes. I write from my point of view, the way I see the world, and the people I've met and know. And I've known a lot of ethnically diverse people.

Back when I was in college, I was the personal assistant to the head of the international studies department. As such, I became the unofficial student ambassador to all the foreign exchange students. And as a consummate people watcher, I found their cultures and customs ridiculously fascinating. I loved it when they pointed out things that I did that weren't as mundane as I thought. But the ultimate lesson learned from that experience is that no one fits into a mold. Everyone is different and unique. We just have to learn to see ourselves that way and stop expecting others to fit into categories too.

And fuck if it isn't fun researching curse words in other languages.

Finding out that the Velvet Revolution just happened to be in the same year as Maddie was conceived, felt kismet. It wasn't planned prior to writing this book, but it was such a perfect piece to the puzzle that I'm not sure I could have written this story as realistically without it. And those are the moments writers live for. Those tiny moments of magic that make us feel like the world is conspiring with us to plot the story.

This book, however, was about so much more for me. Starting out as a new author and only putting out series after series is a rough path to take. I'm pretty realistic though. I know readers don't want to get invested when I haven't proven that I'll be around long enough to finish it. And some of that sketchiness is because I haven't proven to readers that I have what it takes to deliver an awesome ending. It's going to be at least nine books into my career before I can deliver the massive happily-ever-after we all want. It's coming, and I hope you will find it as amazing as I do. And I hope the end of this book brings you some measure of confidence in that promise.

Writing this book was also an adventure in self-discovery. I began to realize that between my first book Providence (which I don't have plans to publish right now), the Duet, and this book, that there's a certain style unique to me. From the way you slowly get to know characters, the awkward funny moments, strong men that aren't threatened by a strong female, the fact that every story has to carry a psychological theme, to just the fact that I'm so addicted to and in love with expanded world stories. Plus the fact that this book is considered dark. The fact that people labeled the Duet dark. Believe me when I say that it is an utter surprise to me that I write dark books.

Maybe I just have a fucked-up mind, but I always set out with the intention that I'm going to write a romantic comedy. It just never turns out that way. I mean, why the fuck doesn't everyone find dead bodies, international spies, assassins, and lurking killers funny?

The other thing that my lovely editor asked when inspiring me to write this was how I keep coming up with such unique characters and storylines. My answer: I have more baggage than a Transatlantic flight. If I give one issue to each character, then I can write for decades to come. And I do. Every one of my characters holds a piece of me. And yes, they are also inspired by other people I know, but in the way that those people relate to me. The common bond that made us friends, to begin with. That gateway that allowed me to understand them on a deeper level.

Though, Rosie, out of all my characters is the closest I've ever written to myself. No, my mamma didn't go to prison, but I too have always wanted to be a photographer. That bit about Ansel Adams and his black-and-white photos, why she wanted to take pictures, was almost like writing a journal entry. Though I've never sold a photo in my life, so I can't assume the title, I've been toying around with cameras far longer than I've been writing.

But this book was such a hard one to write for precisely that reason. Not because it was particularly complex or twisty. But because the heart of this book deals with depression. More specifically, situational depression—the kind that can't be treated with pills and is most often unrecognized by the affected. It was hard because, as I was writing this, I realized the reason it was such a huge struggle was that I was depressed.

Now, I know that it's called situational depression, but it's not something that can be pinpointed down to one reason. Often, it's a perfect storm of factors that weigh on you every day and you don't even recognize that it's happening. You don't see it until you've developed a pattern of destructive habits that halt your forward momentum. Even when it feels like you're still making progress. It's like finding out you're on a treadmill when you thought you were on a trail in the woods. You think you're running forward and making progress, but you're really just running in place, moving inches forward to only be drug right back to where you started.

That's what happened to me with this book. I was still writing every day. I was still posting on social media. I was still selling books. I was handling my business. But every day it got harder and harder to do. And one day I woke up and realized that I didn't even want to get out of bed. I felt like such a failure. I had promised this book to be delivered by a certain date and I missed it by four months. Four fucking months. And the larger that number grew the harder I was on myself for not getting it done.

Plus, as anyone new to any career, you try to go in without expectations, but it's just fucking human nature to create them. You see all the people who started at the same time as you and their paths are more fruitful... you start beating yourself up for all the things you did "wrong" and the reasons why you're not where they're at. Factor in my ongoing divorce and the struggles inherent in that venture, and you have all the right ingredients.

And when it came down to it—when I finally realized what was going on. I realized it was my own expectations that were getting in the way of my progress. I expected things to be a certain way and when they didn't live up to those expectations, I internalized them as failures.

When I finally realized that all I needed to do was cast out those expectations, I wrote the rest of this book in six days. *Six fucking days.*

I've learned my lesson though, and it's this: *Don't fucking dwell on your differences, your hardship, your successes, or your failures. Just keep moving forward.*

Anyway, back to the backstory of this story…I've been there more than once with situational depression, so I knew that was what I was in for when it came to writing a character that has it. But even knowing the pitfalls, it was so fucking hard to do. Because she can't realize why she feels a certain way, it has to be something that the reader can pick up through subtext. And if you ask my editor and betas, I'm the queen of subtext. The vast majority of my edits are clarifying shit that readers aren't picking up on their own.

This story was no different. The biggest issue was that people expected her to be a reliable narrator. That if she said she had no friends, then she didn't, and when it turned out that she did, they were so confused. All this to say that I hope we fixed it. That I made it clear enough in the end.

Because one of my motivating factors for writing this story was that I want people to know that if you are depressed, it's not the end of anything. It doesn't mean life will pass you by. You can still fall in love, find your purpose for living, chase your dreams, and find your happily ever after. And if you just happen to be writing books, you can still finish the goddamn story.

Until then, be you. Stay original.

Rebel

ACKNOWLEDGEMENTS

This is the part of the book where I say thank you to all the important people who helped me get this far. And I get it, unless you're one of them, you probably don't give two shits about who they are. But I really hope you'll read it anyway, you might be surprised in the end, so I'll try to keep it short and sweet.

Thank you to everyone that helped me make the difficult decision to revamp this book and help it reach the readers who are going to love this story. Kristi Webster, Marley Valentine, Cassie Sharp, Julie Joyness, Tasha Lewis, Kelley Needles, and Charly Player. All of your time putting up with each update and every "Does this look good yet?" saved my sanity.

My editor, Sandra Depukat, at One Love Editing, you're a godsend. Not only did you inspire me to write this story because you're a fan and you want to know all my secrets. Spoilers aside, because you'd probably kill me if I blurted a spoiler. I'm sorry that you had to wait so long to find out what I was up to. You put up with the painstakingly slow process of going through edits on this book a chapter at a time, as I wrote them. And zooming through second-round edits with lightning speed once I was done writing... nothing short of amazing.

To my new beta reader, Charly Player. Thank you so much for

being the most awesome reader an author can hope to have. I know you were slightly embarrassed to send me that synopsis of my Duet. But for an author, knowing that someone, even if it is just one reader, appreciates your words enough to hang on each one and dissect your story for clues... that... that means the world to me. I'm so glad that you have come into my life and I really hope you stick around for more because I love your input and insight into my books. And thank you for having so much patience, for being available to read every new chapter as soon as it was posted.

But you also became my friend in the proces. The fact that you willing volunteer to help me every day is a godsend. Thank you so much for reviewing the revised version of this book for errors.

Cassie motherfucking Sharp, I don't know what I would do without. Thank you for putting up with me. Understanding that I'm not always the best friend on the planet, but still being there when I need you despite that. I know I sucked for putting off reading your book to try and get this book written. The fact that you never mentioned it speaks volumes about your character, even if everyone already knows it. I'm 83% through it now, so you can expect a review soon, and everyone will know how amazing it is. I will shout it from the fucking rooftops. I'm so lucky to have you in my life. To help me make the innocuous decisions when I can't make up my fucking mind, or to beta my books and cheer me on. I did write Xander for you, so you can lick him, and stick him in your pocket. He's yours.

My proofreader, Jenn Wood, from All About the Edits. Thank you for being so flexible with me, wedging me into your schedule over a holiday weekend. Your accuracy at such speed is beyond compare. I am more than grateful.

Cassandra Nelson, thank you for jumping in at the last minute, beta reading and providing crazy insightful feedback all in the span of two short days. You are a lifesaver.

And lastly, I want to thank you, dear reader. None of this would matter without you. I'm so incredibly lucky that you found me. I hope you like this story, I hope you'll want to read more of the crazy shit that sprouts from my mind. I don't think I will be able to thank each of you enough to even come close to match what you do for me. Words will never be enough, but for now, that's what you're getting.

ABOUT THE AUTHOR

ebel Farris is a country girl who's spent far too much time in an urban setting. A gentle, pure soul, who can't speak a word without dropping f-bombs or dripping sarcasm everywhere. She was born and raised in Texas, living a mostly nomadic life before settling down in Austin. When she's not busy being a workaholic, writing the next dark story that fills her twisted mind, she can be found hanging with her three minions and two pups, Thugg Dog and King Pin.

Stalk Me here: links.rebelfarris.com

ALSO BY REBEL FARRIS

STANDALONES
Snapshot

FALLING SMALL DUET
False Start

Pivot Line

SEVEN HUMMINGBIRDS SERIES
(Coming In 2019)

Penalty Kill

Whip

Substitution

Transition

Blocker

Turn Stop

Target Zone

You can find out more about these books at
https://rebelfarris.com/books

SNAPSHOT

SOCIAL MEDIA

I have a group of crazy-ass readers all across the web. You can find us on Facebook at the Rebel's Villains group.

But... no matter what your social media of choice is, you can connect with us by using **#rebelsvillains**.

Stalk me on Social Media...

Facebook: /rebelfarris
Facebook Group: /groups/rebelsvillains
Twitter: @Rebel_Farris
Instagram: @rebelfarris
Pinterest: /rebelfarris
Goodreads: /rebelfarris
YouTube: /AnimalLogicProd
Website: https://rebelfarris.com

If you prefer to skip the social media scene altogether but still want to find out all the latest happenings and get in on exclusive shit. And have it all delivered straight to your inbox, then be sure to sign up for my newsletter here.

https://subscribe.rebefarris.com/

274

SNAPSHOT PLAYLIST

Scene Inspiration Songs

To Bring You My Love by PJ Harvey
Love Is Blindness by Jack White

Xander's Record Collection

The Most Beautiful Girl by Charlie Rich
Kiss an Angel Good Mornin' Charley Pride
Oh, Lonesome Me by Don Gibson
He Stopped Loving Her Today by George Jones
Mammas, Don't Let Your Babies Grown Up to Be Cowboys by Waylon Jennings & Willie Nelson
Stand By Your Man by Tammy Wynette
You Never Even Called Me By My Name by David Allen Coe
I'm so Lonesome I Could Cry by Hank Williams
Good Hearted Woman by Willie Nelson
Crazy by Patsy Cline
I Walk The Line by Johnny Cash

Rosie's Mix Tape

Pictures of Matchstick Men by Camper Van Beethoven
Blister in the Sun by Violent Femmes
Heroes by David Bowie
Love Shack by The B-52's
Stand by R.E.M.
So Alive by Love and Rockets
Whip It by Devo
Hazy Shade of Winter by The Bangles
Sunglasses At Night by Corey Hart
I Melt With You by Modern English
Girls Just Want to Have Fun by Cyndi Lauper
In The Air Tonight by Phil Collins
Kiss by Prince
She Drives Me Crazy by Fine Young Cannibals
Faith by George Michael

Find the Spotify playlist by visiting: **https://links.rebelfarris.com**

www.ingramcontent.com/pod-product-compliance
Lightning Source LLC
Chambersburg PA
CBHW070431120726
47910CB00003B/737